Another Tear

Traci Bee

King George Publishing, LLC
National Harbor, Maryland

Another Tear
Sequel to *Two Tears in a Bucket*
Copyright © 2010

King George Publishing, LLC books may be ordered through booksellers or by contacting:

King George Publishing, LLC
145 Fleet Street, Suite 330
National Harbor, Maryland 20745
www.kinggeorgepublishing.com

Layout and interior designed by: interiorbookdesigns.com

Because of the dynamic nature of the Internet, any Web addresses or links contained in this book may have changed since publication and may no longer be valid.

This is a work of fiction. All characters, names, incidents, organizations, and dialogue in this novel are either the products of the author's imagination or are used fictitiously.

ISBN: 13-digit 978-0-9791795-2-5
        10-digit 0-9791795-2-1

Printed in the United States of America

Dedicated to my first, my last, my everything
George Thomas Brewington, Sr.
aka
"My Daddy Angel"

I love and miss you, Daddy!

Acknowledgments

Acknowledgments are so hard to write. It can take years to write a book and in that length of time, help can come from tons of places, and it's always my fear that I'll forget someone. But never will I forget you, Lord Jesus, for where would I be without you FIRST. I thank you, Father God, for providing me with the words when I sat before the computer fearing there were none and for moving the many, many mountains that seemed to come from nowhere. I trust and believe that ALL THINGS are possible through you!

To my editing team: Monique D. Mensah for her powerful developmental editing; Melody Guy for finding cracks in the story that I would've never discovered; and, Editor Carla M. Dean for going through it all, one last time, with a fine-tooth comb. I thank and love you, ladies!

Leona Romich and Cassandra "Cea Ashe" Ashe – you sugarcoated NOTHING! If it was good, it was good. If it sucked, then it sucked. You don't know how much I appreciate the both of you. From the bottom of my heart, I thank you.

I have met some AMAZING people during my literary journey, authors that support and advise like Treasure Blue, K.L. Brady, Envy Red, Monique D. Mensah, Tamika Newhouse, Azarel, Author and CEO of Life Changing Books, Nakia R. Laushaul, Allison Essence M. Edwards, Felisha Bradshaw, Tanisha Mahogani Pettiford, Rahiem Brooks and so many others. What a powerful force the world of AA fiction would be if we threw away the "crab in the barrel" mentality and united on a regular.

To my family over at Salon Couture, the hottest salon in all of Prince George's County, two-time winner of Steve Harvey's Hoodie Awards for Nails and Hair; Deborah Cardona and the Déjà Vu' Lounge in New York; The Cartel Bookstore in Oxon Hill, Maryland, and The Literary Joint in Forestville, Maryland ~ you all showed *Two Tears in a Bucket* so much support and love. It's one thing for a book to grace a shelf but you and your team helped to PUSH it, and I thank you all from the depths of my soul.

Jeffy Gatsby Willson, The Real DJ and DJ Gatsby Book Club; Weather McCraw and the Systaz N' Sync family; my Facebook family: Tiffany Williams, Carla Towns, Shanneasha Yunglit Eacholes, Natissha Manning

Hayden, Rhylander Phillips, Natash Dafney-Neal, Twana Spencer, Vincent Bell, Jeanette McMillian-James, Denise Williams, Denise Collier, Ciara Collier, Treva Bush, my newfound sister, Faith Rose – man, I could go on and on listing readers who have wowed me with their love and support. You have no idea what it means to me. Without you, where would any author be? So to you, I say THANK YOU!

Shanay Campbell, you are a PRICELESS source! Thanks for answering my plea for help. Hope you enjoy how the information was used.

Damion Penn, Cheryl Bruce, LaChelle Brewington - you're always there, no matter the call of duty. Selling books, helping out at events, heck, babysitting so I could write (Damion ☺), but there are no words. I love each of you as if you were my real sister. Blood couldn't make the love I feel for you any greater!

If my girls hadn't spent the summer in North Carolina with their grandmother, Another Tear would still be in the making. Lord knows I love and thank you, Ma!!!

If you could be a fly on a wall in my house, you would hear someone whispering, "Shhh, Mommy's writing," followed by the sound of keys as the husband ushers everybody to the car just to grant me some privacy. I know you guys are glad it's over, but don't get too comfortable because I'm working on two more! But you already know, the goal isn't just about me. It's about us. I love you.

Praise for Traci Bee's debut novel, Two Tears in a Bucket

Traci Bee is an author to watch and I look forward to reading the sequel to this page-turner! The cliffhanger on this book is a DOOZIE!!
--K.L. Brady, Author of *The BUM MAGNET*

TWO TEARS IN A BUCKET will tug at your heartstrings and leave your mouth hanging agape. This author definitely has a flair for writing.
--Leona Romich, APOOO Book Club

Magnificent and moving. Traci Bee has outdone herself. She has helped African American Fiction stand firm by writing a book that shows that this genre is here to stay and within it real raw talent dwells. "B" also stands for BRAVO!!!!!!!!!
--Felisha Bradshaw, Author of *Eyes on the Pryze*

Two Tears in a Bucket is a great debut novel by Traci Bee. This book has a lot of emotional twists and a shocking cliffhanger that will have you begging for the sequel. Two Tears in a Bucket is full of fast-paced drama that will leave you wanting to read the next book by Traci Bee.
--Radiah Hubbert, Urban Reviews

Traci captures a personal and touching story in genuine fashion with Two Tears in a Bucket. Captivating and sincere, this novel was a great read that lingers long after you read the last page. Great debut Traci!
--A. Kai, Author of *Daughter of the Game*

Traci Bee has taken the reader on an unforgettable ride full of emotions, where the reader will wonder what they would have done if they were faced this certain situations. There was a shocker at the end that has me watching for Traci's follow up!!
--Locksie Locks, ARC Book Club, Inc.

Two nights before the birth of their son, life seemed perfect for Kevin and Simone...

Chapter One

Thursday Night, April 5th

S imone Woodard stood in the middle of the botanical garden, mesmerized by miles of perfect landscape and the emerald waters of Rodney Bay. Softly, the St. Lucia steel drum band began to play. It was her cue. Time for the ceremony to begin.

Torn between joy and pain, Simone glanced toward the heavens for strength and filled her lungs with the tranquil scent of the island before she made her way to the runner stretched across the lavish green lawn. The priest raised his arms. The handful of guests rose from white chairs draped in tulle, roses, and marguerites. "Oohs" and "aahs" were heard as Simone came into view, sexy, yet angelic in a full-length gown that resembled a dress worn by a Greek goddess. The soft chiffon flirted with the tropical breeze.

Two steps into her lonesome stroll down the aisle, Simone surveyed the intimate gathering of family and friends. Her soon-to-be mother-in-law, Beatrice, dabbed her eye with a balled up tissue as she mouthed, "You look beautiful." Battling her own tears, Simone decided to focus straight ahead. Fat Ed, Kevin's God-brother and best friend since child-hood, stood at the altar next to Kevin. The two men dressed in identical black classic tuxedos. A modest smirk crept across Simone's face as Fat Ed gave her a thumbs-up and a goofy smile of approval.

A flash of light flickered from the camera of her brother Stan, who stood next to their mother, Angela. Simone's eyes dotted past her mother and landed on the scar on the back of her step-father Ricardo's head. The scar she had given him when she smacked him with a crystal ashtray many years ago. Simone and Ricardo had never liked each other. To date, little had changed. Now they simply ignored each other's existence. Knowing her mother, she forced her husband to come, which probably wasn't difficult since it was a free trip. A mini-vacation for those in attendance thanks to the six figures, Simone's fiancé, Kevin, had earned from his songs.

Halfway down the aisle, Simone spotted the one person she wanted to avoid. The one person who would trigger the pain she battled within.

Simone didn't want to cry. She wanted to be happy. Today, she was marrying the man of her dreams. But her unescorted stroll and the tear drenched face of her step-mother, Mae, symbolized the absence of her father, Thomas. His unconditional love had helped Simone through the harsh realities of life. No matter her mistakes, her father was always there. He had been her security, her best-friend, her first love and now he was her angel in heaven.

The photographer snapped pictures. The videographer was recording. Though she knew she shouldn't, Simone clutched the bouquet with one hand and fanned her eyes with the other to keep the tears at bay. Blinking back tears, she continued her companionless stride as her husband-to-be made his way up the aisle to escort her.

*****

Under the warmth of the covers, Simone snuggled deeper into Kevin's embrace. This was her favorite part of their wedding video. Kevin shared her pain and had come to comfort her. His need to be at her side and the look in his eyes screamed his love for her.

"I still can't believe we kissed before they pronounced us man and wife," Simone said as she played in the sexy trail of fine hair that ran from Kevin's navel down to his manhood.

"Yeah, I know." Kevin rubbed Simone's bulging belly. "It's hard to believe you were pregnant in this video."

"That's because I was only three months." She rested her hand on top of Kevin's.

"That was a beautiful wedding gift too, baby. I'm surprised you kept it a secret that long."

"It was hard, especially when the morning sickness kicked in."

Closing his eyes, Kevin kissed Simone on the top of her head and inhaled her scent. "Just think. In three more weeks, he'll be here."

"Maybe sooner. The doctor said I've already started to dilate, remember?"

"Man, I can't believe any of this. It all feels like a dream," Kevin said. Simone pulled a few strands of hair from the sexy trail. "Ouch! What are you doing?" he asked, grabbing her hand.

"Now you know it's real."

Kevin guided her hand down to his manhood. "Now, I know it's real," he added playfully. Simone squeezed the bulge in his boxers and applied a tender kiss to his bare chest.

"I promise, baby. I'm going to be the best husband and the best father in the world. Our lil' man will never go through what I went through. He won't have fake ass friends setting him up or dragging him down."

Nobody like James' bitch ass, Kevin thought to himself.

*****

Sixteen years ago, selling street corner pharmaceuticals wasn't how Kevin had planned to provide for his family. But when Simone, who was pregnant with their daughter, Jordan, lost her job, the fast money became a need and not a want. Kevin took to the streets, hustling crack night and day to cover the bills until they found jobs. After a few days, the pressure subsided. With two months' worth of rent in his pocket, Kevin couldn't wait to get home and tell Simone that things were going to be okay. But before he could reach their home, he was robbed of the rent money. Kevin and Simone's world flipped upside down.

A week later, Felicia Payne, James' baby momma placed a frantic call to Kevin in the wee hours of the morning. Toby, a Jamaican looking to take over the drug strip, pounded on her door with a shotgun, looking for James who was nowhere to be found. A sucker for a damsel in distress, Kevin headed to the drug strip to defuse the situation. But things got out of hand when James appeared. Gun shots ricocheted throughout the apartment building. When the smoke cleared, old man Mr. Johnson—Kevin's friend and mentor—lay dead, killed by a bullet from Kevin's gun. Off Kevin went, sentenced to forty years. Although co-defendants were never to be housed together in the same correctional institution, Kevin and James found themselves in the same prison.

James was on a mission to create a reputation for himself. A rumor circulating around the prison had finally made its way to Kevin. Not only had James orchestrated Kevin's robbery but he'd arranged to have Toby robbed as well, which is why Toby pounded James' door with the shotgun. Now Kevin was behind bars because he went to help James' girl. He went to save Felicia from chaos James' ignited. A fire burned inside of Kevin. He wanted revenge. His fake ass best friend had destroyed his life.

Ready to add life to his already lengthy sentence, Kevin approached James in the yard but froze in his tracks when a shadow, larger than Kevin's, stood above James. Blood splattered as James fell to his death after being smacked in the head with a fifty pound weight. Oddly enough, James' brutal death brought Kevin little relief for nothing had changed. He was still confined behind bars.

*****

Simone tapped Kevin on his arm. "What you thinking about?"

Kevin raised his arms, stretching as he yawned. Simone peeled herself from his chest to reach for the universal remote. She clicked off the television and turned on her iPod stationed in the Bose dock on her nightstand.

"I wish we were having twins so our son wouldn't grow up by himself."

"What? You sound like a crazy person. Besides, baby, he'll have us. He won't be alone."

The introduction to Brainstorms' *This Must Be Heaven* whispered its serenade.

"Yes, yes, yes." Kevin said as Simone found her place back in his arms. "This has got to be heaven and I'm lying here with my angel. Simone you've made me the happiest man in the world."

Chapter Two

F elicia Payne snatched a few squares of toilet paper from the roll and wiped the haze from the bathroom mirror to get another glimpse of her new figure. Gone were the rolls that once draped her stomach. Her saggy C-cup breasts had been padded and perked to double-D hotness. The fat that once clung to her butt and thighs had been sucked away. In her eyes, she was finally, a five-star chick.

For six weeks, Felicia had been confined, bored, and trapped in the house, while she recovered from plastic surgery. Three times a day, the girls she employed took turns checking on her, giving her food she'd been advised to avoid while tending to her moans and groans. Now as she admired her body from every angle, the agonizing weeks of pain were well worth the reflection in the mirror.

In her thirty-nine years of life, she'd never felt this sexy. She ran her hands down her plump apple bottom, then broke out in the Beyoncé booty bounce. The pain shot from her tender breasts and ricocheted through her body, bringing the dance to a halt.

"Whew," she moaned as she massaged her rock-like breasts the way the nurse had instructed. "Man, I be glad when y'all feel real."

A pink and black bra and panty set rested on the bathroom's marble counter with the tags still attached. She contemplated wearing the little lacy set to her doctor's appointment, but knew Dr. Gustafuson's nurse would piss a fit about the underwire bra. To avoid being reprimanded like a child, Felicia blew the set a kiss and put on her sports bra and skintight girdle for the last time.

"Don't worry, baby," she said to the lingerie. "Once I leave the doctor's office, it's me and you. Now where the hell is that ponytail holder?"

She stole another glance in the mirror, this time staring in horror at her two-month-old blonde and black micro-braids. Salon Couture was the hottest salon in Prince George's County and she had to get to Tracey's chair quick.

Make-up, cotton balls, a box of opened tampons and a curling iron caked with burnt hair products cluttered the bathroom counter. Felicia fished through the mess in search of something to secure her braids into a ponytail. Frustrated, she put her hands on her hips.

"I know I just seen one."

She headed to her bedroom and stood at the threshold, taking heed of the trifling clutter. Her house was just as trifling as the roach-infested apartment she'd moved from. The girl had moved from the hood, but the hood had yet to move from the girl.

"Damn. I gotta get a maid."

Shaking her head, she made her way through the chaos and spotted a grungy rubber-band wrapped around a thick pile of old mail belonging to her daughter, Mercedes. After securing her braids in a sloppy ponytail, Felicia spotted two issues of *Jet* in her daughter's mail. She parked herself on the unmade bed and thumbed through the magazine in search of the 'Beauty of the Week'.

"I bet y'alls' bodies can't touch this here."

She found the first model's picture and gave her a once-over. She was unimpressed. "Baby, you couldn't even work for me." She flung the magazine to the side and picked up the other issue. "What you working with?"

As she flipped through the pages, the caption 'Love and Happiness' caught her eye. She smiled in envy at the blissful couples.

"What the —?"

Her mouth agape, she stared at the photo as her eyes instantly glossed with tears. Without warning, the photo had stolen the joy from her day and the promises of her tomorrow. Salty tears fell from her eyes and made a puddle in the pocket above her top lip. Her eyes read the blurb under the photo in disbelief. It just wasn't possible.

She combed through the mess on her bed and said, "Where the fuck is the phone?"

She stood up, grabbed the comforter and shook the blanket. Papers and trash tumbled to the floor. There was a thump. She scurried to the side of the bed and picked up the phone, which landed next to the chicken bones and French fry crumbs that had fallen from a styrofoam carryout container. Phone in hand, she pounded her girl, Sanora's number, pacing back and forth while the phone rang for what seemed like an eternity. No answer. She hung up and dialed again. This time, Sanora answered on the fourth ring.

"Hey," Sanora whispered, "I gotta call you —"

"Girl, girl, girl," Felicia managed to utter through her sobs. "I'ma get 'em. I promise with everything in me, I'ma get his ass."

"Felicia? Oh my goodness, are you crying?" Sanora asked, her voice now filled with panic. "What's wrong?"

"It's Kevin."

"Kevin? Kevin, your fiancé? Girl—"

"Girl nothing!" Felicia snapped, struggling to continue through her sobs. "This lying muthfucka is outta jail."

"Yes!" Sanora practically leaped through the phone.

"Yes, my ass. I'm looking at his fuckin' wedding picture in *Jet!*"

"What?"

"You heard me!" Felicia sank to the floor.

"Hold up, Felicia. I'm confused."

"Yeah, well imagine how the fuck I feel. Listen to this shit: Up and coming songwriter Kevin Kennard becomes one—," Felicia paused to hold back tears, "with Simone Woodard, owner of Woodard Real Estate, in an intimate ceremony on the tropical island of St. Lucia." Her voice cracked.

"Wait a minute, Felicia," Sanora stated gently. "I thought y'all were getting married? I mean, he sent you that ring and everything. I'm confused. How the hell is he married?"

"Hell if I know. He's not even supposed to be home yet."

Felicia flipped the magazine over to check the date on the cover. The publication was three months old and didn't disclose when the nuptials had taken place. There was no telling when Kevin had snuck home.

"What I'm gon' do, Sanora?" she bawled. "I ain't never loved nobody like this."

Sanora sighed heavily. "Damn, Fe. I don't know, but with your new body, I'm sure you'll find somebody else."

"I don't want nobody else. I want him!"

"Yeah, but he's married now. You have to find a way to forget about him."

"Forget about him? Bitch, are you crazy? After everything I did for him, now I'm just supposed to roll the fuck over and forget? Forget how I drove his mother and every fucking body else back and forth to the jail for damn near sixteen years? Forget how I accepted them expensive ass phone calls for sixteen years?" She sniffed. "The fuckin' money I put into his account?"

"But Felicia, we do those things when we're in love. We can't take it back when it's over."

"Over?" Felicia chuckled. "Oh no. This shit is far from over."

"But if he's married what can you do?"

"You must've forgot who the hell you talkin' to. Watch what the fuck I do!"

Felicia pitched the cordless phone across the room, unfazed by the gash it left in the drywall as it shattered to the floor in pieces.

From the photo in *Jet*, Kevin and Simone's smiles taunted her. A steak knife had fallen onto the floor with the clutter from the bed. Like a crazed maniac, she clutched the knife and lunged at Simone's image in the magazine.

"I'ma get you! I'ma get you!" Felicia screamed while stabbing Simone's likeness over and over until there was little left of her face in the photo.

Panting, Felicia rocked against the bed. From the corner of her eye, she surveyed the damage. Her rock ceased. She could still detect a hint of Simone's smile. Armed with the knife, she thrust the blade into the page with so much fury, she ripped through the magazine. But Simone was no more.

Kevin Kennard, the six-foot-one, honey-coated, hazel-eyed love of Felicia's life, stood alone on the tattered page. Barefoot in the sand, he was so dapper, so handsome in his black tuxedo. Felicia's tears quickened as she traced his image with her finger. Kevin, her Kevin, was not only home but married to someone else.

"I'm gon' get you." Felicia sniffed. "Bitch muthafucka, I swear…with everything in me…I'm gon' get both y'all!"

Now, Felicia no longer desired his love. She craved his blood.

Chapter Three

Deli trays loaded with sandwiches and wings sat on the kitchen counter. Grocery bags crowded the table and chairs, while streamers, helium balloons, and other party decorations flooded the maple wood floors. A baby shower was in the making.

Tamone, the little teacup Yorkie with the pit-bull personality, trotted from bag to bag, sniffing.

"Kayla!" Simone yelled. Startled by the sudden outburst, the little dog jumped and scurried into the family room. "Come get Tamone and put him in your room."

Kayla, Simone's youngest daughter yelled from the top of the steps. "Come on, Tamone!" The stubborn dog ignored her and crept back to the bags.

"Get out of those bags!" Simone yelled. "Kayla, I said come get him, not call him."

"What is up with you and your dog?" her mother-in-law Beatrice asked.

"I don't want people eating food he's licked on."

"It ain't just that. I've never even seen you pat him," Beatrice added.

"Tamone don't like me. He peed on my side of the bed, chewed up my slippers, and don't let Kevin be around. He'll growl at me. I think the mutt is gay." Simone said, laughing with her mother-in-law as she ripped open a packet of Taco Bell mild salsa. She'd craved the salsa the bulk of her pregnancy and sucked at least twenty packets a day.

Home from college for the baby shower, Jordan sat on the couch in the family room, watching her play aunts, Simone's best friends Melanie and Lavon, argue about where to hang the decorations. Cabinet doors slammed one behind the other as Simone's mother, Angela, her step-mother Mae, and Beatrice searched for pots and platters.

"Where's your crock pot?" Mae asked. "I wanna put the meatballs on low."

"Bottom cabinet under the island," Simone said as she sucked the contents from the seasoning pack. She tossed the empty packet in the trash and reached for another. "I have chafers, too, if y'all need them."

"Okay." Mae strained as she kneeled and fished through the bottom cabinet. "Guess we can transfer the food to the chafers after we cook."

The cluster of bags on the kitchen table was driving Simone crazy. "What do y'all need me to do?" she asked as she unloaded one of the bags.

"Simone, get out of that bag!" Angela yelled. "Why are you even down here? You're supposed to be on bed rest, remember?"

"Big mouth." Simone tossed a small pack of baby shower napkins playfully at her mother. "I'm only on bed rest because the doctor went on vacation."

To watch Angela and Simone, one would never suspect such a traumatic past existed between the two. They laughed, joked, and bickered like any other mother and daughter. No one would believe the lies Angela spun around Simone when she was nineteen years old to steal custody of little baby Jordan. It took sixteen years for the web of lies to completely unravel. Unsure of how to fully forgive her mother, Simone insisted they attend a few therapy sessions, during which Simone learned her mother and Ricardo had lost a baby. They tried to conceive again, but Ricardo's drinking and substance abuse made it impossible. While the unfortunate circumstance was no excuse for the pain Angela had inflicted on Simone, they decided to leave the ordeal in the doctor's office, vowing to never reference it again.

Now thick as thieves, Angela and Simone seemed to have a bond as natural as any other mother and daughter. But the closer they became, the more Ricardo drank and smoked. Reunited with Jack Daniels and marijuana, he had come full circle, the abusive drunk and addict that blacked Simone's eye nearly twenty years ago. Simone begged her mother to leave him, but Angela brushed it off, not wanting to believe that once again, Ricardo was an addict. Yet, when Ricardo backhanded Angela during one of his drunken stupors and broke her nose, no more persuasion was needed. With Jordan away at Berklee College of Music in Boston, Angela packed her things and moved into her room.

"Bed rest? This is news to me," Beatrice said. "Simone told me everything went well at the doctor's office on Thursday."

Angela added, "Well, she's dilated two centimeters already and she's not due for three more weeks."

"Oh my goodness! I forgot to tell y'all. Kevin and I took a pre-admission tour of the maternity ward yesterday. They have baby lojack," Simone shared.

"Yeah, that's been out for a while. Security in most maternity wards is crazy," Melanie said. She grabbed a kitchen chair from the table and carried it into the family room. "Simone, if you've already started dilating, maybe you should go put your feet up. We got this."

"Whatever. Y'all making a big to-do over nothing. I'm full term, so for real, I could push him out right here." Simone squatted, her hands curled into tight fists, she pretended to push.

"Simone!" Her three mothers yelled in unison while Simone shared a laugh with Jordan, Melanie and Lavon.

"We're being serious now. Stop being hard-headed and go sit down somewhere," Beatrice ordered.

Simone caught a whiff of her husband's cologne before he crept up behind her. His hands around her enormous belly, Kevin planted a tender kiss on the nape of her neck. "I know y'all not down here yelling at my baby." Simone smiled and rubbed her hands across her husband's.

"Your baby is in the way," Lavon said. She grabbed a pack of pastel colored balloons from one of the bags on the kitchen floor. Ripping the pack open, she dumped the balloons across the already cluttered table and picked up a pink one.

Kevin frowned. "What you doing with a pink balloon?" Shaking her head, Lavon rolled her eyes as she tossed the pink balloon on the table in exchange for a blue one. "Is this better, big poppa?" She lifted a brow and waited.

Kevin grinned. "That's perfect."

She tugged on the balloon a few times, then placed the latex to her lips ready to fill it with the air from her lungs. She blew, but the balloon was still too tight, locking her jaws as she tossed it to the floor. Her eyes crossed as she grabbed both sides of her face.

"Lord have mercy," Lavon mumbled through fish lips to Kevin and Simone's amusement. "Won't be no got damn balloons if I have to blow them up. Where is Kayla?"

Simone dabbed at the moisture in the corner of her eye from laughing. "I can smell the Carpet Fresh which means she used the entire bottle. She's upstairs vacuuming."

Lavon rose from the chair and yelled, "Kayla! Come here, poo. Let auntie vacuum and you blow these balloons up."

Beatrice leaned across the kitchen island, admiring her son. "You look nice, Kevin. Wherever you going, I hope you're taking your wife with you. She's in the way."

"Yeah, why don't y'all go out to breakfast or something?" Melanie suggested.

Simone turned around to admire her husband. She smiled in agreement with his mother. His outfit, dark denims and a button-up fresh out the cleaners, was simple yet crisp. His platinum diamond wedding ring and Gucci watch lent his normal, everyday duds a quiet, confident swag. Kevin met Simone's gaze and kissed her on the lips.

"You coming with me?" he asked.

"No, I need to stay and supervise these here ladies. There's no way things will be ready by three."

"Simone, it's just after ten o'clock. We got this," Beatrice told her. "Go 'head, Kevin. Get her out of here. Keep her out 'til three if you can."

"She can come with me, but I can't keep her out that long. I have to pick up my baby shower gift."

Riddled with excitement, Simone's grin lit up the room.

"You're buying me a present?" The twinkle in her eye thrilled Kevin's heart. He loved her dimpled smile.

"Of course I am. I gotta get Ed though. I need his help."

"Hmmm. Must be something big and heavy." She tugged on her husband's hand. "What is it? Just tell me, tell me, tell me!" she begged in fun.

Tickled by her enthusiasm, Kevin wasn't budging nor was he offering hints. "Nope. I have to go see my new P.O. first."

"That's today?"

"Yep. Have to be in Baltimore by 11:30."

Simone grabbed her purse from the back of the kitchen chair. "I'm going."

"You sure you feel up to it?" Kevin asked. "That's like what? A forty-five minute drive?"

"Yeah, without traffic," Angela shared. "Shouldn't be any this early on a Saturday, I don't think."

"Well, if she don't go, I'm going," Beatrice added. "You know, showing support is crucial. Did they ever say why you got transferred in the first place? And why the heck they have you driving way down Baltimore? I thought the parole office was in Temple Hills."

"This guy supposedly has two offices. On Saturdays, he takes appointments in Baltimore," Kevin said.

"Why the transfer though?" Beatrice asked.

Kevin shrugged. "I'm not really worried about that. By the time it's said and done, I'll probably have had ten different parole officers."

"Well, I'm going," Simone said. "Then I'll get to peek at my present."

"No, you won't." Kevin grabbed their jackets from the coat closet. "I'm bringing you back as soon as we're done. Grab some more sauce packs. You only have a few left in the truck."

Chapter Four

Kevin followed the directions from the navigation system of his burnt orange Hummer. Tenderly, he caressed Simone's hand in his, rubbing her fingers with his thumb. Reclined in the passenger's seat with a bed pillow at the small of her back, Simone rode in silence, daydreaming out the window. Every so often, Kevin freed her hand so she could rip open another sauce packet. He watched Simone devour what had to have been her fourth packet in less than thirty minutes.

"I still can't believe you crave them things."

"I know. Crazy, right?" She rubbed her belly and pulled the packet from her mouth. "Whew."

"What's wrong? You okay?"

"Yeah, but he's running out of room." She grabbed Kevin's hand and guided it to the knot in her stomach. "Feel right here."

"What's that?"

"I don't know. Could be his elbow, his foot, anything."

"Naw, probably his fist. He trying to dap his daddy up."

Removing his hand from Simone's stomach, Kevin pulled the most recent sonogram picture from the inside pocket of his leather jacket. He kissed the transparent film.

"Man, I can't wait." Tickled like a child on Christmas, Kevin eased the image back inside his pocket. "How you feeling though? You okay? You've been kind of quiet. I'm sure everything will be done by three."

"I'm not really thinking about the shower. Just wished…. you know."

Kevin sensed Simone was on the verge of one of her moments. The moments when she realized their son would never know her father.

"You know your dad is still watching over you," Kevin said as he squeezed her hand gently. "We'll make sure the baby knows him. I still say we name him Thomas Kevin."

"I know, baby and thank you for that. I just couldn't call him, Thomas. That would kill me. Now, Kevin Thomas I can do."

Kevin nodded his head approvingly. "Kevin Thomas Kennard."

Simone had been an emotional roller coaster since her second trimester. She cried at the blink of an eye, got an attitude over the silliest of things and then, like now, there were her bouts of depression. The moments when she realized Lil' Kevin would never know his grandfather. Yet, despite the twists and loops of the emotional rollercoaster, Kevin held onto Simone's hand the entire ride. He loved her more than life itself. And now inside of her, was the off spring of such an intoxicating love.

Kevin needed to get Simone to focus on something else. "Hey, you know this is the big week, right? They're supposed to play the song this week."

"You spoke with Don?"

"Not since—" Kevin caught himself. He'd seen Don a week ago but Simone wasn't to know anything of the rendezvous. "Dag, when was the last time? But I know it's this week. I put a reminder in my phone."

"Go head, Mr. Kennard." Simone smiled. "I'm so proud of you."

Kevin squeezed her hand. "Couldn't have done it without my amazing wife. You were the motivation behind that song, baby."

"I'm surprised a new artist is releasing a ballad first."

"They felt the love, baby. They felt the love."

Led by the robotic voice, Kevin frowned as the navigation system directed his final turn into a residential apartment complex. Puzzled, he released Simone's hand and picked up the business card from the cup holder.

"Damn, how he get an office over here?" he wondered.

Oblivious to April's morning chill and the two cars attempting to get around them, a handful of school-aged kids tossed a football back and forth in the middle of the street. Kevin made his way past them and pulled into a parking space.

Simone's brows grew together as she looked around. "Yeah, this can't be right."

Kevin's eyes darted from the card to the dingy white address stamped across the torn canopy. He sighed and turned off the ignition.

"No apartment number but this is the right address. This is going to be interesting."

"Rashad!" A little girl no more than four hollered from the balcony of a neighboring building, dressed in a pair of mismatched, high-water pajamas. "Ma said get your butt in this house."

"Close that damn door," a woman screamed after her.

Laughter echoed from the hallway of the parole officer's building. Three young men, each appeared to be in their early twenties, lolly-gagged on the steps. Visions from Kevin's past waltzed about in his mind as he eyed the group through the glass door. Twenty-five years ago, that was him, his God-brother Fat Ed and his late, fake friend James, hanging out in buildings because there was nothing else to do but dry hump girls. Boredom had been the threshold to their trouble.

Silence fell upon the trio as Kevin and Simone entered, bringing the nippy temperatures inside the building that reeked of bleach.

"Dang. Ain't it supposed to be warm in April?" one of the teens asked. He blew in his fists and stood up while his friends remained seated on the steps. "Get up, dummies. Move out the way."

Impressed by the boy's manners and leadership, Kevin smiled as the two other boys stood.

A door slammed from above. Footsteps galloped down the stairs. A deep, raspy voice perfect for radio bounced from the cinder blocks.

"Man, I hate McPherson's fat ass."

Kevin studied the young man as he joined his friends. There was something special about his voice. Yet the sternness tattooed on his face, the dusty dreads, and the pants sagging from his butt told a different story; one far too common among young black men. Most would assume he was the bad-ass of the foursome. But Kevin sensed something else.

"What, he violated you again?" one of his friends asked.

"Naw, but he going to. You know I don't have no paystub."

"Tell him you lost your job. He'll probably give you time to find another one. Hell, he did before," the well-mannered ring leader said.

"Whatever. He only gave me time then because shorty did that thang for me." he reminded with both brows raised. "I was gonna try and talk to him but his ass in a funk. He acting like an ol' bitch. He got an attitude 'bout something."

"Excuse me, main man. McPherson, the parole officer? His office is upstairs?" Kevin asked the presumed bad ass who glared at him through narrow eyes.

"Yeah, why?"

"I gotta go see him myself," Kevin replied, unfazed by his attitude.

"Well, for real, this whole building is his office," another volunteered. "Everybody in this building reports to him. That's why this mug smell like bleach. They piss in it on Friday, then bleach it down on Saturday."

"Oh, so this is like a half-way house or something?" Kevin asked.

"Yeah, that's exactly what it is, but only this building. What you gon' see McPherson for?" asked the well-mannered teen.

"He's my P.O."

"Pss," the bad-ass hissed as he gave Kevin a once-over.

"I wish I was joking. I did close to seventeen years. I just came home a few months ago."

"Damn, man," another said. "And you already balling with wheels like that? You must've had a secret stash somewhere, huh?"

"Oh no," Kevin replied quickly. "Lady Luck just granted me a break."

Kevin could tell by the looks on their faces that they weren't convinced. "Seriously, all jokes aside. I'm a songwriter. I've been producing a little music."

"What? You a producer?" the well-mannered teen asked with bright eyes and a mile-wide grin. "We a group. We sing."

The bad-ass sucked his teeth. "Man, whatever. Y'all niggas sing. I rap. Don't get that shit twisted."

Kevin nodded his approval. "So y'all a group? Okay."

The well-mannered teen extended his hand to Kevin. "Look man, I'm Ant."

"Ant? What? That's short for Anthony, Ant Eater, what?" Kevin joked as he shook his hand.

"No." Ant chuckled. "It's short for Anthony. But my friends and now my producer," he said, playfully punching Kevin in his bicep. "They all call me Ant." Beaming with excitement, he introduced his friends.

"This is Fly Tye, Ronnell and this fake wanna-be gangsta' is Smooth, as in Smooth Criminal."

"Fuck you, nigga," Smooth spat.

Ant shook his head. "You hear how smooth the foulness rolls off his tongue? That's why he's the rapper."

"My bad," Smooth mumbled more so to Simone. Looking at her, he did a double take. "Dag, you look familiar."

"I was just thinking the same thing about you," Simone responded.

"What's up, man? You trying to get at my wife?" Kevin asked then playfully tapped the teen on the shoulder.

The light joke softened Smooth's hardened expression. "Naw, but my real name is Daryl. My peeps call me DJ. These fools call me Smooth because I am." He smiled confidentially for the first time, displaying a perfect set of teeth.

"That's cool. That's cool." Kevin shook everyone's hands. "Smooth fits your voice, too. You sound like you should be on the radio or something. Look fellas," Kevin said with his hand at the small of Simone's back. "This is my beautiful wife, Simone, who I need to be getting upstairs so she can sit. As you can see, she's carrying our future superstar."

"Aww, that's what's up." Ant smiled.

"But hey, listen. If y'all still around when I come out, maybe y'all can do a lil' something for me. But if you gotta go," Kevin dug in his pocket and pulled Fat Ed's card from his wallet. "Take this. This here is my partner, Ed. He owns a big time studio over in P.G. County."

"This just gets sweeter and sweeter." Ant beamed. "That's where we live."

"That's what's up," Kevin replied. "He has some powerful connections. He helped some of the local big names get their start so call him up, make an appointment, and we'll go from there."

Beaming with excitement, they chanted "thank you" as Kevin and Simone headed up the steps.

*****

Springs from the cushion-less couch poked Kevin and Simone in their butts. Burnt coffee coupled with the stench of a sour refrigerator lingered in the air as they flipped through the outdated magazines spread across the wobbly coffee table of the living room turned reception area of Mr. McPherson's office.

The first few minutes of the wait, Smooth, Ant, and the rest of the group's practice in the hallway had provided a little entertainment. The group displayed some potential but Smooth's melodious flow seemed effortless, almost magical. Kevin didn't care for his cockiness, but his talent was something to consider. Just when Kevin's creative juices began to stir, Mr. McPherson's hoochified receptionist leaped from her squeaky chair and yelled out the front door, "Y'all shut the hell up and get off them damn steps!" Instantly, practice came to a halt.

Time ticked away and before long, an hour had passed. Smacking loudly on her gum, the receptionist sat at her oak desk positioned directly under the tarnished chandelier of the suppose-to-be dining room with a phone tucked between her shoulder and ear. Engulfed in her conversation and the computerized game of solitaire, she hadn't mumbled a single professional courtesy to either of them. Simone began to fidget around in the chair.

"Baby, you okay?"

"I can't get comfortable in this raggedy chair. It's killing my back but I'm okay." Kevin felt otherwise. He stood from the busted couch and beckoned the receptionist.

"Excuse me," he said.

The receptionist glared in response.

"My appointment was at 11:30. It's almost one. Should I reschedule? My wife's supposed to be on bed rest and—"

"Sir," the receptionist interrupted with a frown as if something stunk. "Mr. McPherson is gonna see you."

"Today?"

Annoyed, she rolled her eyes and mumbled to the caller, "Girl, hold on."

The receptionist dropped the receiver onto the shabby desk as she stood from the squeaky high back chair. She pulled her spandex pants from the crack of her behind, shaking her leg a little to rid a wedgie.

"You better not shake her hand," Simone joked as the receptionist disappeared down the hallway toward the back office.

Biting his lower lip, Kevin sighed heavily and resumed his position on the tattered couch. The broken springs welcomed his return with a poke.

"Shit," he huffed from the discomfort.

Minutes passed and Kevin's aggravation heightened.

"This is crazy. We're the only ones here. What are we waiting for?"

"Kennard!" A man's voice bellowed from the back room.

The apartment floors creaked with each imminent stomp. A floppy-shaped white man with a limp came into view. His hunter green high water corduroys showed off dingy white socks that were slouched around his ankles and covered in specks of lint. He cleared his throat and stood before Kevin and Simone.

"Let me explain some things to you. First off, I'm not going to stop what I'm doing because you walked into my office. Sometimes you're gonna have to wait, okay?"

The receptionist chuckled in victory. Rolling her eyes, she slithered back down to her seat and picked up the phone to resume her conversation despite the presence of her boss.

"We're sorry, Mr. McPherson." Simone struggled to stand. "My husband's worried about me because—"

"Miss." He closed his eyes and held up his hand to silence Simone. "Now," he began as he opened his eyes and stared past Kevin and Simone. "I don't know how much professional business the two of you conduct, but sometimes things happen."

McPherson's rudeness pissed Kevin off. "Hold up, Mr. McPherson. My wife was trying to explain..."

"Kennard, Kennard, Kennard." McPherson sighed impatiently. "I don't know how you and your last parole officer did things but I'm sure I run things a little differently. The first thing you need to understand is I don't cater to ex-cons. I'm not trying to be rude on purpose but you have to understand, you're in my office because you broke the law. So don't come in here expecting any favors or special treatment. Now, if you like, you may come back to my office."

McPherson did an about-face and headed towards the back of the apartment where his private office was apparently located, leaving Kevin and Simone to ponder his blatant disrespect.

"This rude-ass wobbly muthafucka gon' make me catch another charge. How this dirty, fat, bitch-ass cracker..."

"Kevin! Come on, calm down. He's not worth catching a charge. Ignore him."

"Ignore him? Simone, that bitch muthafucka was flat-out rude for no reason. You hear him calling me *Kennard*?" Kevin mimicked McPherson's voice. "That's some prison shit."

"You know you're not in prison. You're a happily married, successful songwriter with a baby boy on the way. That's what you focus on, not him and his dumbness. Let's go back to his office, answer his questions and go home. Besides," she kissed Kevin on his lips, "if you catch another charge, I won't get my present."

Kevin's pout disappeared. "Funny. So that's all you worried about?"

"Umm, oh yeah, and the midnight feedings. I told you I'm not getting up every two hours." She smiled.

"Okay, look. You know how I am when it comes to you so why don't you do me a favor and wait out here."

Simone rolled her eyes. "I'm serious, Simone. I'm not going to let him disrespect you."

"Kevin, please. I'm not thinking about him. I've had clients worse than his fat ass. So c'mon. Let's just go back to his shabby-ass office, listen to what he has to say, and go home. Okay?"

"Yeah, alright." He mumbled. His voice riddled with doubt.

McPherson gestured toward the two chairs in front of his desk. The furnishings in his office were as tatty as the rest of the place.

"Have a seat," he offered uninvitingly. "Kennard."

Kevin glanced at his wife. She met his gaze with a reassuring smile as they took their seats.

"How long have you been home?"

"Almost six months."

McPherson's eyes shot up from the manila folder and fired in on his target - Simone's belly. "You're kidding me, right?"

Simone's lips parted in shock. Kevin addressed his disrespectful comment before she could. "No, Mr. McPherson. I'm not kidding you. What does that have to do with the terms of my parole?"

McPherson reared back in his chair. With a hunch of his shoulder, he redirected his attention back to the folder. "Where are you employed?"

Slouched in the chair, Kevin folded his arms and glared at McPherson. "I'm self-employed. I'm a songwriter. Look in the file. I'm sure everything's there," he added with bitterness.

Seated next to him, Simone bumped him with her knee as McPherson flipped through the file.

"A songwriter, huh? Interesting. Now where's the real job?"

Kevin couldn't help the short sarcastic chuckle. "That is my *real* job. I sold ten songs right before I was released. I gave my last P.O. a copy of the contract. I'm sure if you flip through my file you'll see it."

"There's an extra copy in your briefcase," Simone whispered to Kevin.

"Hand me what you have." Mr. McPherson ordered with his hand outstretched.

Kevin retrieved the file and bypassed McPherson's chubby hand, sliding the file across the desk.

"That's the sales agreement, the deposit slip, and the A & R's contact information."

"A & R?"

"Yes. Don Brandon. He's like a talent scout for the record label. He liked my songs and the label he works for bought them for one of their artists."

McPherson fished around inside his desk for a calculator. His pinkish face turned a shade darker as he tallied up the money Kevin earned from selling his music.

"You mean to tell me you made all this selling music?"

Kevin enjoyed the cloud of envy that hovered around McPherson. Part of him was tempted to share the advance he'd received nearly a week ago. Two of the songs he'd sold to Don Brandon's label were being released as singles, which sparked more interest in Kevin's catalog. But he couldn't mention the money. Not in front of Simone who knew nothing about it.

"Okay. A bank statement.Where's your bank statement?" McPherson asked.

"My bank statement?" Kevin turned to Simone, who appeared just as confused by the awkward request.

"Yes, your bank statements."

Puzzled, Simone said, "I didn't know we needed them. I mean, what purpose would they serve any way? We've never provided them before."

"Kennard, how do I know you have money left? How do I know you're not out there selling drugs because you spent the money on strippers, liquor, drugs and wild parties like every other con trying to catch up on life?"

The fact was, the majority of the money Kevin had earned was gone, spent on Simone's monster engagement ring, the proposal at the arena, treating their family and friends to the lavish wedding in St. Lucia, Kevin's Hummer, and months of living without worry despite the deflate in the real estate market. They weren't broke, but their account wouldn't reflect anything close to six figures.

Simone shook her head. "Mr. McPherson, are you always this pleasant?"

"Look, it's my job to make sure your husband's abiding by the law. Therefore," he said, redirecting his attention to Kevin, "you need to show me proof that at least half of the money is still in the bank or you need to get a real job."

"So the contract's not good enough? That's not proof that my song writing is a real job?"

"The paperwork shows that you came into some money but it doesn't show any consistency with income. So I need statements or pay stubs from a real job. And unfortunately, Kennard, if I don't have it within thirty days, you'll be in violation of your parole. Then you know what that means, right?" Without waiting for a response, McPherson said, "It's back to prison."

Simone's patience had run its course. "I thought one of your roles as a parole officer was to help the parolees."

"No, ma'am." McPherson replied as he made notes in Kevin's file. "My role is to make sure he's not out there violating the terms of his release or breaking the law. By no means am I supposed to take him by the hand and babysit him. Lack of employment or money is often what triggers the behavior that made them convicts in the first place. With that being said," McPherson slammed the file closed. "I need a pay stub or proof that the money's there."

Shit, Kevin thought as Simone fished around in her purse. With the baby coming, he had no plans on getting a job outside of the house. He missed out on the early joys of fatherhood with Jordan and didn't want to be an absentee father ever again. Besides, his song writing career seemed more promising than ever. Once Don returned from Brazil, he promised Kevin he'd work on a deal that would guarantee him a handsome, steady income as writer with the label. But until the deal was made, he needed to produce a stub or he'd have to disclose the money he had hidden in Fat Ed's account.

Simone slapped her business card on the desk. "He'll be employed within twenty-four hours."

"Baby, what are you–?" Simone's glare dared Kevin to continue.

McPherson picked up the card, propped his elbow on the desk and read aloud. "Simone Woodard. Woodard Real Estate."

"Yes. My partners and I were in the process of hiring somebody else and as far as I'm concerned, we just did. Don't worry. It's legit. I'll have his new hire documents faxed to you first thing Monday morning and he'll have a pay stub in two weeks."

"You can keep the documents, ma'am. I only need a stub."

Simone forced a smile. "Not a problem. You'll have a stub. Anything else or are we done?"

"No, I guess that's everything for now. I will need to pop by your home. I'm sure you know that's standard procedure."

"That's not a problem." Simone answered as she wiggled to the edge of her seat. Kevin stood to help her. "Come for lunch."

"Keep the lunch, ma'am. But Kennard, I will need to see you back here in two weeks."

"Two weeks?" Kevin replied.

"Two weeks with a stub. You can make an appointment with the receptionist up front or give us a call sometime during the week."

Kevin and Simone bypassed the receptionist's desk and headed straight for the door. Smooth was walking in as they were leaving.

"Hey, I gotta holla at McPherson but if you can hang around—"

"Naw, man. I'm not gonna be able to listen to y'all today. I gotta get my baby home. But call my partner so we can get y'all up in the studio," Kevin said. "Just tell him I told you to call and he'll hook something up. I'll give him a heads up, too. You got a mean flow."

The compliment was music to Smooth's ears. "So make sure you call."

"A'ight man," Smooth replied with a nod of his head. "We'll call him today."

*****

McPherson pulled his cell from his hip, scanned through his list of contacts, and placed his call.

"Hey," he said as he stood in the window, watching Kevin help Simone climb inside the truck. "This is not gonna be a piece of cake like you thought. I tried ruffling his feathers a bit. I made him wait over an hour, I told him I couldn't accept his contract as proof of employment, I asked for bank statements, I mean, I did everything. He got a little heated but that's when she stepped in. She has his back for sure."

"We have a deal," the caller replied.

"Hey, I'm not giving up. It's just gonna take me a little longer to find a reason to violate him is all I'm saying. Just give me a little longer and he'll be back in the slammer."

McPherson flipped his cell closed and returned to his desk. He jumped when he realized he wasn't alone.

"What are you doing in my office?" he barked, unsure of how much Smooth had heard.

"I came to talk to you. I lost my job, so I don't have a stub." Smooth replied. "And the girl from the last time not talking to me no more. So, I can't hook —"

"Mr. Harris!" McPherson bellowed, cutting him off. "You're in violation of your parole and you know what that means."

"Hold up! Let me call around. I can find another lil' —"

"Mr. Harris," He interrupted again. "You have twenty-four hours to turn yourself in; otherwise," he said as he shuffled through the papers on his desk. "You'll be a wanted fugitive."

McPherson watched as Smooth stormed from his office, mumbling unpleasantries under his breath. He pulled his cell from his hip again and redialed the last number.

"Yeah, some knucklehead overheard part of our conversation. He knows some things about me and well, you know."

"Can he prove it? Did he see you in the act?"

"No, never."

"Then he's not your problem, but I am. So get your focus straight," the caller advised and hung up.

Chapter Five

"Wow, your new bod has made you popular already." Dr. Gustafuson chuckled. "You look like a celebrity hiding from the paparazzi in those dark shades."

"No, it's not that," Felicia mumbled. "I don't feel good. That's why I canceled my appointment yesterday."

"I'm sorry to hear that. You're not having complications are you?"

"No, no complications. Just allergies and a little bad news."

Seated on a small stool in an examination room of his private practice, Dr. Gustafuson whistled along with the music playing throughout the office surround sound system as he waited for Felicia to peel herself from the girdle. She twisted her hips and grunted with each tug until she'd finally worked the garment passed her thighs.

"Today's my last day in this monkey suit, right?" she inquired, looking at him through her dark shades. "This itchy ass thing been pinching the hell outta me."

The wheels squeaked as Dr. Gustafuson slid across the floor on the stool. "Let me take a look. Hopefully today will be your lucky day."

Applying light pressure to Felicia's stomach, Dr. Gustafuson examined the scar from the tummy tuck and the small incisions scattered about her hips and thighs from liposuction.

"Both your stomach and the scar from the abdominoplasty appear to be healing well as are the scars from the liposuction. Your breasts," he said as he squeezed them gently, "are still a bit firm, which isn't uncommon. Just continue to massage them in the circular motion we showed you during your last visit. Soon the implants will feel natural. As far as getting out of the girdle, when was your surgery?" He reached for her file and shuffled through her medical records.

Felicia placed a hand on her hip. "You ain't gotta check, Dr. G. It's already been six long painful ass weeks, and you said that's all the recuperating time I needed."

Dr. Gustafuson pulled an expensive looking pen from the pocket of his lab coat and scribbled notes. "Well, you don't have to wear the girdle every day, Miss Payne. However, I would recommend wearing it while you sleep, at least for the next two weeks. Otherwise, your goal has been accomplished. You look like a new woman. Your fiancé's in for quite a surprise." Dr. Gustafuson's narrow pink lips curled into a smile as he closed the file. "When's he coming home?"

"I don't know. It was supposed to have been January," Felicia replied spiritlessly.

"Wow, that's less than a year away. You should be completely healed by then."

"Yeah, how 'bout that," she mumbled more so to herself.

"Boy, I tell you, I can remember my time in the military as if it was yesterday. The Air Force did everything in their power to get me to re-enlist. Twenty five years was enough. How long has your fiancé been in?"

"Sixteen years."

"What branch?"

"Umm… the Coast Guard."

"Ah." Dr. Gustafson approved with a nod. "Where's he stationed?"

Fuck, Dr. G. Why you asking me all these got-damn questions? Felicia thought to herself. *Shit, I don't know.*

"He over in that mess."

"Which mess? They're a bunch of them."

"I don't know. Over there with them crazy-ass suicide bombers, I guess."

Felicia read the bewildered expression on Dr. Gustafson's face and realized she probably sounded ignorant. But she didn't care. She reached for the girdle. "Look, I gotta go, Dr. G. Are we done?"

He rose from the stool. "My apologies, Miss Payne. I forgot you weren't feeling well."

"It's cool, Dr. G. Thanks for everything."

"No, thank you, Miss Payne." He headed to the door. "And remember, lipo doesn't come with a free pass to the buffet. I did my part, and you'll have to do yours."

Felicia sucked her teeth. "I don't eat at buffets, Dr. G."

"You know what I mean, Miss Payne. Congratulations in advance on the nuptials."

Before the door could close, Felicia headed to the bio-hazard container, stomped on the foot pedal, and tossed the skin tight girdle inside.

"Sleep in this thing, my ass. I wish I would wear this itchy muthafucka again."

*****

The nippy breeze of April swayed the trees from side to side. Draped in a cashmere wrap, Felicia headed to her Range Rover unfazed by the chill. Her mind was too busy calculating the thousands of dollars she'd drained from her savings to buy the house and the thousands she'd accumulated in debt changing her lifestyle just to impress Kevin. For years, she'd collected the fast money. She transported and stashed drugs for the neighborhood dealers, pimping her little ring of escorts and turning tricks — and for what?

The truth of the matter was she hadn't heard a peep from Kevin or his mother, Beatrice, in sometime. But it was cool. Kevin had been up front and shared that the few visits and handful of calls he was allotted were now reserved for Jordan, the daughter he'd never had the pleasure of knowing due in part to his incarceration. Felicia knew that meant Kevin was probably spending time with Simone, Jordan's mother, but instead of allowing the what-ifs of the family gatherings to drive her insane, she decided to devote her time and energy into herself. Besides, as long as he was behind bars, his love remained untouchable, reserved in layaway just for her.

While Kevin played daddy, Felicia went on a mission. Her goal: to secure her place as Mrs. Kevin Kennard by becoming the baddest bitch he had ever laid eyes on. To stay motivated, she bought a cheap little diamond ring and told everyone who inquired that Kevin had purchased the token of love from the prison commissary. The lies didn't stop there. As far as anyone knew, Kevin still called and she still visited every chance she got. And in between those chats and visits, she prepared a life for the two of them.

Gone was the rinky-dink, roach-infested apartment in Capital Heights. Home was now a pricey 4,000-square-foot, four-level townhouse in the heart of Annapolis, equipped with a two-car garage in a ritzy gated community. If the upscale neighborhood far from the hood didn't impress Kevin, then Touchsations, the luxurious day spa she opened in a strip mall off Crain Highway would surely do the trick.

A few weeks after she'd purchased the townhouse, Felicia racked her brain trying to think of the right business venture for her and her girls. On more than one visit, Kevin had made his plans clear. He wanted no parts of anything illegal ever again. But tricking and managing dancers was all Felicia knew. As she and Sanora sat unpacking boxes, it had hit Felicia the second she blew the dust from Sanora's Master of Science in Nursing Degree. A degree Sanora had tossed on life's back burner as she hustled drugs and a six-figure income from strip clubs.

For days, the idea simmered. What the hell did she know about a spa? Even with Sanora's degree, there were so many things to consider. But when a prime location fell in her lap, Felicia tossed caution to the wind. A few doors down from the hottest rim shop in the Washington D.C. metropolitan area, a place where all the true ballers gathered to trick out their vehicles, was an elaborate store front for lease.

Man, fuck a spa, Felicia thought. *This could be my brothel. A fake-me-out bunny ranch disguised as a spa.*

The mortgage banker who'd handled her loan for the house surprised her when he shared her credit history was one of the best he'd seen. Absent of any credit card debt, Felicia had financed a number of vehicles for herself and a drug boy or two. Every vehicle had been paid off with a perfect payment history. She called her mortgage banker again, to inquire about a business loan. He referred her to an associate and seventy-two hours later, she had a check. Touchsations Day Spa opened a month later.

Word spread fast. The spa was an overnight success due in part to its location. In a month's time, sex, illegal prescriptions written from the stroke of Sanora's pen, and a legitimate massage or two brought in more money than Felicia and Sanora could've imagined. The spa was a gold mine. But then, out of the blue, Sanora just up and left. Six months later, she had yet to return.

Business was fine at first but Felicia quickly felt the pinch from Sanora's absence. Rent, the business loan, the girls' pay – there were so many expenses. She needed Sanora back; the lack of prescriptions could eventually become the spa's demise.

Despite the strain in her finances, Felicia went ahead with her final mission — her body —financed through her new American Express. An impressive home in a ritzy community, a successful legitimate business and the best body money could buy — everything in Felicia's life was where she wanted it to be. Yet the picture in *Jet* said it had all been done in vain.

After driving forty-five minutes, Felicia sat at a traffic light, waiting to turn into her gated community. Tucked in the first row of townhouses visible from the main road, she glanced toward her house and noticed what appeared to be a handful of her uppity neighbors gathered a few feet from her house.

"Aww, what the fuck," she mumbled as she turned into her community.

From the corner of her eye, she noticed the guard nod hello but she rolled her eyes. She hated the way he grinned in the white peoples' faces like an old Uncle Tom. Besides, she needed to find out what she'd done to become the topic of discussion amongst her neighbors once again.

Nasty grams from the homeowner association flooded Felicia's mailbox on a regular. Her screen door hung from the hinges, a huge dent from a night of driving drunk decorated her garage door, and despite the three warnings she'd received, a floral-printed bed sheet still swayed from her living room windows. Today's issue: her trash. The trash she sat out two days prior to the scheduled pick up had blown up and down the street.

"Fuck y'all and that damn trash," Felicia mumbled as she pressed the remote, opening the garage.

Despite the damage, the door still functioned which in Felicia's eyes lessened the importance of getting it fixed. Before turning into her driveway, she slowed and glared in her neighbors' direction. The daggers she shot dared them to utter a sound, which they never did. They communicated with Felicia through their nasty grams.

Parked in her driveway, she climbed from her truck. Without an apology or backward glance, she strolled through the garage she used for storage. Her truck would probably fit, but between the deep freezer, storage boxes, and the smelly bags of trash that often lingered in the hot, closed in garage for days, she figured the driveway was best.

Through the garage, she entered her basement. Silence and the scent of filth greeted her as she walked up the steps. Living alone had never been the plan. At first, she despised Sanora and her daughter, Mercedes, for leaving her but she quickly forgave them when she realized, the love of her life would be home soon. Surely, he'd be staying with her. With Sanora and Mercedes both gone, Felicia and Kevin could have free roam of the house, christening each room with their lovemaking. What a fool she'd been to have thought such a thing.

With the death of her fantasy, she longed for Sanora's loud music or to smell the incense Mercedes would light in an attempt to camouflage the undeniable aroma of weed. Once upon a time, the house had been filled with life. Now, it was simply Felicia and four walls of loneliness.

Up the steps, Felicia's eyes drifted to the room that up until three months ago belonged to her daughter. Felicia turned a blind eye to the weed smoking and even the condom wrappers she found in Mercedes' room on several occasions. Hell, she was a teenager, and teenagers experimented with marijuana and sex. But Felicia caught a case when she discovered her daughter was turning tricks.

Two weeks after opening the spa, Felicia and Sanora had decided to throw a Client Appreciation Day. White balloons filled with helium floated throughout the spa, servers dressed in tuxedos ensured the crystal flutes stayed topped with Cristal, and the baddest DJ had been hired to keep the party going in the reception area where a handful of the girls would perform. For the clients who desired a more risqué celebration, the rooms were open and ready to house whatever they desired. But the day of the celebration, Sanora received an emergency phone call from her mother who had been diagnosed with cancer. Immediately, Sanora gathered a few of her things and high-tailed it to Richmond, Virginia. Pissed, Felicia needed air and decided to take out the trash.

The dumpster directly behind the parlor overflowed with boxes and garbage from a shipment sent to one of the spa's commercial neighbors. The landlord had been penalizing the retailers of the strip mall with hefty fees if trash from their establishment littered the alley. The last thing Felicia intended to do was waste a dime of her money on fines. Forced to carry the trash to another dumpster, she spotted an old champagne-colored Buick Regal parked in the alley. As she got closer, she noticed a head bobbing up and down in the front seat. Immediately, she assumed one of her girls was trying to get over. She dropped the trash, stormed over to the car, and pounded on the hood.

The white man opened his eyes and said, "Who the fuck is pounding on my car?"

Mercedes sprung up from his lap. "Oh God," she cried, wiping her mouth with the back of her hand. "It's my mom."

Glass shattered as the driver side window came crashing in. Filled with the devil, Felicia snatched open the door and dragged the man from the driver's seat with his pants still gathered around his ankles. Unable to secure his balance or defend himself, he tried to block Felicia's monstrous blows to his head and face with his arms but fell to the asphalt where she stomped and kicked the part of him he'd stuffed in Mercedes mouth. Felicia had no idea who called the police, but they saved the man's life. Felicia celebrated Client Appreciation Day locked up in the county jail. Lucky for her, attempted murder had been thrown out in exchange for assault and two years' probation. The white man got off scot-free because at eighteen, Mercedes was a consenting adult.

Two days after her release, Felicia purchased a one-way ticket to

Mobile, Alabama and sent her naïve daughter to live with her grand-parents in the country. *Who in their right mind would give head in a car around the corner from their mother's business? she thought.*

Screw the county police. In Felicia's eyes, the white man was a rapist and a pedophile. Determined to file some kind of charge against him, Felicia tracked down good ol' FBI Agent Andre Perkins. She hadn't seen Andre since their run in at the post office when he spotted the letter she'd planned to mail to inmate Kevin Kennard.

Andre had proven to be of little help with her daughter's case. She hadn't heard a peep from him since she'd called him about the ordeal. Then she wondered, why Andre hadn't told her Kevin was home. Like a ton of bricks, it hit her. The day she called Andre, he had asked her if she'd seen her boy.

I thought he meant had I been to the jail. Damn, he probably thought I knew Kevin was home, she thought as she continued up the last few steps until she stood before the pigsty that was her bedroom.

Her wrap and purse thrown on top of her bed, Felicia kicked off her UGG outdoor slippers and headed for the bathroom. She had to get out of the house before she went crazy.

Buttons ricocheted across the bathroom as Felicia ripped open the jean dress she'd worn over top of the body girdle she left at the doctor's office. She caught a glimpse of herself in the mirror. The reflection warranted a smile but when she realized it had all been done in vain, her heart ached.

Months ago, she called Beatrice's cell but the number had been disconnected. She contemplated going by her home but wanted to wait until after her surgery. Now she realized the entire Kennard clan had played her for a fool.

Your precious daughter-in-law probably sold you a house, huh?

The thought of leaving the house to flaunt her new body lessened with each depressing minute. Felicia headed to her bed, folded back the covers and climbed in. She was ready to spend the rest of the weekend trapped in the funk of her room, plotting revenge.

"He didn't even have the fucking decency to call and just say, 'Hey bitch, I'm home.'"

She flipped back the top of the decorative knick-knack nestled on her nightstand and pulled out the ticket to peace. She lit the joint, pulled back a long drag, and held it in before sending a faint cloud of smoke through her nostrils.

"The ungrateful bastard didn't say shit."

Her eyes swelled with tears as she fished around the rubbish on her bed for the remote control. She drew another hit from the joint. Soon peace would befriend her and drain away her sadness. There was no time for a pity party. Felicia needed a clear head.

Bed pillows propped behind her back, she surfed the channels and found a marathon of motivation. Back-to-back episodes of *Snapped*, a documentary series chronicling the crimes of women gone mad with rage. Comfy and cozy, she reached in the top drawer of her nightstand, grabbed a rat-tail comb, and began taking out her braids.

"Yeah, I need a crazy white bitch to give me some ideas, 'cause I swear, if it's the last thing I do, I'm gon' get these muthafuckas."

Chapter Six

H and in hand, Kevin and Simone rode home from McPherson's office in silence. Kevin suspected Simone's mind flitted back and forth between the baby shower and Mr. McPherson's rudeness, while his mind marveled over the amazing woman he'd married. What had he done to deserve such an angel? She had been his heaven on earth the moment she graced his life with her presence. Faithfully, she stood in his corner, supporting and encouraging his goals and dreams while expecting nothing in return.

A successful business-woman, a prison fling wasn't on Simone's agenda. Her goal was simply to unite Jordan with the father she'd never known. Unlike the other women in Kevin's past, Simone's intentions were pure and unselfish. Those attributes, coupled with her beauty, made him fall in love with her more and more every day — just as he had done when they were teenagers.

Kevin and Simone pulled into the garage at 2:30 p.m., giving Simone just enough time to transform into the belle of the ball. Entering the house, they froze. The chaos they'd left hours ago had been transformed into a baby shower. Teary eyed, Simone stood speechless. Her family had out-done themselves without her supervision.

Silvery streamers dangled from the kitchen and family room ceilings. Balloons were scattered about the foyer, living room, dining room, family room, and kitchen. Large pastel-colored balloon bouquets graced nearly every corner. The tables were dressed, the food was ready, and the place was simply amazing. A white wicker basket sat in the middle of the table reserved for party favors. Pacifier, bottle, breast pump, and an array of other baby items were written on nametags.

"What are these for?" Kevin asked.

"Name tags," his mother replied.

Simone explained the game. "Every guest gets a nametag and a baby blue clothes pin. We have to call them by whatever's on the nametag. If we mess up and call them by their real name, they take our clothespin."

"Oh, so whoever has the most clothes pins at the end wins?"

"Yep."

"You notice we don't have cups, right?" Angela asked. Kevin looked around. There was a punch bowl but no cups like his mother-in-law said. "We're using baby bottles for cups."

Kevin couldn't help but laugh.

"You playing the games, Kevin?" his mother asked.

He glanced at his watch. "I still have to scoop up Ed and go pick up my baby's gift."

Simone said, "Kevin, you know technically you don't have to get me a gift. I mean, the shower is for our baby. The gifts are for him."

"This gift will be for him, too."

"But why do you need Ed?" Simone probed. "We pretty much have the big stuff. I mean..."

"You being nosey and I gotta go. Hopefully, I'll make it back. What time is it over?"

"Invitation said three to six," Beatrice replied. "So you better get to getting."

"Yeah, I wanna see y'all play some of these games." Kevin grabbed Simone by the hand and led her into the living room.

"What's wrong?" Simone asked.

Kevin pulled her into his embrace and they shared their first real kiss of the day.

"Don't start no stuff, won't be no stuff," Simone joked.

But Kevin didn't share in the amusement. Instead, he cupped Simone's face in his hands and said, "I love you and I'm about to show you how much." He kissed her on the forehead and headed out, allowing his words to linger.

Chapter Seven

Nothing could erase the lotto grin plastered on Kevin's face as he maneuvered through the weekend traffic. To help celebrate the moment, he shuffled through the tunes on his iPod in search of a song that would mirror that joy.

There it is, he thought to himself. He turned up the volume, and cleared his throat, preparing to sing along.

"Come on Kevin, man, really?" Fat Ed cried from the passenger seat as the introduction to Donny Hathaway's "This Christmas" blasted through the speakers. Fat Ed reached over and powered the stereo off.

Kevin laughed. "Just one time, Ed, I promise. I know it ain't Christmas yet but that's what it feels like."

Kevin powered the system back on and started the song over. He used the control on his steering wheel to increase the volume.

"Oh my goodness," Fat Ed mumbled. He rested his head on the window as Kevin began to sing.

"I'm sorry, man but I can't wait to see my baby's face tomorrow."

Kevin had scooped up Fat Ed and headed straight to the bank to make the withdrawal to pay for Simone's gift.

"You want the whole thing?" Fat Ed asked as they stood in line inside the bank.

"Yeah. Put it in two separate cashier's checks. One made out to the dealer, the other made out to the wife."

"Can I help you?" the teller said through the glass.

Fat Ed stepped up to the window. "How you doing? I need three cashier's checks."

Kevin corrected him. "No, just two."

"I have to get something for someone else."

The teller smiled. "Three cashier's checks?"

"Yes."

"Okay, Mr. Jones. I'll need you to write out the payee information." The teller passed Fat Ed a thin stack of post-it notes.

"What's the other check for?" Kevin asked as he stood off to the side watching Fat Ed scribble Simone's name.

"It's for none-ya," Fat Ed joked. He peeled off the first post it note and passed it back to the teller. "That's for the first two checks."

"Okay. And the third?"

"Damn," Fat Ed mumbled to himself as he wrote the dollar amount for the withdraw on the post-it. "I can't remember the chick's last name."

"I bet you know her stripper name." Kevin chuckled.

The receptionist smiled.

"Don't pay that unemployed comedian no mind," Fat Ed told the teller as he placed the remaining post-its through the opening. "Let me just get that in cash." Tapping his fingers on the counter, he said, "Now she'll know I'm serious."

"How you serious about a chick and you don't even know her last name?" Kevin shook his head. "Then you're giving her ten grand? What the hell is up with you?"

"Long story, man. Long story."

Kevin lifted a brow, taken aback by the generic response. Their entire life, they'd always shared everything.

Four hours later, Kevin couldn't stop grinning. A bit disappointed that he couldn't afford the Mercedes SL 65 AMG, the white convertible 550 was still a force to be reckoned with. Since the deal had been made late in the day, the car couldn't be delivered that night. Shiny as a new copper penny, the manager promised to give the Mercedes a thorough spit-shining and deliver the gem bright and early the next morning, big bow and all.

Man, I can't wait to see your face tomorrow morning, Kevin thought to himself, so proud of the purchase.

Over and over again, he pictured Simone sitting on the couch, her long silky tresses swept into a messy up-do. First, she'd unwrap the brown Gucci box that contained the expensive diaper bag she had "oohed and ahhed" over.

"Get it." Kevin had suggested.

"It's nice but we're not Will and Jada. I'll buy Gucci purses and brief-cases because I can carry them for years, but a diaper bag?"

Kevin chuckled as he imagined her fussing, but the keys to her convertible Mercedes would be buried deep inside the bag in the brown tissue paper.

"What you over there giggling about?" asked Fat Ed.

"I'm just picturing my baby's face."

"Yeah, I thought you out-did yourself with that crazy ass ring but that car is vicious, man. What you gonna get her for Christmas? A new house?"

"Damn, that would be the bomb, too." Fat Ed shook his head and continued to gaze out the window.

A white Honda Odyssey pulled up alongside of Kevin as he proceeded down the three lane highway in route to Ed's house. The yellow rectangular "Baby on Board" sign dangling in the back window caught Kevin's eye.

"Yes indeed." Kevin reached inside his jacket and pulled out the sonogram picture.

"Hey, did I ever show you this?" Kevin extended the envelope to Fat Ed.

Fat Ed removed the image from the envelope and glanced at the picture.

"The doctor said your God-son could be here any day. Simone's already dilated and everything."

"Oh yeah?" Fat Ed offered seemingly uninterested. He placed the picture back in the envelope, passed it back to Kevin, and resumed gazing out the window. His lack of enthusiasm shocked Kevin.

"Is that all you have to say?" Kevin questioned as he returned the envelope to his jacket. "Damn, I thought you'd be a little more excited than that."

A week after the wedding, Kevin and Simone announced they were expecting. Fat Ed rejoiced right along with them, immediately proclaiming himself the undisputed "God-father," and rightfully so. He was Kevin's God-brother and the two had been the best of friends, as close as brothers, from as far back as either could remember.

Sixteen weeks into the pregnancy, the doctor recommended an amniocentesis due to Simone's age. Four days later, Kevin and Simone's prayers were answered. Not only was the baby perfectly healthy but it was the little boy they'd been hoping for.

Thrilled with the news, Fat Ed had dropped five grand into a savings account for his God-son and his generosity didn't stop. He'd insisted on tagging along with Kevin and Simone four months later to pick out furniture for the nursery. After bouncing from store to store, Simone had finally found a set worthy and elegant enough for her little prince. Once the sales person tallied up the tab for the espresso coated nursery set - complete with a sleigh-styled lifetime crib, armoire, dresser and changing table - Fat Ed had whipped out his black card.

"Ed, are you crazy?" Simone had protested.

"Yeah, we can't let you do that," Kevin had added.

But 'no' wasn't an option as far as Fat Ed was concerned. He was taking his God-father role seriously. Yet the excitement he displayed in the earlier months had dwindled. Lately, the mere mention of the baby seemed to depress him.

"What's up with you, man? Everything alright?" Kevin asked.

"Yeah, I'm straight. Why you ask that?" Fat Ed replied.

"I don't know. You just seem a little distant. I got time for the long story."

"The long story?" Fat Ed questioned with a raised brow.

"Yeah, about the girl you got the ten grand for. You said it was a long story."

Fat Ed sighed. "You wouldn't believe it if I told you."

"Try me."

"We'll talk. We'll talk."

Kevin shook his head. Fat Ed had brushed him off again.

"Did them youngins call you today?"

"What youngins?" Fat Ed asked.

"That group I told you about earlier. Smooth and Anthony. The ones I met this morning at my P.O.'s office."

"Oh yeah, yeah. They left a message. I have to call them back."

"What about Jordan's demo? You mix it yet? Don is ready to shop her around."

"Kevin, you can do that."

"I would have had I known you weren't going to do it."

"I'ma get to it, Kevin, man. I promise. Tell Jordan I'm sorry, but I got her."

"See, that's what I'm talking about. You keeping secrets and you distracted from the studio. The studio?"

"Look, I just got hit with some life changing shit that I'm trying to get a grip on. It sucker punched me but it ain't gonna kill me. Shit, for real, it's gonna end up making me better. I'll finish Jordan's demo by the weekend, and I'll check them youngins out. But after that, I'ma take some time off."

"Hey man, I don't know what you got hit with but I'm here if you need me. Don't shut me out."

"It's cool, Kevin. You're kind of my inspiration right now, man. I'm thinking way different than I used to because of you." Fat Ed managed a smile for the first time that evening. Through a stretch, he added, "Who knows? I may mess around and get married."

Wide-eyed, Kevin said, "Just make sure she climbs down from her pole and puts some clothes on first."

Fat Ed chuckled. "Damn, you know me too well." He eased up in the seat and pulled a business card from his back pocket. "Look, I planted a few dollars in this new spot. Let's go toss back a few shots. You'll need a drink for this long story."

Kevin glanced at the card. "The Gentleman's Bar. A strip club?"

"Man, it's a bar like the card says."

"Yeah right. If you planted dollars in it there's some asses shaking. I don't have to leave home for that. I can see that for free."

"Free my ass. How much that car cost?"

Kevin grinned, so proud he had the means to do something wonderful for Simone. "Shit, I feel kinda bad 'cause I been gone for hours. I missed the shower and everything. Let me make sure Simone's straight." The battery light on Kevin's phone flashed. He fumbled around the console for his car charger. "Dag, Jordan got me again."

"What?"

"Jordan lost her cell phone charger so she's been using mine. My phone's about to die." Kevin held out his hand. "Let me see your phone so I can call and check on Simone. Then we'll go."

"Naw, it's just after seven o'clock. It's too early to go now. We can meet up later, like ten or eleven."

"That's too late. You know I don't be running the streets."

Fat Ed shook his head. "Meeting me for a drink ain't running the streets. Hell, you been home damn near a year."

"Hasn't been a year, man. Only been six months." Kevin corrected.

"Regardless. We still haven't sat down and had a drink. Give Simone some air." Fat Ed glanced at Kevin. "The car's coming in the morning. Let that erase any guilt you feel."

"Whatever, man. I'll be up there by ten and I don't want to hear no shit about you coming out the closet either."

Chapter Eight

Angela, Jordan, Kayla, and Melanie shuffled through the stack of boxes scattered across the family room. Bows and gift wrap were all over the place. Tamone pranced around, toying with a spiky-looking bow from one of the gifts.

"Goodness gracious," Kevin said. He strolled into the family room and leaned against the arm of the sectional as he took in the stroller, high chair, swing, bassinet, and a mountain of disposal diapers.

Angela opened a pack of onesies and placed them in a pile with the other items she'd planned to wash. "Now all you need is the baby."

"Yeah, I see." Kevin replied. He counted the boxes of disposal diapers. There were twenty in five different sizes starting with newborn. "Where in the world are we going to store those diapers?"

"We just put ten boxes of the larger sizes in the closet in the basement!" Melanie shared.

"What?"

"Yeah, one of Simone's favorite clients had them delivered." Angela said. "Don't think you'll have to worry about pampers. They left the receipt, too. Sometimes babies can't wear certain brands but you won't know that until the little boo-boo gets here."

"Wow. Where's Simone now?"

"Lavon got her a Kindle so she's upstairs in the tub reading," Angela told him.

"Should've known Lavon wasn't going to buy a baby gift." Kevin laughed.

Melanie quickly agreed. "Right. She wouldn't know what to buy any way."

"I'm mad I missed it. So how was everything?" Kevin said as he prepared to head up the rear stairs located in the family room.

"The last guest just left maybe ten minutes ago." Angela replied. "We recorded it so you can watch it whenever you want. There's a ton of food left if you're hungry."

"I'll get something after I check on Simone."

"Daddy, how'd your shopping go?" Jordan asked.

"Perfect."

"So what'd you get her? Where's it at?" Kayla questioned.

Kevin winked. "You'll know in the morning."

*****

The bathroom door opened. Simone turned her attention toward the door. An apple in one hand and her new e-reader in the other, she smiled from the tub full of bubbles as her husband strolled inside.

"Hey baby. I should've gotten one of these along time ago," she said as she bit into the apple. Kevin planted himself along the ceramic ledge of the Jacuzzi.

"Melanie just told me Lavon got you a Kindle. What you reading?"

"Lavon loaded this thing up with books. I got *Harlem Girl Lost 2* by this author named Treasure Blue. It's really, really good. She told me to read *Inside Rain* by Monique D. Mensah next and then, *The Bum Magnet* by, hold up." Simone went to the home page of her Kindle. "K.L. Brady. She put a bunch of books on here, and she got me this cute little leather case with the built in light. See?"

Kevin glanced at the gadget, then picked up the magazine resting on the ceramic. His expression turned sour when he discovered it was *Jet*. Simone noticed the expression.

"Kevin!"

He answered with an arched brow.

"Get over the picture already. It was a wedding gift."

"No, it was an announcement that I'm home. Then they added that stuff about being a successful songwriter." Kevin shook his head. "You know I didn't want anybody to know when I was being released. That's why I lied about when I was coming home."

"But what's the big deal? Who you hiding from?"

"Everybody from my past. The niggas from back in the day. Rhonda, Felicia –"

"Who's Felicia?"

"You know who Felicia is. She use to bring my mother back and forth to the jail. She brought Jordan the first time, too."

"So what's wrong with her knowing your home?"

"A bunch of reasons."

"Like?"

"For starters, I know she's in all types of illegal mess. We use to cook coke up her apartment back in the day while she tricked."

"The prostitute?"

Kevin was surprised. "How you know?"

"You don't remember the argument we had a hundred years ago in the apartment?"

Kevin's bewildered expression clearly said he didn't remember.

"I was fussing about you not coming home on the weekends, and I asked where you slept once the crack-heads disappear. You said a bunch of y'all slept at her house. Matter of fact, I went out with Lavon and Melanie that night 'cause I was pissed that you'd be gone another weekend. When I came home, I found a note from you."

"The note with the bullet?" Kevin smiled.

"Yes. Your crazy ass thought I went out with a dude." Simone laughed. "That was kind of sexy crazy."

"I don't know 'bout the sexy part, but yeah, I did do some crazy shit back then. It went with my environment. But that's why I want to keep them knuckleheads from my past in the past. Most of them, with the exception of Ed, are still doing the same thing."

"So this Felicia person, is she still a prostitute?"

"Naw, I think she manages escorts or some shit. But on top of that, all she talked about for years was me and her getting together once I came out. I told her it wasn't happening but I don't know. I just don't want anything to do with her or anybody else from back then."

"Interesting. So basically, she wants some ding-ding. Hmm..." Simone said. "Wonder how much she'd pay for a night?"

"Funny, funny. But that's why I don't care for the picture being in *Jet.*"

"I was a part of your past, too."

"And my today and my tomorrow. It's cool though, baby. I mean, what's done is done. I just wished Ed would've asked before he did it."

"Well, I love it. Makes me feel famous. Plus," she said as she bit into the apple again, "it's the closest I'll get to being featured as the 'Beauty of the Week.'"

Kevin placed his fingers in the tepid water and swirled it around. "You're the 'Beauty of my World,' baby. That's better than being the 'Beauty of the Week.'"

"Whatever." Simone chomped on the apple. "I feel like I'm your whale. Can you believe I'm almost a hundred ninety pounds? I've gained forty freaking pounds."

"That's because our son is growing inside of you and to me that makes you the most gorgeous person alive."

"Well if I'm gorgeous, what would you call Beyoncé, Tyra Banks, or Jada Pinkett?"

"A singer, a model, and an actress."

"You should be in politics."

"No, politicians lie. I'm being serious."

"So what if they were to walk into this room, butt-naked. Then what?"

"Then I don't know. We'd have four naked superstars in the bathroom. One pregnant, soaking in the tub, smacking on an apple."

"And one horny, drooling songwriter."

Simone placed her Kindle on the ceramic surrounding the tub and took another bite from the apple. Chewing her final bite, she reared her head back and aimed for the trash can. Kevin held out his hand.

"I might be star stuck and I may try to sell Beyoncé some of my songs, but I wouldn't be horny and I wouldn't be drooling. Besides..." He took two back-to-back chunks from the half-eaten apple. "...my dick don't control me. I control him," he said with his mouth full.

"Oh, whatever." Simone rolled her eyes and splashed Kevin with water.

"Simone, I'm being serious." He slid across the ceramic in a failed attempt to block the water that landed on the thigh of his jeans. "My heart wouldn't allow him to get excited over anybody but you." He stepped from his shoes, rose from the ledge, and unfastened his pants. "I don't think you realize how much I love you."

As hard as she tried not to, Simone couldn't help but smile. He chomped away at the rest of the apple then shot the core into the bathroom trash. His hands fully free, he took off his jeans, boxers, and socks.

"What are you doing?" Simone asked.

"You wet my pants," he said as he unbuttoned his shirt. "Plus, I feel like I haven't seen you all day. I want to get in there with you."

"You know how long I've been in here?" She held up her hands, pruned to the fingertips. Kevin stood naked, proud of the body he'd chiseled while incarcerated. "My back has been hurting all day, so I came up here to soak in some hot water. I know I've been in here over an hour."

"Why didn't you tell me your back was hurting?"

"I don't know. I'm okay, though."

"Well, come on out before you turn into a raisin." Naked, he strolled to the towel rack that hung from the back of the bathroom door and pulled down Simone's towel.

The water gurgled as Simone lifted the stopper. She grabbed both sides of the tub and attempted to pull herself up.

Kevin slung the towel over his shoulder, stepped inside the tub, and helped Simone to her feet. "This is why I been in here so long. Getting out ain't easy."

"I didn't mean to be gone that long. How was the shower? Did you have fun?" Kevin stepped onto the cream shag area rug before assisting Simone. He draped the towel around her back and began to dry her off, starting with her breasts.

"Had a ball. Did you see the stuff?"

"Mmm hmm," he replied as he patted her breasts dry with the towel.

"So what did you get me? Is it downstairs?"

"Not 'til tomorrow."

He massaged her breasts through the towel. Simone placed her hand underneath Kevin's chin and directed his attention from her breasts. His hazel eyes twinkled as he smiled his million dollar smile.

"What? I wanted to make sure they were dry."

"You're giving them too much attention, which could possibly lead to trouble."

"Trouble? I like the sound of trouble." Clutching the ends of the towel, he moved in as close as her belly would allow.

"Kevin, we can't."

"The doctor didn't say that."

"Yeah, but we shouldn't."

"The doctor didn't say that either."

Simone tugged the towel from his grasp. "I'm already dilated though. If we do anything, it'll open me more." She could feel Kevin's eyes on her as she turned to hang her towel back on the rack.

"Make it bounce for me baby."

"Yeah right," she said as she folded the towel and draped it across the metal bar. "Feed me more ice cream, and I'll make it thunder."

Kevin laughed. "Yeah, that cookie dough had you going, boy."

"Yeah, baby boy might have some lactose issues."

Kevin crept up behind her. The warmth of his breath skimmed the back of her neck. The heat from his fully naked body felt good. She could feel his nature rising.

Slowly, her eyes closed as Kevin placed tender kisses along the nape of her neck, causing her to moan. He eased his arms around her and placed his hands back on her breasts.

"Kevin." She sighed.

"What?" he whispered in her ear. "I can't hold and kiss my wife?"

"Yeah, but when you kiss me like this, things happen."

He grabbed her hand and guided it to his erection. "Already happening."

She turned to face her husband. The love and passion in his eyes mirrored her feelings. No longer could Simone ignore the heat of passion that throbbed between them. She bought his lips to hers. There was so much hunger in their kiss.

Panting, their lips finally parted. Kevin nodded toward the bathroom vanity. Simone smiled. She turned around, leaned her pregnant self against the vanity and waited for her husband to slip inside.

"You sure, baby?"

"I'm positive."

There was something about being able to see each other in the mirror that drove them crazy. Kevin knew he couldn't keep Simone in that position for long. Normally he'd ask her if she were ready for him. But today would have to be different. Sweat beaded Kevin's brow. Breathing heavily, he filled her with his love.

He eased from Simone and leaned against the dual sinks to catch his breath. Washing between her legs, Simone smiled; watching Kevin as he turned on his sink and gulped down handfuls of cold water. The water off, he grabbed Simone's hand and led her to the bedroom.

In the bed, Kevin took his time, pleasing his wife until her legs began to quiver. Shortly thereafter, her satisfaction rained. Cuddled in the spoon position, the twosome drifted off to sleep but Simone's back pain returned, more intense than before, waking her minutes into her slumber.

Oh my God, she thought to herself. *Those aren't back pains. I've been having contractions.* She laid there using the clock on the cable box to time the pain that seemed to come every fifteen minutes. Smiling to herself, she rubbed her tummy.

"Come on, my sweetie. Mommy can't wait to meet you."

But I'm not going to the hospital until the pain is unbearable.

"What you say, baby?" Kevin mumbled, kissing her on her bare shoulder.

"I was talking to the baby."

Kevin rubbed his eyes. "Damn, what time is it? Feel like I only slept for maybe ten, twenty minutes."

"Thirty actually. It's almost nine."

"Shit," Kevin hissed.

"Why? What's wrong?"

"I told Fat Ed I'd meet him for a drink around ten or eleven. Something's up with him. He said he'd fill me in tonight."

"Is he okay?"

"Yeah, I guess. He's just been acting different. Real distant."

"Well, it's nine, baby." Simone climbed from the bed and headed to the bathroom. "So, as your momma says, you better get to getting."

"Hell, I'm tired. I'll get up there some time tonight, I guess."

Kevin grabbed his cell from the nightstand and sent Fat Ed a text: I'LL BE UP THERE SOMETIME TONIGHT BUT NOT BEFORE 12.

He placed the phone back on the nightstand while it charged.

Under the warmth of the covers, his hand accidently skimmed the puddle in the bed from their lovemaking. It took a lot for Simone to get comfortable and he didn't want the wet spot adding to her discomfort. He rose from the bed to yank off the sheet but froze at the pinkish stain. He rushed to the bathroom.

"Hey, baby you—"

Simone stood in the middle of the bathroom floor, water trickling down her leg as she clutched her stomach in pain.

"Oh my goodness."

Kevin hurried to her. "What baby? What is it?"

"Another contraction."

"What you mean *another* contraction?"

"I think those back pains were contractions. And well," Simone stared down at the puddle beneath her. "My water broke."

Kevin's face was riddled with panic. "What do I do, baby?"

"Call the doctor while I wash up."

"Shit, Dr. Covington's on vacation."

"I know. Dr. Peterson will have to deliver him."

Chapter Nine

Never again would Sanora second guess the age-old myth. Full moons did in fact spark labor. Her second night in the delivery ward confirmed it. Five babies and a set of triplets had been delivered in the last four hours. The hospital staff was down three nurses, which made things even more chaotic. The hustle and bustle was the perfect distraction from Sanora's personal issues. Yet, once her shift ended, the problems would still be there to smack her in the face, including the biggest one of all: Felicia Payne.

Why the hell did I answer the phone yesterday? she thought to herself. She pushed through the double doors to the supply room to grab a catheter but instead plopped in a wheelchair, oblivious to the stack of folded towels beneath her.

Sanora's life had changed dramatically and there was no room for Felicia and her foolery. She was going back to school, to become a doctor like she'd originally planned. The paperwork for the Physician Assistant Program had been submitted. She'd written the hell out of her personal statement and had obtained three letters of reference from professors who'd passed her with flying colors years ago in exchange for sexual favors.

"You're a beautiful woman. One with many talents," Professional Hayman said from behind his desk three weeks ago.

Silver hair blanketed his head and connected to a full beard. He was distinguishingly handsome yet reserved and professional. But beneath that layer of poise was the kinkiest man Sanora had ever entertained. She wanted to scream when she recalled some of the vile things she'd done with him. There was something about the warmth of urine that sent him over the edge. Then he'd lie on his back, shivering, as Sanora licked off her urine mixed with his semen.

With the right high, Sanora was down for whatever, especially if the benefit was right. Boy, the places her mouth had been for a few extra dollars. Her first drug of choice had been alcohol. The next day, there was no recollection of the disgusting things she'd done. But liquor made her sloppy and the clients often complained about her lazy, amateurish performance. So Felicia band her from drinking and turned her on to weed.

The ganja worked magic. Not only did it relax her, it made her feel like the sexiest woman alive. She would love it all the more if only it would black out the nights' events as alcohol had done. She would hurl in the commode when she recalled some of the places her mouth had been. The thuggish dudes always wanted their ugly toes sucked or their nasty asses licked.

"The Physician Assistant's Program requires several hours of patient care. Do you have the hours, Miss Goldstein?" Professor Hayman had asked.

"No, not all of them. I'm looking for a job."

Professor Hayman leaned back in his chair. "How's your background?"

"It's fine. I mean," she lowered her eyes, "I'm not proud of some of the things I've done but my background as far as criminal activity is spotless."

Professor Hayman picked up a pen to sign the letter of recommendation. "There are several nursing positions open at a few of the hospitals. I can make some calls."

Surprised by the lack of a response, Professor Hayman peered over his dark framed glasses and watched Sanora's lips twist in an uneasy smile. She fidgeted in her seat and avoided his eyes. Professor Hayman corrected his relaxed posture, rested the ink pen on top of his desk, and cupped his hands.

He cleared his throat and said, "Miss Goldstein, there's no need to camouflage the obvious. While I have enjoyed your company," he said with a hint of sarcasm, "I'm glad you've gathered your focus and decided to further your career in the medical field. I believe you'd make a fine physician. That is what my recommendation will be based on."

Barely two weeks later, Sanora was on her second day at the job. A job Professor Hayman practically placed in her lap. It killed her to return to Maryland. She had hoped to find a nursing job closer to her mother's house in Richmond, Virginia. Anxious for the patient care hours, she took the job with her mother's support, but kept a watchful eye on the classifieds for a nursing position in Richmond.

The first few hours of Sanora's shift, the devil sat on her shoulder whispering how crazy it was for her to even consider working a real job, especially one as hectic as the hospital's labor and delivery ward.

Maybe I can still write illegal prescriptions, she thought as she sat in the wheelchair. "No. I can't go back," she sighed with her head in her hands. "I'm not going back."

On any given day, Sanora wrote close to twenty prescriptions at a hundred dollars a pop when she worked for Felicia. Money she and Felicia split equally. If the grand wasn't enough, hundreds awaited her alter ego, Tootie, at the strip club. Her flawless beauty - olive skin compliments of her biracial ethnicity, sea-green eyes, silky auburn tresses lengthened by extensions, a lean 5'7" frame flattered by voluptuous curves, coupled with the grace she acquired from years of training as a dancer, made Sanora the main attraction whenever she graced any club with her presence.

Over and over, the devil reminded her of the thousands of dollars she foolishly allowed to fall through her grasp. Yet too much had happened, and life for Sanora was no longer the same. Despite everything, her feelings for Felicia hadn't dulled. She loved her like the sister she never had. But as she sat in the supply closet, she couldn't help but wonder how her life would've been had she minded her own business that day in the jail almost seven years ago.

*****

"You get three chances to clear the metal detector and that's it. As of today, we're no longer frisking or using the wand," the officer advised.

"That's some bull," Felicia said. "How was I supposed to know that?"

He nodded toward the two signs plastered on the entrance door. "Signs have been posted throughout both the waiting room and visiting room for weeks. Inmates were supposed to inform everyone as well."

"Well, I never noticed the sign and the *inmate*," Felicia said with sarcasm, "never said nothing."

"Oh well," the sergeant said and shrugged his shoulders.

"It can't be 'oh well' after I drove two hours in the rain to get here. I got metal in my bra so it won't make sense for me to go through this thing again 'cause it's just gon' beep. Then if I take my bra off, we got a whole 'nother issue."

The sergeant shuffled through papers. Without a glance he said, "No, you can't take off the bra."

Felicia threw her hands up in the air. "That's what I just said. So what am I 'pose to do?"

"I don't know, ma'am. I guess you need to invest in some sports bras."

Steaming hot, Felicia fought to maintain her composure. The last thing she wanted to do was piss off the guards and get banned from the jail altogether.

"This is some bull," Felicia barked through clinched teeth. "I hope you don't have wire in your bra cause if you do, your ass ain't getting in," she said to the young lady who stood in line behind her.

"I think I do," the timid voice replied.

Irritated, the sergeant glanced up from his stack of papers. The words he'd planned to speak sat silent on his tongue. A sly grin cracked his hardened expression as he stared into Sanora's sea-green eyes. He leaned across the counter.

"Wow, anybody ever tell you that you look like that supermodel? Hey!" He yelled over his shoulder to another officer. "What's that black girl's name? The one who was on *Sports Illustrated*?"

"I don't know her name but I know who you're talking about," the officer replied.

"I know one thing, you could be her little sister. What you doing here at the prison anyway? I hope one of these worthless knuckleheads ain't your boyfriend."

"No. I'm trying to see my brother."

Felicia watched the interaction.

The officer licked his lips and reached underneath the counter for the wand.

"I'll tell you ladies what," he said eagerly. "Since there's no one else in line, I'll go ahead and use the wand this time." He made his way from around the counter. "Now there is no female officer present but if you don't mind, I'll do a quick pat down and wave the wand over you just this once with your consent. But next time, be prepared. Somebody as nice as me may not be at the desk."

Two hours later, Sanora stood outside in the blazing sun with her car hood up. Her hooptie wouldn't start. Felicia spotted her in the parking lot and headed in her direction.

"Hey, thanks for earlier. He'd have sent my ass home with the quickness if it weren't for you. He couldn't wait to get his hands on Tyra's little sister." She chuckled. "What's wrong with your car? You need a jump or something?" Felicia studied the rusty little bucket Sanora drove. "What you doing driving crap like this any way? I can't even tell what it is 'cause your damn symbols are gone."

"Yeah, it's not much but for the most part, it runs and gets me where I need to go."

"And where is that?"

"Where is what?" Sanora asked.

"Where do you need to go? I mean, what? You still in school?" Felicia asked.

"Yes, I'm in school."

"You graduate this year?" Felicia probed.

Sanora laughed. "No, I'm in college. I hope to be a doctor someday. I work at the hospital part-time and I teach dance to young girls, too. My *bucket* gets me to all those places."

"Get the fuck out of here. I thought you were a senior in high school."

"No, everyone thinks that." She smiled bashfully. "But once I finish, then," she said as she eyed the beat up vehicle beside her. "I'll get a new car. Right now, it's kind of a struggle."

"You ain't gotta struggle cause you in school. A lot of the girls that work for me go to school and they ain't driving buckets."

"Buckets?"

"Yeah, you know. A bucket? A hooptie?"

"Oh, no. I don't know." Sanora smiled and shrugged off her naiveté.

"You teach dance to little girls, huh? So you dance, too?"

"Yeah, all my life. Just doesn't pay well."

"That ain't true. The dancers I know make a killing. If you worked for my company, you'd be out of that car in a month, if that long."

"Really? How's that?"

"Let's go somewhere and grab a bite to eat. I'll call a tow for your car."

Overnight, Sanora went from rags to riches. Her look, her style of dress, and even the hooptie she used to get around in had been upgraded at Felicia's expense. It was easy to enhance Sanora's look, but preparing her for the next stage took a lot of work. Just when Felicia was getting ready to give up and send Sanora back to Richmond, she remembered ganja's magical powers.

In no time, Sanora become Felicia's number one stunner, her real moneymaker. A virgin to the streets, the glitz and glamour of the fast life became addictive. Soon, her grades began to slip. But it was nothing a lap dance or a meaningless tussle in the sheets couldn't cure. Gone was her dream of becoming a doctor. Instead, she utilized the credits she'd earned, settled for a master's degree in nursing, and bid farewell to school.

A product of her Caucasian mother's backseat fling with a Jamaican she'd encountered one night at a local bar, Sanora was ridiculed by her white family members and friends for her biracial ethnicity. Behind closed doors, her Caucasian brother and cousins would taunt her with names like mutt, oreo and zebra every chance they got. Her olive-toned skin appeared dirty next to the white, pale skin of her family. Their hair was blonde and straight and their eyes were blue. Sanora's eyes, in their opinion, were a muddy green and her hair was an explosion of auburn frizz. Sanora's white stepfather couldn't bear the sight of her and left with her brother when she was barely six, leaving her and her mother to fend for themselves.

A year later, John John, Sanora's Jamaican dad moved in with his sixteen year old son, Harvey. Unlike her wicked Caucasian brother, Harvey adored his little sister as did her father, who was seldom around. A career criminal, John John spent more time in jail for petty crimes than he did seated at the head of the table. Financially, things were difficult for Sanora's mother whose one goal in life seemed to be repairing her daughter's self-esteem. Days were spent in the dark while Sanora's dance lessons, modeling classes, and private school tuition took precedence over the utility bills.

Determined to help with the finances while his father served time, Harvey stumbled upon illegal employment with some rednecks at a chop shop and quickly learned stealing cars brought in the big money. It was the beginning of his career as a criminal.

The money Sanora's mom invested in her timid daughter had seemingly gone to waste until Sanora met Felicia. The hours spent training as a classical, modern dancer were now being spent on drunks who longed to know the goddess better and paid handsomely for it. For two years, things between Felicia and Sanora were great until Harvey came home from prison. Free for barely thirty days, he was already in trouble.

"Hey, I need your help to get me outta a little mess." Harvey stated after Sanora had treated him to a steak at her favorite five-star steak-house.

"Damn, Harvey. Is the ink even dry on your release papers?" She hissed. "Why do you and dad even waste the parole board's time by getting released when all you're gonna do is go back?"

"How you gon' say some shit like that when you don't even know what happened?"

"Whatever, Harvey. Moving back to Jamaica was the best thing dad did. Maybe you should go."

"Maybe you should ask me what happened."

"Okay, Harvey. What happened?"

"This dude fronted me some product so I can get on my feet. Shit was going good 'til I got set up. I owe him five grand."

Sanora stared at Harvey with a blank expression. She wasn't buying it.

"Look, it ain't like I'm asking you to dig into your pockets and give me the money."

"I hope not 'cause I don't have five grand. I mean, I could get it but—"

"You ain't even gotta get it. I got a way that I can put money in your pocket, too."

"Hell no, Harvey! I'm not messing with you."

"Sanora, I'm serious. I can get us both paid but the shit won't work without you. You gotta help me."

"Help you how, Harvey?"

"You can't say shit to your girl."

"To who, Felicia?" Sanora grew agitated. "Why not? I tell her damn near everything. She's cool, Harvey. She's like my sister."

"She's your pimp is what she is. I mean, look at you!" Sanora's extensions traveled to the small of her back. Her boobs were pushed up so high they nearly touched her chin. The make-up, the lashes, the tight clothes and the suicide heels screamed that she was for sale.

"Harvey, I dance. That's it."

Harvey toyed with the broccoli on his plate, unable to look at his sister. "It's me, Sanora and you know damn well I know better. I just hope you not doing half the shit that she does." He rested his fork on his plate, shaking his head as he recalled his sexual encounter with Felicia his first day home from prison. She'd made his toes curl, which was fine. He just hoped his sister wasn't as raunchy.

"Look, all I'm saying is for this here, for our scheme, the less people who know, the better. Shit, I'm talking about putting five g's in your pocket in one night."

"Five thousand dollars? In one night?"

"In one night." He reiterated without as much as a blink. "You just have to let me know when you meeting with one of your caked up clients."

"Now see, this is the nonsense I'm talking about. First you call me a hooker and now you want me to set up one of my clients so you can rob them."

"I didn't call you a hooker. I said I hope you aren't doing half the shit that Felicia does. Secondly, I'm not gon' rob them the way you think. It's just a white collar crime."

Sanora shook her head.

"All you gotta do is let me know the next time she hook you up with one of them fancy-dancy muthafuckas. Can't be a regular client. Has to be somebody you've never met. Preferably somebody old."

"And then what?"

"Give me the particulars about y'all meeting like the place and how long you think it's gon' — "

"Okay, okay." Irritated, she tossed her napkin on the half-eaten steak. "And then what?"

"Then I'm gon' knock on the door looking for my little sister."

Sanora sat in silence, waiting for him to finish but he said nothing else. "Okay, Harvey and then what?"

"I don't know." He shrugged. "How young do you think you can pass for? Fifteen, sixteen? Then it's up to them. I'ma threaten to beat their ass and call the pigs on him 'cause they messing with a juvenile."

Sanora sucked her teeth. "Harvey, that sounds dumb."

"Dumb, really? The waitress thought you were my daughter. Do I look old enough to be your father?"

She studied her brother. A low, even haircut and goatee both trimmed by the barber hours before dinner graced his smooth, dark oval face. He reminded her so much of a giant, thuggish-ass Taye Diggs.

"No, you look thirty-three."

"Exactly. Sanora, you look like a teenager playing dress up."

Sanora sighed. "Look, we only gotta do it once. She tells you the particulars on the cats, right?"

"Yeah, she tells me everything about them."

"On down to the money they make, right?"

"Yes."

"Bet. The next time you meeting with one, let me know. You can pick the victim. Just make sure he's a caked up old head."

A week later, Sanora stood in front of a full length mirror analyzing herself as Harvey's idea marinated. Despite being twenty-three, she could easily pass for a high school student, especially if she peeled off the lashes, washed off the make-up and pulled her hair into a ponytail like her brother had advised. *Five thousand in one night...*

Tempted by the money, Sanora finally decided to give the scheme a try with new client and old head, Linwood Harris. A recently windowed real estate investor, he seemed like the perfect victim.

Sweat poured from Linwood. Grunts accompanied his every hump. Minutes later, he collapsed on top of Sanora and drifted off to sleep. Pinned beneath him as he snored, Sanora waited for Harvey who was taking forever. She shook Linwood gently to get him off of her, but to her surprise, he woke up fully aroused.

"Damn." He'd said as he removed the old condom. "I was wondering when that pill was gonna kick in." He grabbed another condom from his wallet on the nightstand and passed it to Sanora.

"What pill?" Sanora asked. She opened the wrapper with her teeth. For some reason, that seemed to turn a few of her clients on.

"Viagra, baby. Bosslady gave it to me." He grinned like a Cheshire cat as Sanora eased the latex down his shaft. "Now taste it, baby. It's strawberry flavored."

Sanora couldn't wait to get her hands on the five grand. She deserved a tip after all the tricks Linwood requested. He'd put a hurting on Sanora. There was no way possible Felicia just gave him Viagra. Linwood, the sixty something year old suddenly had the stamina of a horny, adolescent teen. Finally, he'd had enough. Knocked out in the bed, Sanora jumped in the shower wondering where the hell her brother was.

The second she wrapped the towel around her body and stepped from the bathroom, Harvey pounded on the door damn near giving Linwood a heart attack. He shot up. Tossing back the covers, he threw his legs over the bed and reached for his tighty-whities.

"Who the fuck is that?"

"Sanora, open this door. I know you in there."

Sanora tiptoed to the door and peeked out the peephole. "Shit. It's my brother," she whispered in a panic.

"What the fuck does he want?" Linwood asked as he stepped into his pants.

"I don't know!"

"Sanora, open the door. Open it now!"

Shaking his head, Linwood reached for his undershirt as Sanora undid the locks.

"What the fuck you doing?" Linwood asked.

"I gotta open it or he'll call the police."

"Call the police? Call the police for what?"

Harvey pushed the door open, storming inside with fire in his eyes. Sanora flinched when Harvey raised his hand to slap her.

"What did I tell you about this shit?" He shot his attention at the old man getting dressed. "Did you fuck that old ass bastard?"

"Look, man," Linwood said, "I don't know who you are, but—"

"But?" Harvey growled through clinched teeth. "Here's a but for your old, nasty, perverted ass. Look at her!" Harvey snatched Sanora by her arm and shoved her in front of the old man like a rag doll. "Mutha-fucka, look at her real good. You like fuckin' little girls, you old dirty bastard! You like sticking your rusty dick in sixteen year olds? Where the fuck is the phone?"

"Sixteen?"

Linwood stood speechless as he took a good look at Sanora's face, who was now free of the make-up washed off in the shower. She looked every bit of sixteen. Harvey pushed Sanora down on the bed and stepped toward Linwood.

"I don't know if I should beat your old ass or call the muthafuckin' police."

"Hold up, now. Hold up." Linwood inched back with his hands up. "I didn't know she was sixteen."

"Look at her, man!" Harvey screamed, pointing at Sanora sprawled out on top of the tussled linens.

"Shit, I can see that now."

Harvey pulled a gun from the small of his back. Tears welled up in Sanora's eyes. Instantly she regretted her willingness to participate. Harvey was taking things too far.

"What are you doing?" Sanora asked.

"Maybe I should fuck you up *and* call the police. I'm sure they'd understand. That's my muthafuckin' baby sister, man."

Visibly shaking, Linwood said, "Look, man. I'm telling you I didn't know. I wouldn't mess with no sixteen-year-old. Please man. Let's work this out."

Things worked out just as Harvey had planned. He picked up the ten grand in cash, just as he and Linwood had agreed. The five thousand dollars Sanora pocketed didn't feel good. So, she put it in a cashier's check and sent every penny to her mother.

Harvey didn't settle his five-thousand-dollar debt. Instead, he blew his portion like the man he was: a convict fresh out of prison. Broke, he decided to call Linwood a few days later and demand another ten grand. But blackmail was a deadly game.

The ten grand Linwood had paid initially was supposed to squash the entire ordeal. But Harvey wanted more and it was obvious to Linwood that he'd keep coming back. Flipping properties was a lucrative business that required quite a bit of upfront money. Upfront money that Linwood received from his sons' notorious drug game. It was those same sons that supposedly met Harvey with his second demand for money.

A fight broke out and Harvey was killed, shot in the head. When Sanora heard what had happened, she was terrified. Scared that Linwood would sic his sons on her, she went running to Felicia. She shared her brother's whole cockamamie scene.

"I set you up with Linwood, right?"

"Yes, but I gave you your money," Sanora cried.

"You gave me my money," Felicia mocked. "Are you really that fuckin' stupid? Are you that fuckin' green and gullible? Bitch, if I set you up with Linwood, that means I set him up with a dumbass minor! Me!" She leaped from the couch. "Did you ever fuckin' think that they'd come after me?"

Felicia set up a meeting with Linwood. In less than an hour, the entire ordeal had been settled and not a single dollar had been repaid. The five grand Sanora sent to her mother had covered the cost of Harvey's funeral.

Rooted in the secrecy of Harvey's blood, Felicia and Linwood formed an alliance. A 'no questions asked' type of partnership. Despite the grief Sanora felt from the loss of her brother, she was eternally grateful knowing she could have been laying in a pine box next to him for her part in the scam. With a bleeding heart, she turned to drugs even more.

Little had changed between Felicia and Sanora. After all, Sanora was her true moneymaker, and as far as Sanora knew, she was alive because of Felicia. Things were okay up until a few months ago.

*****

"I should've never answered the phone yesterday," Sanora said aloud.

The supply room door swung open. The nurse gasped then clutched her chest, startled at the sight of Sanora seated in the wheelchair.

"Girl, you scared me." She chuckled nervously as she grabbed a few bags of IV fluids. "You okay? You in here talking to yourself?"

"I always talk to myself, just never listen."

The nurse shared a half smile. "You're new, right?"

"Yeah, it's my second day."

"Well, I think they're looking for you. I think you just got a new patient or something."

"Okay. I'm coming out now."

"And just FYI. This ain't a good place to hide," the nurse shared as she pushed through the doors with Sanora trailing behind. "They'll find you in there."

"The doctor needs your help in 305," the nursing supervisor advised as she passed Sanora the chart. Sanora placed it on the counter and opened it up to review the patient's information.

"I got it," another nurse said. "I've already been in there."

The supervisor glanced over her shoulder and studied the dry erase board. "You sure? You have five patients already."

"It's cool. She's in the room between my two other patients. I may as well take her, too. Plus, I like working with Dr. Peterson." She said as she rushed down the hallway. "I'll come back and get her file in a second."

"Okay," the supervisor said as she turned to add the newest patient to the board.

"Penn was mine. She delivered. She's in her room now so you can erase her," Sanora shared.

"Thanks. Oh and I have your file right here. Personnel has more forms for you to sign. You can take it and just bring it back before your shift ends."

"Okay," Sanora replied through the surgical mask.

"Hey, I'm sorry. I can't remember your name. Hell, it's so crazy in here I can't remember my own name." She chuckled. "Look inside that file for me please and give me the new patient's name. The one in 305," the supervisor requested with her back turned.

"Umm, Kennard," Sanora said. "Simone Kennard."

Chapter Ten

There were a couple things that the *Snapped* marathon reiterated to Felicia over and over again. Don't leave clues and don't tell your business. And damn near anything could be traced – cell phones, tire prints – anything. But as far as ideas, she wasn't impressed. Hell, her existing criminal repertoire outshined any of the women featured on that show. Where the hell were the thorough bitches of the world like Lorena Bobbitt or Alex, Glenn Close's character from the 1987 blockbuster *Fatal Attraction*? Now they knew how to get revenge, and Felicia wanted to do something just as memorable.

Maybe I should chop off your dick and boil your pet, Felicia thought to herself.

She contemplated calling one of her goons. Finding where the precious Kennard family lived wouldn't be hard. She could have somebody blow up their house or maybe even put a hit out on Simone but that was too easy - too *Snapped*. A bone chilling pain is what she wanted to induce. One that would shatter Kevin's heart into a million little pieces the way he'd shattered hers.

Close to seven at night, Felicia's high began to subside. She flipped back the lid to the knick-knack box on her nightstand in search of something more potent than plain old weed. She thought about dipping a joint in some PCP but opted for the white stuff in the plastic bag. As she prepared to snort away her blues, her phone began to ring. The caller I.D. said the call was coming from Wakefield hospital. She snatched up the phone.

"Hello?"

"What's Kevin's last name?"

"Hello?" Felicia shouted. "Who is this?"

"Fe, it's me, Sanora."

"What the hell you doing at the—"

"FELICIA!" Sanora growled into the phone. "I need to know Kevin's last name? It's an emergency."

"It's Kennard but what you—"

"I think he's here at the hospital."

"What?"

Sanora knew she had Felicia's undivided attention now. "His wife name's Simone?"

"Sanora, why you calling me—"

"Because if it's Simone, they're here at the hospital! She's having a baby." Sanora interrupted abruptly. "Felicia, it's a crazy house up here. At first, she was supposed to be my patient, but this other nurse took her because she's cool with the doctor or some shit. But I saw the file with their names and was like, no fucking way. Ain't that some shit?" Felicia was silent. "Hello... Felicia?"

"I'm here," she whispered.

"Oh my goodness, Fe. Shit, I'm sorry. I thought maybe you'd want to come up here and talk to him. I wasn't trying to upset you."

Felicia sniffed. "Naw, it's okay. It's all good. Has she had the baby yet?"

"No, she was just admitted. It may be awhile. I don't know what's going on with her or anything, but I can make arrangements for you to see him and try to talk to him."

"Yeah, that's a good idea. I need to see him. Let me get dressed."

Felicia hung up with Sanora and prepared to call Linwood. Then she remembered. From this day forward, there could be no evidence, no clues. Kicking back the covers, she rushed from her bed and headed straight for Sanora's old room to pack her bag. Once she'd gathered everything she needed, she'd drive to Linwood's spot.

*****

Sweat beaded on Felicia's forehead. She didn't know if it were her nerves, the pill she'd popped less than ten minutes ago, or the leather seats of the silver Toyota Camry. *Why get leather in a Camry?* she wondered as she pressed the button to lower the window.

From the car, she watched Linwood's grandson pussyfoot around the gas station as if searching for a gas container killed him. His excessive girly-ass bitching was annoying the hell out of Felicia and went against the image he projected with his continuous sulk paired with a hostile vibe, long dusty, unkempt dreads, and jeans that sagged from his butt. Shaking her head, she couldn't believe how hardcore he'd become in five years.

After paying for the gas container, Linwood's grandson hopped back in the front seat and passed the can to Felicia. She nodded toward the backseat and extended two hundred dollar bills. He tossed the can in the backseat and glared at the money.

"What?"

"I forgot. I need two of them cheap pre-paid phones."

Smooth slapped the steering wheel and laid his head back on the headrest. "Why can't you go in the store?" he asked with attitude, his eyes on the ceiling.

"Because I can't. Plus, your grandfather has my phone. So here."

She slapped the money on his thigh. Smooth crumpled the money in his hand, hissing under his breath as he headed back inside the store. Being Linwood's grandson had saved him his front teeth. Felicia wanted to take the cold piece of steel she had tucked deep inside her large duffle bag and bitch-slap him right in his mouth. Smooth knew not to try Felicia. He'd seen her in action.

Linwood owed Felicia in a major way and tonight had been declared payback time. Hell, she'd proven herself as an asset on more than one occasion. Their drug game stepped up a notch thanks to Felicia's ingenious street hustle. Linwood's sons now had a smorgasbord of narcotics, street and prescription drugs, to satisfy the craving of every class of addict. Felicia got a pinch off the prescriptions Sanora wrote, then turned around and sold them to Linwood's sons for double. Thirty days after the spa opened, she'd tucked a quick twenty-five grand into her wall safe; fifteen grand came from the prescription drugs she'd sold to Linwood's sons alone. But Sanora's absence was threatening her gold mine.

But the hook up with the prescription drugs wasn't why Linwood owed her. Hell, she was getting a cut off it so it benefited them all. Linwood and his sons owed Felicia for saving the life of Big L, Linwood's oldest son.

Linwood had called Felicia hawking acid through the phone after the event with Sanora. Felicia had not only set him up with a minor, but the young girl's brother was blackmailing him. Too embarrassed to tell his son, he'd paid the initial amount and disregarded the whole ordeal as a lesson learned. But when Harvey called back, Linwood knew it wouldn't end.

Felicia was beside herself. If Linwood had been a real O.G., there wouldn't have been a phone call. A bullet would've been lodged in three heads: Sanora, Harvey, and her own. She knew the cockamamie scheme was Harvey's idea and insisted on tagging along to the meeting place. Linwood gave her the address but didn't trust her enough to tag along.

Big L had big balls. He was supposed to bring his other brother, but instead he came with his teenage nephew. Huge mistake. Harvey was a thorough-ass, big dude. Felicia pulled up just in time to witness Harvey beating the shit out of Linwood's oldest son.

A light flicked on inside Big L's BMW 745 li. Inside, a teenager fished around in search of something. Felicia crept up to the window, scaring the teenager whose face was drenched with tears and mucus as he fumbled with the gun. In the dead of winter, she put her gloved finger to her lips and summoned for him to roll down the window.

"Give it me," she had mouthed nice and slow.

He passed the gun with a trembling hand. Five minutes later, Harvey lay dead. She'd saved Big L. When Sanora found out her brother had been killed, she came running to Felicia. As bad as Felicia wanted to follow Linwood's suggestion and blast a hole in her friend's head, she didn't. Instead she gave her a performance fit for an Oscar. Smooth had driven well over an hour, complaining constantly.

"Man, pops ain't tell me I was takin' a fuckin' road trip. I had things to do. We been driving for over an hour."

Felicia had finally had enough. "Will you stop cryin' like an old bitch?"

"Shit, I had things to do. My father's lazy ass could've drove you around."

"What did you have to do?" Felicia asked sarcastically.

"I was supposed to go see my girl. I gotta turn myself in tomorrow for parole violation. I was tryin' to — you know." He said with a shrug.

"So what? You want me to suck your lil' dick?"

"What?"

Felicia rolled her eyes. "Do you want me to suck your dick?"

There was nothing Smooth could do to camouflage his grin. "For real?"

Digging inside the duffle bag, Felicia mumbled, "Yeah, for real."

"Shit, alright."

With one hand on the steering wheel, he unzipped his jacket. He reached to unfasten his belt but Felicia's hands were already there.

"Pull to the shoulder, but don't turn the car off."

"Naw, I can drive while you do that shit. My girl does it all the time."

"I'm not an amateur like your girlfriend. Pull over," she ordered as she undid her seatbelt. "Plus, you may miss what I'm looking for."

Smooth slowed and pulled onto the rocky shoulder like Felicia requested. "It's gon' take me a minute, and you know these shoulders be hot. We can't sit here like that."

Felicia ignored his warning. "Lean your seat back a bit."

Reluctantly, Smooth did as he was told.

"Use this so you can watch." She handed him a mirror that she'd pulled from her bag.

"Damn. What barbershop you steal this from?" He laughed, clutching the handle. "I don't need a mirror to watch. I can see."

"All you'll see is my head. Hold the mirror, and you can see what I'm doing to you. You'll come faster if you watch, trust me."

"Shit, alright. Hand me some napkins out the glove compartment."

"For what?" Felicia asked as she freed him from his boxers. He was already fully erect.

She took him in, all of him, pleasing him as if he were her highest paying client. Smooth began to moan and fidget. His body stiffened as he beat the steering wheel with his fist.

"Damn, girl," he moaned through his teeth. Not even five minutes in, his satisfaction erupted. "Okay, okay, okay," he whined like a girl as Felicia chased every drop, licking him clean. Speechless, Smooth stared at Felicia in amazement.

"How often does your girl do it?"

"Not that often and never, *ever* like that."

Felicia fastened her seatbelt. "You sour. Probably too much damn carryout. Eat more fruit like pineapples or bananas."

"What?" He chuckled.

"It'll change the taste of your semen. Maybe she'll do it more."

He shook his head and placed the car in drive. "I see why my grandfather fucks with you. You gangster and got a mean ass head game."

Traffic was light as they headed south along the dark highway. Smooth hadn't uttered a single word since Felicia worked her magic. It was the peace and quiet she needed as she thought out her plan.

"Ooh, right there," Felicia said. "Pull over behind that car right there on the shoulder and hit your lights." She dug inside her duffle bag and pulled out two pair of plastic gloves, placing one pair in Smooth's lap. "Then put those on."

He did as instructed.

Opening the car door, Felicia said, "See if there's a front plate while I get this one off the back."

Smooth got out and jogged around to the front of the car. Sure enough there was a front plate. He needed no further instructions. He reached in his pocket, pulled out his extra set of keys that housed a miniature screwdriver, and removed the plate.

Back in the car, Felicia said, "Hit the next rest stop, and we'll change the plates."

"For what?"

"Too many cameras at the hospital. Can't take no chances. That's how most of the chicks on *"Snapped"* got caught."

"Huh?"

"Don't worry about it. Just hit the rest stop and we'll make our way back."

"What's at the hospital?"

"Your grandfather don't ask questions. You shouldn't either."

Felicia pulled a plastic bag full of pills from her purse. She grabbed an E-pill and bit it in half. She dropped one half back in the bag and chased the portion in her mouth with a loud gulp of water.

"The rest stop is coming up. You still going to see your girlfriend?"

Grinning like a cat, Smooth nodded. "I'ma stop and get some bananas and pineapples, though. The pineapples in the can work?"

"Yeah, they work." She passed him the other prepaid phone. "Here, before I forget, take this. I'ma text you on that phone so be listening for it. I'ma need you to meet me on 301 later. And put some gas in that container."

"Gas?"

"Yeah, and bring it with you."

Chapter Eleven

Beads of sweat formed along Simone's forehead. Gasping for air, she fell back on the bed, thankful that the ordeal was over. Kevin stood off to the side, lost in the wonder and the miracle of life he and Simone had created. The on-call doctor snapped the band around the baby's ankle and swaddled him in a blanket.

"Time of birth?" the doctor asked.

"12:07," the nurse replied as she scribbled the time on the clipboard.

Seconds later, the doctor cuddled the baby boy in her arms and asked, "Now who wants the little prince?"

Kevin chuckled nervously. "My wife can hold him first. She did all the work."

"No, Kevin." Simone responded. "You hold him first."

Kevin stood there, lost and confused, his eyes darting between Simone and his son. He'd never held a newborn before.

"I don't know how to hold a baby. Plus, I mean, he's so tiny, I don't —"

"Here, Mr. Kennard." Dr. Peterson forced the glider from the corner with her foot. "Just sit here."

Kevin lowered himself into the chair with uncertainty scribbled over his face. Ignoring his uneasiness, the doctor placed the baby in his stiff arms.

"Now, just relax and cuddle him in your arms like a football. A football you cherish with your heart. Let him feel your love. You're his daddy."

Squirming in Kevin's arms, the baby's eyes slowly blinked open.

"You should see him, Simone," Kevin shared as he stared into the eyes of his son. "His eyes look gray."

"Gray? Uh, oh," Simone said. "Must be the cable man's baby."

Beaming with pride, Kevin began to relax. Gently, he moved the glider back and forth. "My eyes were gray when I was first born, too."

"It'll take a while for his true eye color to come in. But, in the meantime, how are you feeling?" Dr. Peterson asked Simone. A faint cloud of powdery dust flew about the air as the doctor snatched off the latex gloves, tossing them in the trash along with her surgical cap.

"I'm glad that part is over," Simone said, her voice quivering. "But these cramps are killing me, and I'm freezing."

"Well, as uncomfortable as the afterbirth pains may be, they're a good sign. It's a natural response from your body that'll keep you from hemorrhaging."

"I may want to take my chances with the hemorrhaging," Simone replied. She shifted just a little, in an attempt to find comfort.

"Dr. Peterson," a nurse stuck her head inside Simone's room. "316 is ready to push."

"Wow," Kevin said from the rocker. "It's crazy in here."

"It's what we've come to expect when there's a full moon." The doctor headed to the door.

"Doc, what about the baby lojack? When are they going to install that? The other hospital said it was done right after childbirth."

"Baby lojack?" Dr. Peterson chuckled. "That's a more advanced mobile system. This hospital hasn't received funding for that particular mobile device yet. They do have alarm bands that will be installed once your son has been examined. They'll take his footprints and pictures, too. His I.D. bracelet is wrapped around his ankle for now."

Kevin unraveled the blanket. The bracelet was around the baby's pale little ankle just as the doctor said.

"See, it matches your own bracelet."

"So when does the examination take place?" Kevin inquired.

"Someone from the nursery will be down to get your son momentarily. They'll do everything there. Shouldn't be too much longer. In the meantime, I'll get someone to bring your wife something for pain and a nice blanket from the warmer. Okay?"

"Yeah, thanks doctor Peterson."

"Congratulations, you two."

Cradling the baby in his arms, Kevin eased from the rocking chair and planted himself on the bed next to Simone.

"Did I tell you how much I love you?" he asked.

Simone squirmed and bit down on her lip.

"Damn, baby? It's that bad?"

"My God, I still feel like I'm in labor. I'd take the epidural now if they would give it to me."

"Here, can you hold the baby? I'll run out there and light a fire under somebody's butt."

"Okay."

Kevin placed the baby in Simone's arms and headed out the door, determined to find his wife a remedy for her pain.

"Hey, sweetie," Simone cooed. She attempted to inch back the receiving blanket to get a glimpse of her son, but a sharp pain ripped through her stomach. "Mmm, mmm, mmm," she moaned as she threw her head back on the pillow.

"Knock, knock, knock," a nurse chanted in a singsong voice. She entered the room, pushing a bassinet across the floor. "Hi, I'm here to take the baby to the nursery."

Simone glanced up at the nurse, disturbed by the hooded gray sweat suit underneath her white lab jacket. The nurse followed Simone's eyes.

"Oh, yeah, I know," she said with a wave of her hand. "It's been crazy in here. I'm a nurse for labor and delivery, and just as I was about to leave for the day, they begged me to stay and help out for another hour or so. See, here's my badge."

She brushed back her jacket to allow a quick glimpse of the ID dangling from the chain around her neck.

"Okay." The explanation made sense. Everyone had complained about how busy the hospital had been.

"I thought they wanted me to help with labor and delivery, but they have me helping with the nursery, too."

"Think you can find me some drugs for this pain?" Simone passed Lil' Kevin to the nurse.

"Sweetie," she replied as she placed the baby in the bassinet, "it's your lucky day. I have that, too."

"Wow, they have you playing double duty for real, huh?"

"Gets like that on occasion," the nurse replied.

"If you see my husband at the desk, can you tell him — Damn!" The nurse yanked Simone's arm down with unnecessary force.

"I'm sorry, I'm sorry," the nurse said. "My last patient was a cry baby. We had to practically hold her down. I'm so sorry." She tied rubber tubing around Simone's arm, then pulled a syringe from her pocket. She pushed the air from the needle and injected Simone with the contents.

"You didn't wipe my arm with alcohol."

"You didn't wipe my arm alcohol," Felicia mimicked sarcastically as she snatched the band from Simone's arm. "Bitch, fuck you."

The drug raced through Simone's veins and began to take effect. "What did you call me?" she slurred.

Felicia dropped the needle in the front pocket of her lab coat. She grabbed the edge of the bassinet and quickly pushed Lil' Kevin out the door, heading in the opposite direction of the nursery.

Simone patted the side of her bed for the buzzer, but gave up when the pain seemed to vanish. All of a sudden, there was calmness. Minutes later, Kevin tip toed back in the room and stood before his wife.

"Hey, baby. Did somebody make it in here yet?" he asked.

Fighting to keep her eyes open, Simone's head wobbled back and forth as she swatted the air, fishing for Kevin's hand.

Kevin caressed her hand. "You okay?"

She moved her mouth, but there were no words.

"Hi, I'm so sorry," a nurse interrupted as she rushed inside the room toting a Dixie cup and a blanket draped across her arm. "I have her painkillers and a nice warm blanket fresh out the oven."

Kevin studied his wife, watching as her eyes blinked slowly. "She's trying to say something."

The nurse who assisted Dr. Peterson with the delivery approached the bed. "Oh, she's just groggy. Looks like someone already gave her the pain medicine. Let me check her chart." The nurse rested the warm blankets on the bed and placed the Dixie cup with the pills on the hospital tray. The chart that normally hung from the bottom of the bed wasn't there, nor was it in the chart holder by the door. "Let me see who has it."

"But if you're her nurse, who gave her pills?"

"When it's crazy like this, we help each other out. I'm sure they documented it in her chart. I'll buzz the desk and have them bring it to me." She pressed the call button on Simone's bedside remote to summon the nurse's station.

Kevin caressed Simone's hands and stared at his wife. A tear fell from Simone's eye as she forced out her words, "The baby."

The nurse was puzzled. "What she say?" But Kevin had heard her loud and clear.

"She's asking about the baby."

"Oh, he's in the nursery. They have to clean him up and count his fingers and toes. You can go down to the nursery, if you want."

"The baby," Simone repeated, her voice light and frail.

Kevin hated the feeling gnawing away at his gut. Something wasn't right. "Where is the nursery?"

"Go out the door, make a right, and follow the signs. You can't miss it."

"Okay," Kevin said as he looked back at Simone. "Why do I feel like something's wrong?"

The nurse offered Kevin a reassuring smile as she pressed the call button again. "She's okay, Mr. Kennard. I'll be here for a few minutes. I need to check her bleeding to make sure she's not hemorrhaging." She pulled back the covers to peek at Simone's pad. "Then I'll find her file if I have to go room-to-room. Go to the nursery. Everything's fine. I promise."

Chapter Twelve

Kevin followed the nurse's instructions and headed towards the nursery. "Here it is," he said as he pressed the doorbell. The elderly nurse inside was taking forever to open the door.

"Hi, can I help you with something?" the nurse asked as Kevin made his way inside.

"Yes, I'm here to check on my son."

"Do you have a bracelet?" Kevin extended his arm.

"Hmm...Kennard," the nurse read aloud.

Kevin followed her eyes to the dry erase board on the wall and scrolled down the long list of names.

Jacobs, DeChavez, Ford, Lincoln, Hampton, Byrd, Brown.... Where the hell is Kennard? he thought to himself.

"We don't have a Kennard, sir."

"Okay, maybe I'm in the wrong nursery."

"Your baby was premature?"

"No, well I mean, he wasn't due for three more weeks but—"

"No, that's full term. The other nursery is for our preemie babies or babies with complications. Were there any complications?"

"No, none that I know of."

Kevin strolled through the rows of bassinets, scanning the nametags taped to each one.

"Well, we don't have a Kennard yet. What's the mother's last name? Maybe he was registered under her..."

"Miss." Kevin sighed, trying to snub the uneasiness swelling inside of him.

"Sir, it's possible that it's under the mother's name."

"She's my wife which makes her last name Kennard."

"Well, who's your doctor? I can page them to..."

Before she could finish her sentence, Kevin pushed through the nursery doors and rushed back to his wife's room. Something was wrong and Simone was trying to tell him.

Calm down, Kevin. Calm down. Maybe he's back in the room with Simone.

Back inside Simone's room, Kevin hurried to her bedside. He had to wake her. He went to scoop her in his arms and noticed the front of her grown and the blankets were saturated with vomit. Scooping her in his arms, he shook her.

"Simone, baby, wake up."

He grabbed her hand and gasped. It was cold and clammy.

"What the fuck," he mumbled. "SIMONE!"

He shook her and yelled her name repeatedly until he was scream-ing. Still, she remained unresponsive.

"Oh, my God, baby." He checked her pulse only to find a faint throbbing.

Kevin laid her back on the bed and frantically pressed the call button over and over again. He ran to the door, screaming at the top of his lungs.

"I need a doctor in here! I need a doctor in here now!"

Hearing his frantic pleas, the nurse rushed from the patient's room next door.

"Mr. Kennard, what's—"

Without a second thought, he snatched the nurse from the rubbery soles of her feet and pressed her into the wall of Simone's room.

"What the fuck did you give my wife?" he yelled as he wrapped his hands around her neck. "What did you give her?"

The nurse clawed at Kevin's hands while gagging. "You're choking me!"

"Bitch, I'ma do more than choke you," Kevin threatened as he tigh-tened his grip. "WHAT THE FUCK DID YOU GIVE MY WIFE?"

"Nothing," she struggled. "Nothing."

Kevin loosened his grip, allowing the nurse to fall to her knees as others hurried into the room. Seeing the chaotic scene, one nurse yelled into the hallway, "Call security!" as she rushed to the aid of her co-worker.

"I didn't give her anything. I went to find her file," the nurse managed through her coughs.

"Oh my God!" another nurse cried as she stood at Simone's bedside. "Code Blue in room 305! She's going into cardiac arrest! Code Blue in 305!"

Chapter Thirteen

S anora had another patient, a fifteen-year-old girl, six months pregnant in preterm labor. She headed to the supply room to gather IV fluids. Her pace down the heavily populated hallway turned sluggish at the sight of Felicia, who stood at the elevator dressed in a red wig and oversized hoodie. With a large duffle bag draped over her shoulder, Felicia stared at the ground like a bashful child.

That's not what she had on earlier when she came up, is it? Sanora wondered.

Felicia stole a quick glance to her right, then her left and spotted Sanora. Wide-eyed, Felicia bit down on her lip, looked over her shoulder, and summoned Sanora with a nod. Sanora hurried in Felicia's direction. She stood before her and shook her head.

"Hazel contacts, Felicia, really? And what's with the whole sweat suit get-up? You were supposed to be flaunting your sexiness."

Felicia pressed the elevator button a few more times as if to hurry it. "Yeah, yeah, I know."

"So what happened? Did you see him?" Sanora reached to remove her surgical mask.

"No." Felicia grabbed her wrist.

"What are you doing?" Sanora asked, snatching her hand away.

"Leave your mask on."

"Leave my mask on? For what?"

"Germs." Felicia raised the duffle bag up on her shoulder. "I shouldn't have come."

"Why? What happened?"

The elevator dinged, announcing its arrival. "Come on. Walk me downstairs," Felicia said as the doors parted.

"Felicia, I can't. I have a fifteen-year-old in preterm labor. I need to start her IV."

Felicia tucked her arm through Sanora's and pulled her inside the elevator. "Just walk with me real quick so I can tell you what happened."

Sanora sighed as she headed inside the elevator.

"Don't you have a key or something that'll make the elevator go straight down without stopping?" Felicia asked. With her back to the doors, and her head hung low, Felicia pulled the hood over her head and eased on the dark shades she pulled from the pocket of her fleece hoodie.

Sanora pulled her key badge from the pocket of her pink uniform. "What floor? Where you going?"

"The garage."

Sanora swiped her badge and pressed level "G." She studied Felicia as she stood facing the wall with her hoodie and dark shades.

"Felicia, is everything okay? Something don't seem right."

The hospital intercom beeped to alert the staff and visitors of an announcement: "Attention hospital staff. Code Blue in L and D. Code Blue in L and D."

Sanora fumbled for her key badge. "Oh shit."

"What?"

"I have to go back. They called a Cold Blue in Labor and Delivery."

Felicia snatched the key badge from her. "What are you doing? I have to get back upstairs," Sanora told her.

"I need your car," Felicia said as she stuffed the key badge inside her pocket.

"Felicia, I have to get back upstairs."

"I. Need. Your. Car. My ride left me."

Sanora sighed. "Your ride left you? Why didn't you drive?"

"Because I didn't."

The intercom beeped. The announcement rang out again.

On the verge of panicking, Sanora said, "I don't even have my keys, Felicia and I really need to get back upstairs."

"I have a key to your car, remember? Just like you have a key to my house."

Felicia's queer behavior suddenly made sense. She was high. Off what, Sanora hadn't a clue but she understood the need to tread with caution.

The intercom beeped again. "You know, Felicia, take my car. Just give me my access key so I can get back upstairs."

The elevator stopped. The doors parted. Felicia turned, but her focus remained on the floor as she prepared to step from the elevator.

Sanora pointed. "My car is over—" Felicia grabbed the bottom of her shirt and pulled her from the elevator with more force than needed. Sanora stumbled into the duffle bag.

"Show me," Felicia said. She pushed Sanora in front of her.

The faint whimper of a baby seemingly came from nowhere as Sanora led the way to her car. Sanora peered over her shoulder, but quickly refocused when Felicia barked, "Hurry up."

The intercom beeped again, this time with a different code. "Attention all hospital staff. Attention hospital staff. Code Pink. I repeat Code Pink."

The baby's wails heightened. "My car is right there." Sanora's voice quivered. Felicia reached in her pocket and disabled the alarm and locks.

"What the fuck is a Code Pink?"

Sanora turned to face Felicia, her face wet with tears. "It's a baby abduction." She wiped her eyes. "Give me the baby, Felicia. He didn't do anything to you."

Felicia bypassed Sanora, purposely bumping into her shoulder as she headed to the blue two-door BMW convertible. She folded back the front passenger seat and placed the duffle bag on the quaint backseat.

"Shhh...." she hissed, then popped open one of the baby bottle tops sealed in plastic. "You got some tissue or something?"

Sanora stood there, shaking her head. Her teary eyes pleaded with Felicia as the intercom beeped yet again.

"Did you hear me?"

"Felicia, please. Give me the baby. Don't do this." Felicia raised the back of her hoodie and revealed the gun tucked in the small of her back. "Now wipe your face and get the fuck in the car."

"What!?"

"You have two choices, Sanora." Felicia wrapped her hand around the gun. "Driving or dying. Which would you prefer?" Sanora burst into tears. "I ain't got all day."

Felicia waited until Sanora was inside the car. When Sanora's door slammed, she fished for a bottle of water from the duffle bag and tossed it in the passenger seat.

"Pass me a piece of napkin or something." Sanora reached inside the center console and handed Felicia a tiny pack of tissue.

"Ain't I supposed to fill this nipple?" Sanora's shoulders shivered as she nodded her head.

Felicia ripped the tissue, stuffed it in the nipple to block the air, and placed it in the baby's mouth. She had to get him to quiet down if they had any chance on making it out of the garage.

"We won't be able to get out," Sanora said as Felicia hopped in the front passenger seat and closed the door. "Within ten minutes of a Code Pink, the gates and entrances are locked."

"It ain't even been five minutes, so let's go."

Sanora started the car. "Here." Felicia handed her the bottled water. Sanora accepted the water but stared at the pill resting in the palm of Felicia's hand. Her days of getting high were over.

"I don't do drugs any more, Felicia."

"Take it," Felicia ordered. "You can go back to being drug-free later. But right now, you need to calm the fuck down. Take the pill."

Sanora stared at the pill. E was something she'd taken a million times before but not within the last six months.

"And get rid of those tears," Felicia further ordered as Sanora swallowed the pill with a gulp of water.

Sanora wiped her eyes with the back of her hand and backed from the parking space as another Code Pink rang out from the intercom. She headed to the gate, her heart thumping wickedly. Felicia peeled off the dark shades and rested her head against the window. Her eyes closed, she pretended to be asleep and threw her hand over her face.

"Bitch, you better win an Oscar," Felicia mumbled.

The gate was usually down. To exit, employees simply inserted their access key while patients inserted their parking tickets. But because of the Code Pink, the gate was up. Two guards, one black and the other Indian, stood outside of their glass booths checking the interior of cars with flashlights. Sanora pulled into the line with the black guard who she'd known briefly for a few months now. She undid her bun pinned at the crown of her head and allowed her auburn tresses to flow over her shoulders as she watched the guard search the cars ahead of her. She opened her center console, pulled out her tube of MAC gloss and shined up the remnants of her lipstick. She glanced in the rearview mirror. Her eyes were already red.

"Shit," she mumbled. She was up next. "Okay, okay," she said aloud.

"Will you stop talking to yourself and get it together?" Felicia said through tight lips.

Rolling down the window, Sanora yawned and then offered a subtle, yet sexy smile. "Hey," she damn near purred to the guard.

Unfastening her seatbelt, she pulled off her uniformed top, giving the guard a front row peek of her breasts, which were lifted high thanks to the tight little tank she had on underneath.

"Hey." He smiled, unashamed of the open gap in his teeth from years of obvious thumb sucking. His uniform, a pair of black slacks and a black shirt with *Grant Security* embroidered in yellow, were too big for his petite frame. "You leaving already?"

"No, I'll be back. Just have to run my co-worker home right quick. What time you get off?"

"Don't know now. You seen anything suspicious?"

"No, thank goodness. Man, I hope y'all catch them before they get too far."

"Yeah, me too. Can you imagine how you'd feel?"

"Yeah," Sanora laughed nervously.

"You know, I can't believe you work here now. Those days you came up here for those doctor appointments, man. I know I dreamed about you for days." He laughed.

At a loss for words, Sanora pretended to laugh along.

"So how's lil' man doing?"

"Ah, he's fine." She glanced in her rear view mirror. "Hey, you better get back to work. I'll see you in a minute. Will I be able to get back in?"

He stepped away from the car. "Yeah, you should be okay unless the police take over. They on the way now."

"Wow, okay. See you when I get back."

"I can't wait." Sanora pulled off.

With her head still resting against the window, Felicia said, "that muthafucka look like he got hit in the mouth with a dick."

"Where am I going?" Sanora asked, not the least bit amused.

"Hit the beltway and head to the spa. Somebody's going to meet us on 301." Sanora pulled from the garage and headed toward the beltway. "So your lying ass been working up here for a minute."

"No, I just started yesterday."

"Then what the hell was he talking about? You turning tricks while you helping your super sick mother?"

"No, I was bringing her back and forth to the doctor."

"Speaking of your mother, here." Sanora glanced at the prepaid phone. "Call here. She'll probably see the shit on the news. Let her know you okay. Block that number, too."

Sanora took the phone, hit star 6-7 and dialed her mother.

"And who's lil' man?" Felicia asked.

"My nephew. My white brother's son."

Chapter Fourteen

T rapped in the darkness, Simone fought to free herself. She hated when her body became immobile but her mind remained fully conscious. Normally, when she hallucinated in her sleep, her surroundings seemed clear. But this time, a still blackness haunted her. Finally, after a fluster of forced blinks, her eyes opened. Slowly, the objects around her began to take form beyond that of their initial blur.

An older Caucasian man stood two inches taller than Kevin. A head full of salt-and-pepper curls, a slowly aging face of soft wrinkles, and his lean build clothed in an expensive-looking navy blue suit; everything about him screamed money. His mouth moved, yet silence flowed as he chatted with her husband. Pain was etched in Kevin's face as he listened, his back resting against the wall to support his feeble stance as he stared out at nothing. Angela sat in a chair, black mascara smeared around her eyes. Dried-up tears stained her cheeks.

Kevin's lips moved. She knew his lips well and read what seemed to be "Still no word on..." The doctor's nod cut Kevin off before he could finish asking his question.

What's going on? Simone questioned. She couldn't hear a thing. Nothing but the continuously, annoying beep from the heart monitor. *Is that machine for me? I'm in the hospital?*

She grunted and pulled, but couldn't move. Something held her down. Yet, her surroundings were too vivid for it to be a hallucination.

The doctor took a step toward the door. *No, don't leave!*

Simone grew frustrated. *Wait a minute!* Her ears popped. Her hearing had returned. Relieved, she called after the doctor. *Doc!*

Kevin leaned against the wall with his hand on his forehead. "Doc."

Thank you, baby, Simone said.

Though Kevin's voice was muffled and seemingly as weak as hers, he was closer to the doctor. Lifting his head, he stared at the doctor through red eyes stained from crying.

"There's really nothing you can do? I mean, suppose she was the president? What would y'all do then? I can't take fifty-fifty, Doc. I need something more concrete. I need you to tell me she's going to be okay."

The doctor sighed as he searched for the right words of comfort.

"Unfortunately, Mr. Kennard, we've done everything we can. Pulling through something like this is up to the patient. It just depends on their will to live."

I've pulled through, doc. Kevin, I'm up. It's okay baby, Simone said.

"Can she hear us?" Kevin asked.

Yes, I can hear you. You can't hear me? Simone cleared her throat. *Is that better? Can you hear me now?*

"In most cases, they can," the doctor shared. "So talk to her. It can only help."

Okay, I have got to get out of this bed.

Simone tugged. She pulled. But no matter her attempt, she couldn't free herself from the bed. To gather strength, she relaxed and filled her lungs with air. Fueled by determination, she gave another powerful tug until finally, she sat up in bed.

It happened in slow motion. Angela's gut wrenching, boundless wails bedeviled the room as her body gradually descended from the chair to the floor. Kevin's eyes bulged in fear as he and the doctor leaped across the room to Simone's bedside.

Simone turned to the heart monitor. The continuously, annoying beep was gone. In its place: a flatline.

Chapter Fifteen

Nervous energy flowed through Felicia's veins as she snatched off the oversized sweat suit. Dressed in her bra and panties, she frantically searched the bureau in her office for a change of clothes. But thanks to the plastic surgery, everything was too big.

"Shit, now what am I gonna put on?" she mumbled.

Unable to sit still, Sanora paced back and forth, dancing to the tune playing in her head. "Clothes? You just blew up my fuckin' car and you're thinking about clothes?" The image of her 2005 BMW convertible up in flames sent her to the black leather sofa where she sat next to Lil' Kevin.

"I always wanted to do that shit, too." Felicia chuckled. "I saved your tags, though. I have your keys, too, but you ain't getting them."

"Ha ha ha."

"But seriously. What choice did I have? The wig, those glasses, all that shit had to be destroyed. It was evidence."

"You should've kept your wig." Sanora said. Felicia's hair was a mess. Nappy, tangled braids on one side, and her natural, matted baby bush on the other.

"Fuck you, bitch."

"Damn, I feel like a good fuck, too. All them pills ever make you wanna do is dance and fuck."

Sanora had to do something with herself. She rose from the couch, smacking her lips. "Damn, my mouth still dry as hell."

She snatched the office door open, waltzed out to the lobby, and grabbed two bottles of water from the small refrigerator. She took the top off the first and guzzled it down without a breath.

"I'm glad to see you remember your way around," Felicia yelled from her back office.

Felicia parked herself in the high back chair behind her desk to think. To hell with clothes, for the time being. Now that she had the baby, what was she going to do with him and Sanora for that matter?

Felicia glanced at her watch. Sanora had taken the pill almost two hours ago. She'd be antsy for hopefully, another two. Felicia knew she had to keep Sanora high and under tight surveillance until everything was figured out. By now, the authorities had probably identified Sanora as the missing nurse. Nine times out of ten, the Virginia authorities had been notified and a team of detectives were en route to Sanora's mother's house, which would turn up nothing.

Sometime within the next forty-eight hours, Felicia knew the cops would be heading her way, which didn't faze her too tough. Hell, what could she tell them? Sanora had quit months ago. Sure, they chatted on occasion. Felicia could even share that Sanora called her from the hospital the night the kidnapping took place to see how her appointment went with Dr. Gustafuson. And that would be all she knew. Investigating Felicia would be another dead.

As far as becoming a suspect herself, Felicia wasn't worried. The layer of clothes beneath the baggy sweat suit gave her the pounds she'd rid herself of weeks ago. In addition to her disguise, she kept her head down to avoid the cameras. If one of the cameras happened to catch a glimpse of her, it would reveal nothing more than an overweight, dark skinned chick hiding behind long, flowing red hair, dark shades and a hoodie. She was dark skinned yes but she wasn't big. And besides, her cell phone records would prove she wasn't anywhere near the hospital. She was at Linwood's house, chatting for hours with her daughter, Mercedes.

"Whew, I need to dance!" Sanora yelled from the lobby.

Minutes later, Sanora's favorite CD shot through the spa's surround sound system, which she accompanied with finger snaps. Felicia rose from her chair and tiptoed down the hallway. Her hand over her mouth to contain her giggles, she peeked around the corner to watch Sanora grind to the reggae dancehall. Felicia had to give it to her. Sanora's Jamaican blood was alive and well. The girl still had moves like few she'd seen. But after watching for a few minutes, Felicia got pissed. Her number one moneymaker was in the middle of the floor putting on a show for no one, inside the spa that suffered financially because of her absence. Dressed in her bra and panties, Felicia stormed to the system and shut the music off.

"What you do that for?" Sanora asked.

"I need to think," Felicia yelled over her shoulder as she headed back into her office. "And that shit is distracting."

Sanora followed Felicia back to the office. Lil' Kevin laid on the couch whimpering.

"See we couldn't even hear him for that bullshit. I thought you had to tend to your so-called dying mother?" Felicia plopped back in her chair.

Ignoring Felicia's question, Sanora sat along the edge of the couch. She scooped the baby up in her arms and eased back the receiving blanket to get a glimpse of him. Instinctively, he turned his pinkish face toward her breasts.

"Hey, handsome," she cooed, then absentmindedly started humming "Murder She Wrote" by Chaka Demus and Pliers, the last dancehall song that had played.

Felicia sucked her teeth. She rose from her high back chair and sat on the couch, inches away from Sanora. "Give him to me. Shit. I should be his mother for real any way." Sanora was hesitant. "Give him to me," Felicia demanded and pried the baby from Sanora's arms.

"Yeah, you gon' be a cutie just like your fine ass father. You already got them funny color eyes," she commented as Lil' Kevin whimpered. "What's wrong? You hungry?"

"That and he probably wants his mother," Sanora said.

Felicia sat on the couch mesmerized. "That's okay." She reached behind her back and toyed with the hooks to her bra.

"What are you getting ready to do?" Sanora laughed as Felicia tried to unfasten the hooks. "Girl, ain't shit in those fake, rusty ass titties but dust." Sanora reached inside the nursery gift that Felicia stole from the hospital and grabbed a ready-to-feed bottle. "Give him here. I'll feed him."

Felicia handed the baby back to Sanora. She stood from the couch and began her own pacing back and forth across the carpet. Sanora sat on the couch, humming as she fed the baby. Unable to sit still, she said, "Okay, here Fe. You gotta feed him. I need to move around, dance, or something."

Felicia held her arms out for the baby. "Your ass done picked up some weight. You lookin' a lil' thick," Felicia said as Sanora placed the baby in her arms.

Ignoring Felicia's comment, Sanora snapped her fingers and moved to the imaginary tune.

"You know what? Maybe you should go dance. Hell, you still got a rack of shit in your office. A new spot just opened a few weeks ago right on the Bowie, Crofton line. I gotta get up there and holla at them about getting some dancers in there. Some real ones. I need more money since your ass bailed out on me." She rolled her eyes at Sanora.

"Damn, matter of fact, you could grab some mad ass tips and an alibi. Them drunk-ass niggas won't remember what time you got there. They'll just remember that Tootie's fat ass was there and they're open 'til four on the weekends."

Sanora stood in the middle of the floor. "So what? Go? You telling me to go dance at the club?"

"Yeah. You can get dressed here. Take my old Honda. It's parked out back. You should get there in time to snatch the finale spot. Me and the baby will stay here tonight. I ain't trying to go nowhere 'til I map this shit out."

"So where do I go when I'm done?"

"Just come back here."

Holding the bottle with her chin, Felicia slid open her top drawer and placed a cash box on top of her desk. She popped it open. Inside was the ticket to every possible high imaginable. She grabbed the baggie loaded with pills. "Take a few of them with you. Matter of fact, pop one before you go."

Sanora snatched a tissue from the box of Kleenex on Felicia's desk and placed three pills inside.

"Take one," Felicia repeated.

"Damn, can I go get my shit and some water first? Please and thank you." Sanora turned to head back out to the lobby.

"Hey!" Felicia shouted after Sanora, stopping her before she set foot outside her office.

"Yeah."

"A few rules. First, no cell phone calls."

Sanora shifted her weight and held out her hands with a crazed expression as if to say, duh. "Felicia, I don't have a phone any got damn way. My stuff—"

"Second!" Felicia bellowed. "Don't get any ideas or I promise you," her narrow eyes sent daggers across the room, "your mother will be laying right next to your brother."

Sanora said, "Burp him."

"What?" Felicia shot back with a look of pure evilness.

"Burp. Him." Sanora replied. "You just fed him so now you have to burp him."

"Get your high ass out my office."

*****

Slow down, slow down, Sanora told herself. Speeding would summon unwanted attention. Crain Highway was often flooded with both state troopers and county cops.

Like a bat out of hell, she'd fled from the spa. She rolled down the window and spit out the pill tucked under her tongue. She'd swallowed the first in the hospital parking garage but had no intention of popping any more, especially now that the high was beginning to subside. Months ago, she depended on the pills to get through some of the vile things men asked her to do. She remembered the way the pills made her feel, the way they made her act. Mimicking the behavior was easy.

The radio beeped. The Emergency Broadcasting System was rendering an AMBER alert. An infant had been abducted from Wakefield Hospital. Stones from the heavily graveled shoulder flew into the blue Honda Accord as Sanora pulled over. Before the car was in park, she burst into tears.

"Why did I call you? Why did I call you?" she cried.

Never in a million years could she have fathomed that her phone call would ignite a wave of crime that would spark her fame on *"America's Most Wanted."* Deep down, Sanora hoped getting Kevin and Felicia into the same room would rekindle their relationship. Kevin would be in awe of Felicia's body and everything she'd done just for him. No sparks would jump off that night, but it would give Felicia something else to focus on.

"You were probably lying the entire got damn time." Sanora mumbled through tears. "How were you going to see him if he was home and married?" She cried.

Felicia wasn't what most men considered attractive and it wasn't because of her midnight complexion. Beautiful women came in every shade. But Felicia's nose spread the width of her face. Her teeth were tiny and gapped in the front, which looked extremely odd considering the size of her thick lips. She seldom smiled, which made her thuggish demeanor seem evil and stern. On the rare occasions when she did chuckle, she covered her mouth with her hand. However, the biggest turnoff, the 225 pounds that once graced her 5'5 frame, had been demolished.

But Sanora had no idea how distraught Felicia was. She'd taken Felicia's quest for Kevin's blood as an idle threat spilled from a broken heart.

In the rearview mirror, headlights beamed off in the distance.

Sanora's heart began to thump. She wouldn't be surprised if Felicia had decided to follow her. Tears would prove Sanora wasn't as high as she pretended to be. Smacking away the tears, Sanora placed the car into drive. The tires spun amidst the gravel, creating a cloud of dust as she skidded from the shoulder to the main road. Dancing had always relaxed her. Once she was relaxed, she could think of a way to save herself and the baby she'd placed in harm's way.

*****

A little after three, the Gentleman's Bar parking lot was still pretty full despite the fact it closed in an hour. Sanora circled twice to get a feel for the money inside. There were a few Buicks and Nissans, but the Mercedes, BMWs, and Porsches were plentiful. No doubt, big money awaited her inside.

"Damn. Valet parking," she said through her sniffles as she drove past the attendant's booth.

She pulled into an empty parking space toward the back of the lot. Her high was dwindling fast. The little common sense she had left questioned the whole dancing thing and suggested she call the police. But she was scared. There was no telling where Felicia or one of her spies lurked.

A car door slammed, startling Sanora as she searched the parking lot. The engine started. A black Acura backed from a space a few cars away. Her nerves were shot to hell. Another pill would calm her but she tossed the notion aside and opted for a drink from the bar. Inside, she would feel safer.

Chapter Sixteen

F at Ed sat at the bar, his lip curled in a smile as he swished around the caramel colored liquor in his shot glass. He'd made up his mind. It didn't make sense to hide it anymore, anyway. It had been official for three weeks. It was time to share the news. He'd planned to tell Kevin over a toast, but where was he?

Fat Ed pulled his phone from his hip and dialed Kevin's number again. But like the times prior, Kevin's voice mail greeted him.

"Damn, man. What happened? I've been up here since midnight. Thought you were coming up? Look, hit me in the morning. Need to talk to you. It's important."

The bartender mopped a white terry-cloth rag along the marbled counter. "What's up? Did you reach him yet?" he asked over the loud music.

"No, and I know he ain't coming out now. Shit, y'all close in an hour right?"

"Yep."

"I know he cuddled up with his wife. Can't be mad at that. All he thinks about is his family and music. I'm happy for him, though. He finally living the life he dreamt about."

"Damn, that's what's up. I hope I find me somebody special like that," the bartender replied.

Fat Ed tossed back the shot swishing around in his glass. "You should see them together. They always touching and kissing on each other. They make you feel like you in love and you ain't even got no damn body."

He stared into the empty shot glass, wishing he could have the evening back. He would've told Kevin earlier, and right now, they would have been celebrating.

"Man, this place seems to be picking up," Fat Ed said as he glanced around the room.

"Yeah, man. I wasn't feeling the valet, but these fools love it," the bartender replied as he gripped the bar.

Fat Ed pulled a wad of folded bills from the inside pocket of his black mink jacket and placed a hundred dollar bill on the counter.

"You know niggas lazy. Once y'all get a better class of dancers up in here, things will really jump off."

The bartender spotted the money. "C'mon, Ed. You know your money ain't no good in these parts."

"XO ain't cheap." Fat Ed eyed the bottle nestled on the top shelf. "And I put a little dent in that bottle."

"Yeah, don't too many people come in here asking for that but you. That's like your own personal bottle."

"I got Kevin on that XO, too. One day, I'ma get his ass in here to have a drink."

The bartender slid the bill back across the counter to Fat Ed. "Can't wait to finally meet him. In the meantime, take that back. You've invested enough already, so get that outta here."

Fat Ed grabbed the rejected bill and placed it back inside his pocket. He glanced at the plasma mounted on the wall behind the bar and narrowed his eyes to read the alert scrolling across the screen.

"Hey, what's that scrolling across the screen? A storm coming or something?"

"No. It's one of those AMBER alerts. Think a baby got kidnapped from a hospital or something.

"Damn, man. White people crazy," Fat Ed mumbled to himself. "Alright, man. I'll holla at you one day next week."

Reaching across the counter, Fat Ed and the bartender exchanged a brotherly handshake. A sharp pain ripped through Fat Ed's stomach as he swiveled around on the stool to leave. There she was, as radiant as ever despite the absence of make-up. His eyes roamed her body, then made a face at the black leather mini dress that cherished her every curve. A hint of her butt cheeks peered from underneath the hem, while the deep V-cut opening in the front exposed the plumpness of her breasts. Fat Ed heard one of the patrons at the bar ask the bartender, "Is she dancing tonight?" She had the attention of every man around her. After a quick scan of the room, she spotted him.

He noticed her bloodshot eyes. Based on her attire, she'd not only come to dance, but she was high. Instantly, he felt like a fool. She hadn't changed at all.

For three weeks, he had beaten himself up about doing the right thing. Now he was glad Kevin had been a no-show. He was even more thankful that he'd gotten the ten grand in cash as opposed to a cashier's check. Cash always made for an easy deposit.

She smiled at him but Fat Ed didn't return it. He eased from his stool and strolled in her direction. The closer he got, he could tell something was wrong. There was a pinkish undertone to her exotic looking olive-colored skin. He watched her chest deflate from a deep sigh before she ordered a shot of Hennessy. Elbows propped up on the bar, she closed her eyes and massaged her temple as she awaited her drink. Tears glistened through her lids. As hard as Fat Ed tried, he couldn't deny his concern. This wasn't the Sanora he cared so deeply for.

"Oh, so you do see me?" She opened her eyes and grabbed a cocktail napkin from the stack in the holder to dab at the moisture in the corner of her eyes.

The bartender placed her shot in front of her. Before Sanora had a chance to scoop it up, Fat Ed pushed it back and gestured toward the cognac on the top shelf.

"Every man in the room sees you." The light touch from his hand made her jump.

The bartender placed the shot glass filled with the top shelf cognac on the counter. Fat Ed watched as she gulped it down, growling from the harsh burn, then coughing to clear her throat. The bartender placed the bottle and another empty shot glass on the counter. Despite the burn, Sanora slammed two additional shots back to back. Fat Ed stopped her at the fourth.

Leaning against the empty stool, he said, "Sanora, come on. Talk to me. What's wrong?" He tugged on the strap of her dress. "I thought you were changing your life around."

"I was. Things were —," she shrugged and glanced around the room, "one person away from being perfect."

He followed her gaze. "I thought staying away was your plan. I mean, why come back?"

"I fucked up, Ed. I fucked up big." She tapped a rhythm-less tune against the side of the shot glass with the tips of her French manicured nails.

"Anything I can do?"

She turned to him. Her sea-green eyes were unsure, yet pleading. "Have a drink with me?"

They held each other's gaze. Fat Ed broke the stare and climbed on top of the barstool.

Minutes filled with idle chatter and laughter ticked away the tension and the time. To each other's surprise, more time was spent chatting than sipping on the top shelf liquor. Still through the few smiles Sanora displayed, Fat Ed knew something was wrong. Despite the relaxing toxin in her system, she was jumpy and constantly looked over her shoulders. If silence lingered for more than a minute, her tears threatened to surface.

"Sanora, is somebody after you or something? Why you keep looking over your shoulder?"

"I'm fine," she lied.

The bartender moseyed over to Fat Ed and Sanora with his jacket folded over his arm.

"Damn." Fat Ed looked around. The music had stopped long ago. Engulfed in each other, they'd lost track of time. The place was empty with the exception of the three.

"Thanks for keeping me company, though." The bartender smiled.

"How much do we owe you?" Sanora asked.

"You with my man, so you good. Don't worry about it."

Fat Ed placed the hundred back on the counter. "Take it, man. If the drinks were free, your service wasn't. Take it as a tip."

With a wide grin, the bartender grabbed the bill and placed it in his back pocket. "Thanks man. Listen, I'm going to check these other doors and make sure they're locked."

"Okay," Fat Ed said as the bartender strolled off.

Sanora stumbled from the barstool. Standing, the liquor hit her.

"Okay, you won't be driving," Fat Ed said. "Where you going?"

"To hell I'm sure."

"Well, before then?"

She hunched her shoulders. "It's late. I hope you not in trouble."

Puzzled, Fat Ed turned to face her as she stood, swaying. "In trouble for what?"

"I'm sure your girlfriend or whoever is probably pissed."

He shook his head, laughing to himself. She leaned against the corner and looked him in his face.

"Are you in love?" Her voice had begun to slur.

"Actually, I think I am."

She forced herself in between his legs as he sat on the barstool. Piercing him with her sea-green eyes, she tossed an arm over his shoulder, while her other hand rubbed his cinnamon brown face. She kissed him. He welcomed her lips that tasted like a night of cognac. Her drunken lust echoed his own. Never did he bother to pull away like a man in love should do. But few seldom pulled away from Sanora.

Finally, she peeled her lips from his, yet they remained entwined, kissing like Eskimos as they inhaled each other's liquor scented breath.

"Let your bitch know that your baby momma loves you, too," Sanora whispered.

"Oh really?"

"Yes, really."

Inching from her, Fat Ed said, "Well, let me call and tell that bitch now." Baffled, Sanora watched in disbelief as Fat Ed pulled his cell from his hip and placed a call.

"Typical fucking man."

She grabbed her purse and attempted to storm off on unstable legs. Fat Ed climbed from the stool, surprised by his own uneasiness. But he'd consumed more than his fair share of liquor, too.

"Damn," he mumbled as he found his footing. He chased after Sanora and grabbed her arm before she broke her ankles running drunk in her stilettos.

"Get off of me." She tried to pull from Fat Ed's grasp, but he wasn't letting her go.

"Where's your phone?" he asked while holding her arm.

"Please, Ed. Just let me go," she said. The tears she battled for hours trickled down her face.

"Sanora, look at your phone. I was calling you." He held out his phone. She stopped fighting long enough to stare at the screen. It was her cell that he'd called. Her mouth agape, she gawked at him.

"You got your stuff?"

She answered with a nod.

"Come on. I'll take you where you need to go. You can't drive no damn way."

The bartender surfaced from the back.

"Hey, you good?" Fat Ed called out to him.

"Yeah, man. Y'all go 'head. I'm leaving in five minutes."

"Alright, man." Fat Ed tossed up a nod then pushed open the door.

Daylight and the crisp morning breeze greeted them as they stepped from the club. Sanora went into a frenzy, shocked by the start of day.

"Oh my God, what time is it?" she asked. She stumbled around in circles, surveying her surroundings.

Fat Ed glanced at his watch. "It's a little after five in the morning. Why?"

She kicked off her heels and ran to the black Navigator on her tiptoes. She tugged on the passenger door handle. "Open the door. Please, open the door."

Fat Ed disarmed the alarm and quickened his pace to the driver's seat while she climbed in.

"Sanora, what the hell is going on?" He said as he slammed his door. He placed the key in the ignition. The radio blared. He reached to turn it down. "Look, I know I acted like an ass when you told me you were pregnant."

"Ed, drive. Please, just drive," she cried.

"No, we're not going anywhere until you listen."

The broadcasting system's alert beeped through the radio. Sanora reached over and powered off the system.

"Ed, please just—"

"SANORA! WILL YOU LISTEN."

Sighing in frustration, Fat Ed said, "Look, I know I haven't been there for you and I'm sorry for how I acted when you told me you were pregnant. After you left, it hit me. I knew that I was in love with you. I got the paternity test results three weeks ago and I've been racking my brain on how I can make this right."

Sanora sat in the passenger's seat combing through her hair with her hand as her tears splashed onto her breasts. Fat Ed opened up his center console and handed her the bank envelope.

"I got this out the bank earlier today for you and the baby. It's ten grand." Sanora didn't flinch. Fat Ed grabbed her clutch from her lap and put the envelope inside. "I want to make this right, baby. I want you to trust me." He reached over and rubbed her shoulder. "I know you in some kind of trouble." She dropped her head into her hands. Her quiet sobs erupted into wails.

At a loss for words, Fat Ed started his truck. "I'm going to get us a hotel room down the street."

Sanora shot up. "No! No hotel rooms."

"Well, we can't sit here. I'm okay to drive a little ways, but not to my house. That's too far."

Sanora fished inside her clutch for the set of keys to the Honda. She searched the ring and found the key she was looking for. "I know where we can go. It's only fifteen minutes from here."

Chapter Seventeen

K evin's mind went stir crazy as the chaotic scene unfolded before his eyes. Simone's gown was ripped from her lifeless body as a team of doctors worked to resuscitate her. In a matter of seconds, the metal bars on her bed were latched into place, and Simone's unresponsive body was whisked off.

For hours after the announcement of the Code Pink and Code Blue, detectives swarmed the scene and shut down the hospital. Uniformed officers were planted at every entrance. Only critical patients were admitted to the emergency room. A baby had been kidnapped and murder had been attempted. Everybody in the hospital was a suspect, including Kevin.

"Mr. Kennard," one of the detectives said to Kevin as he sat at Simone's bedside with his face buried in her bed, refusing to release her hand. "I'm going to need you to come to the station to make a statement."

Kevin didn't budge. His wife had gone into cardiac arrest and flat-lined both within a matter of hours. Parting from her side was the furthest thing from his mind. He wished he could make everyone disappear so he could crawl into bed with his wife and breathe love and life back inside of her.

"Mr. Kennard, you have a very impressive criminal record."

Kevin lifted his head and stared angrily at the detective through painful eyes tinted red from tears.

"You think I did this to my wife? You think I kidnapped my own son?"

"Everyone's a suspect, Mr. Kennard. We can eliminate you if you come down to the station and answer a few questions."

"What more could y'all possibly ask me? I've already answered questions from two other detectives. If y'all leave me the hell alone, maybe you could find my son and the muthafucka that did this shit."

"We have officers aggressively searching. Mr. Kennard, there's a wave of information on the internet. We checked you out and saw your wedding picture in *Jet*. You and your wife live a pretty lavish lifestyle."

"Lavish? The wedding picture was a gift. Wasn't like we had folks from the magazine following us around. And what's so lavish about our lifestyle? We drive decent enough cars and live in a decent house just like everybody else in Prince George's County."

"Have you written any of the inmates that you were incarcerated with?" the detective asked.

"No, not one. My wife and I wrote one of the lieutenants, Lieutenant Newsome. But I haven't written any inmates."

"What did the letter say?"

"I mean, she helped us with a misunderstanding once. We wrote to thank her and sent her a wedding picture."

"Did you mention your songwriting deal?"

"I said I'd sold some music, yes. Damn," Kevin said more so to himself. He knew where the line of questioning was leading.

"Where'd you and your wife get married?" the detective probed.

"In St. Lucia."

"And the picture—"

"Yes, it was from the island," Kevin replied. "So what, you're thinking Lieutenant Newsome may've showed them off and word got around and... ah, man." Kevin shook his head.

"It's possible she showed a guard or two who may have said something to an inmate and things could've been exaggerated. But, like I said, it's just one of many avenues that we're pursuing. We've already requested a list of the inmates recently released who were incarcerated with you. Nine times out of ten, Mr. Kennard, they aren't living like you. In the meantime, I still need your official statement. Every little bit helps. Your wife will be in good hands. We have an officer at the door."

"Look, Detective—"

"Ward." He reached inside his khaki-colored trench and passed Kevin a card. "Detective Ward." Kevin took the card and placed it on Simone's bedside table without giving it a second glance.

"I already told you everything that I know. The doctor confirmed it. The nurses confirmed it. Ain't nothing gon' change if I go to the station. Your questions gon' be the same and my answers gon' be the same."

The detective sighed. "Mr. Kennard, if I have to, I'll obtain a warrant."

"Then file the papers because I'm not leaving my wife. Not like this."

Detective Ward closed the small note pad and eased it into his back pocket. While heading to the door, he added, "You are aware that your failure to cooperate could be viewed as violation of your parole."

"I think a judge might understand."

"I'll give you twenty-four hours, Mr. Kennard. Then I'll have to file the papers."

Andre Perkins took advantage of his authority. Flashing his FBI badge to the officer at the door, he strolled inside Simone's room and stood over top of her bed, staring at her lifeless body connected to machines. Slowly, her chest heaved up and down thanks to the assistance of the plastic tube inserted down her throat. IVs probed her hands. Gently, he planted a tender kiss on Simone's forehead while Kevin sat on the opposite side of the bed, completely unfazed by Andre's presence or gestures.

"You know," Andre cleared his throat to ward off his grief, "this is your fault."

"What?"

It was one thing for the detectives to view him as a suspect, but Andre? The man who had taken Simone's hand in matrimony, only to guide her through years of misery. Simone had shared the horror stories about the women, the strippers, and Andre's comings and goings throughout the night. She'd shared how they'd argued like strangers in a heat of road rage, calling each other things that folks couldn't imagine. There was a heap of things Kevin could've thrown at Andre.

"Simone wouldn't be in this bed fighting for her life if she was still married to me."

Kevin locked eyes with Andre. The disgust each man felt for the other was obvious. Out of respect for his wife, Kevin bit down on his bottom lip to keep from saying what he wanted.

"I wonder if your P.O. knows that a warrant is being prepared for you. What's your P.O.'s name?" Andre snapped his fingers. "McPherson?" He said it as if a light bulb went off.

Kevin nodded his head. "Yeah, that's his name. You want his number? You can call him and whoever else you need to call. But, do me a favor: Make those calls outside of my wife's room."

Andre stood at Simone's bedside seemingly stung by Kevin's words. Simone was Kevin's wife now.

Andre's sulky look hardened as he strolled to the door. Before he made his exit, he said, "Let's see how long she stays your wife once you go back to prison."

Chapter Eighteen

Tipsy as hell, Fat Ed and Sanora stumbled inside Felicia's town-house. The stench greeted them.

"Damn, whose funky ass spot is this? I thought you were staying with your mom's?" Fat Ed asked as they staggered up the steps.

"No, it's a friend of mine. She's out of town." Sanora lied as she led him upstairs to Mercedes' room. Pushing the door open, she sighed in relief. A pigsty by some standards, Mercedes' bedroom had always been the cleanest bedroom in the house.

Inside, she tossed her clutch on the pillows, dropped her stilettos to the floor, then closed the bedroom door. Alone with Fat Ed, she felt safe. But, the alcohol and the love he'd confessed had her feeling horny. Barefoot, she strolled toward Fat Ed with lust in her eyes.

"Get this dress off of me."

Happy to oblige, Fat Ed eased the piece of material she called a dress from her shoulders and tugged it down her hips. Underneath the dress was nothing but her au naturel.

"Damn, girl. You carry that baby weight well. You still phat as a mutha."

Her short manicured nails on his chest, Sanora backed him to the queen size bed in the middle of the room until he had no choice but to sit along the edge.

"Hold up, baby." Fat Ed removed his mink and tossed it on the black and pink high-heel shoe shaped chair. He placed the gun nestled in the back of his waist on the nightstand next to the bed. Sanora screwed up her face.

"Since when you carry a gun?"

"I ain't got time to be fighting these young bammas out here. What? It bothers you?"

"No," she replied as she rubbed the sexy stubble sprouting from his face. "It makes me feel safe."

Resting on his elbow, metal clapped together in a rhythmless jingle as Sanora unfastened his belt. She undid his pants, lowered his zipper, and reached inside his silk boxers for that short, plump erection she'd craved the past few months.

"Damn, I forgot how thick he was."

Fat Ed eased from his elbows to pull the cashmere sweater over his head. "I hope you ain't forget how to ride that muthafucka."

Minutes later, the room was filled with squeaks from the bed. Their cries of drunken lust rang out for nearly an hour as they christened their newly confessed love.

Drenched in sweat, Sanora climbed from him, pulled back the comforter, and crawled up to the pillows, accidentally sending her clutch behind the head of the bed. Change fell from Fat Ed's pockets as he kicked his pants from his ankles to the floor and crawled up to the pillows with her. Pulling the comforter over their nakedness, he stretched out his arm and invited her into his embrace. He kissed her lightly on her forehead as she made herself comfortable in his arms.

"You ready to tell me what's going on?"

"No, not yet. I just want to lay here and pretend like everything's okay. Just for a few more minutes."

"It will be okay. I meant what I said, Sanora. I love you, and I'm going to make everything up to you and our son. I promise."

Sanora laid there in silence.

"What you think about us moving in together? You know, actually being a family. You wouldn't have to work, unless of course you wanted to. But, not no fucking strip club."

"Ed, what are you saying?"

"I'm saying I can get you out of this shit. I can take you away from your troubles."

His words lingered in the air as he waited for a reply from Sanora. But instead of the joy he expected, he felt her tears against his chest.

"Okay, that's it. You been jumpy all evening, crying and carrying on. Talk to me, baby. What's wrong?"

Buried in Fat Ed's chest, her muffled voice said, "I've been trying to get out of this shit and get away from these fucked-up ass people and this fucked up ass life."

"Sanora, listen to me. Fuck your past and fuck this game. We'll just move away from it all. I can do music from wherever. Shit, we can go to Georgia or some damn where. Won't a soul know us."

In the back of Sanora's mind, she often wondered how life would've been had she continued on her original path. If she had simply walked away from the metal detector and went to visit Harvey another day. Maybe, just may, he'd still be alive. Would she be the doctor she'd set out to be with a loving husband and kids living comfortably in a house with a white picket fence? What ifs flooded her mind on a daily basis as the detour she'd taken swallowed her alive and boarded-up every exit.

Once upon a time, she figured marriage would never be an option for her. What good man would want a relationship with a tricking stripper as popular as Sanora? A year ago, it seemed that one of her private fantasies was coming true when a condom ripped during a round of heated sex with Fat Ed, her new caked-up regular who she acquired without Felicia's connection.

She'd seen him in the clubs here and there. Normally, she wouldn't have given him a second glance. She'd never been into fat dudes. Big, thick, and muscular—yes. Fat, no—unless of course they were paying for her services; then she didn't care what they looked like. But there was something about this Fat Ed person. His presence commanded attention. From the stage, she watched as even the big-time ballers stopped to dap him up and show him love. The next step most of those big-time ballers took was to the stage where they placed fifties and hundreds inside the g-string of the grand finale they called Big Booty Tootie. But, this Fat Ed person never paid her any mind.

One night, Sanora headed outside to her car, only to find him leaning against her hood.

"Them fake-ass ballers be lined up to get to your ass, huh? Why don't you come make some real money and have a good time at the same time? Only thing I ask is that my dealings with you, be just with you. That bitch you work with can't know shit about us. You can't even mention my name."

"Why? You know her?"

"Yeah, I know her. I ain't never did shit with her, though. She's just a grungy bitch, trust and believe that."

"Can I ask you a question first?"

"Go 'head."

"Why would somebody like you need to pay?"

"I don't. I can get pussy out the ass, but I don't have time for the rules and games. I'm a busy man, baby. When I want to go, I want to go."

Fat Ed delivered on his promises. Sanora had a blast with him. He took her out to dinner, to the theaters, and on weekend getaways to romantic bed and breakfast establishments where they chatted into the wee hours of the morning. It killed Sanora to take his money at the end of their rendezvous, for it was a constant reminder that she was nothing more than a hired hooker.

Five months into their arrangement, she couldn't shake the feeling stirring inside of her. She loved him, and in the fantasy that dwelled in her mind, he loved her, too. Why else would he spend so much time with her? Why else would he treat her like a lady, pulling out her chair, opening and closing her car door? He even helped her with her coat. And while he paid to be pleasured, he took his time to pleasure Sanora, too. Every time he paid, and paid handsomely, she wanted to give the money back. He was the first man, besides her father and Harvey, to make her feel loved. But a weekend trip to Paradise Island in the Bahamas changed everything.

The condom ripped during sex and Fat Ed went ballistic. Repeatedly, he asked Sanora if she had any STDs which made her feel dirtier than she'd ever felt in her life.

"You know I don't have anything, Ed. Why would you even ask me that?"

"You take the pill, though, right?"

"Yes," she lied. She'd stopped taking the pill and cut off her other clients two months after their arrangement begun.

For six weeks, Sanora waited for her period but it was a no-show. She peed on the plastic stick and got the news she'd secretly longed for. Elated by the results, she didn't want to jinx it. So, she kept it hush-hush, knowing her history with drugs and the number of abortions she'd had could cause her to have a miscarriage. Close to five months along, the weight gain was becoming obvious. It was time to share the news with Fat Ed. He hit the roof. Chivalry became a thing of the past.

"That could be anybody's muthafuckin' baby! How you gon' put that shit on me?"

"I haven't slept with anyone else since we really started hanging tough. And the condom ripped with you in the Bahamas. Do the math. Count the months."

"Do I look like Sam Sausage? I know I ain't the only muthafucka to bust a nut in you."

And just like that, their relationship went dead. Her heart ripped from her, Sanora used the tears triggered from her argument with Fat Ed to sell Felicia on her mother's fake illness. She packed her bare necessities and fled to her mom's house in Richmond. Three months later, Michael Edwards Jones, Fat Ed's first and middle name in reverse, was born a month premature barely weighing five pounds.

A month after his birth, Sanora requested a paternity test. Not for financial support, but because she wanted her son to enjoy all that life had to offer which included a father. A week later, the test revealed what Sanora had already known. Fat Ed was the father. Deep down, she hoped it would change things between her and Fat Ed. Maybe, just maybe, they'd raise their son together. Now finally, he'd spoken the words she'd longed to hear.

Sanora sat up in the bed. "Are you serious?"

"As a heart attack. I mean, it ain't like either of us is getting any younger, so why not? Shit, let's get married, move away from the bullshit, and do the right thing for our son."

Sanora kicked back the covers and climbed from the bed. "Okay. If that's what you really want, then we have to leave tonight. We have to go to my mom's to get her and the baby."

"Sanora, we can't leave tonight."

"Yes, we can. Hell, I have money and you have money. We can stay in hotels until we figure it out."

"That's no way to live with a baby. We'd have to plan it out."

"We can plan from the hotels. Just please, let's go." Her tears surfaced again.

"Where?"

"Shit, Georgia like you just said. Or we can go wherever. I don't care. Let's just go, please."

Fat Ed sat up and turned his attention to the door. "Do you hear that?"

Antsy, Sanora replied, "Hear what?"

"Your friend got a cat?"

Sanora sighed heavily. "No, no. There's no cat in here." She pulled a thong and a pair of leggings from her bag and eased them on while mumbling to herself. She had thrown a bag together at the spa and searched inside for a shirt. "Shit," she hissed, "I know I packed one."

"You know you gon' have to cut that shit out."

"What you talking about?"

"Talking to yourself. That's gon' drive me crazy." Fat Ed chuckled. "You always do that shit."

Sanora turned around and waved off his comment, still focused on a shirt. She didn't want to put the dress back on.

"Now that's some sexy shit right there." He said as he admired Sanora topless in the tight fitting pants.

"Ed, come on. Put your clothes on."

He chuckled. "Damn, we ain't even washed our asses."

"Who cares? We'll be funky together."

"And sticky and itchy."

"Who cares?"

"I do."

"Look, baby. We'll take a shower together later, I promise."

"Mmm, I like that. We'll do that shit every morning?" he asked.

"Every morning, every night, and throughout the day."

"I'm liking this shit already. But, you know, you still haven't told me what's up?"

Sanora dropped on the bed and kissed him quickly on the lips. "Look, I'm in some big trouble. I mean, big, big trouble. The sooner we leave, the sooner I can make it right."

"Is somebody after you?"

Sanora tugged on his arm. "On the way to my mom's baby, I promise, I'll tell you everything."

"Okay, alright. But the second we get into the truck you have to start talking."

A load of bricks had been lifted from Sanora's shoulders. For the first time in years, she felt everything would be alright. Not only would she rid herself of the life but her and Fat Ed would marry. And even before that happened, she would turn Felicia's ass in and reunite the baby with his parents. She wasn't sure what her charges would be, but she'd face them knowing wholeheartedly that her soon-to-be husband would be by her side.

"How far is your mom's house from here?"

"I don't know. A couple of hours."

"Shit," Fat Ed fell back on the bed. "I'ma have to get some No Doze and a couple of those energy drinks."

"There's probably something here that I can give you. Let me go see. I'll be right back." Sanora opened the bedroom, but swung it closed just as quickly as she'd opened it. Her heart raced.

"See, you heard that shit! It's a cat in here."

"Okay, okay," she said pacing the floor. She held her hands to hide her sudden nervousness. "We'll just stop by a gas station."

"That's fine, but go make sure that muthafucka is put up somewhere. I can't stand cats. Somebody threw one on my head back in the day and that muthafucka scratched the shit out of me. I've hated them creepy muthafuckas ever since."

"I'll kick it if it comes out, I promise."

"You won't get a chance to. I'll shoot your friend's place up. Just go make sure he's up. While you out there, see what she has. I'm tired as hell. I might fall asleep the second I get inside the truck."

"Okay, okay." Sanora opened the door.

"Hey," Fat Ed yelled after her. "Where the bathroom at? I gotta pee like shit."

Chapter Nineteen

Sanora burst through the double doors that led to the master bedroom. Felicia leaned over top of her bed, changing Lil' Kevin's diaper.

"Why the hell is his shit black? Babies doo-doo supposed to be black like that?"

"Felicia, what are you doing here!? I thought you were staying at the spa."

"I changed my mind," she replied over Lil' Kevin's wails. "What you doing here? And who you in there turning out? You got that muthafucka screaming like a first-time faggot."

"Yeah, I gotta get him outta here."

"Well, hold up one second." Felicia refastened the snaps to the baby's long sleeve undershirt and attempted to swaddle him in the receiving blanket. She gave up trying to fold the blanket and turned to Sanora. Her head snapped back as she stared into Sanora's reddish, sunken eyes. It was evident she'd been crying. "You been running your mouth?" Felicia questioned through tight lips.

"No, I haven't said shit."

Felicia's hands curled into fists. "Sanora, I can tell you've been crying."

"And? Doesn't mean I said anything."

"Fix the blanket while I grab the bag with the bottles. I left them in my truck."

"Felicia, I'm covered in this nigga's sweat and shit."

"Well, I can't take the baby outta the room!"

Sanora shooed her off. "Fine. Leave him, but hurry up."

Felicia left to fetch the bottles, while Sanora twitched nervously in the middle of the floor watching Lil' Kevin whimper. Pacing back and forth, she ran her hands through her hair. The bedroom door slowly opened. Sanora gasped.

"What are you doing in here?" she asked him.

"I had to piss." He smiled and pointed his stubby finger to the baby on the bed. "Why didn't you tell me he was here?"

"No, no, that's not him," she said barely above a whisper. "It's my girl's grandson."

"Why you letting him cry?" He took a step toward the bed. Her bare breasts jiggled up and down as she rushed into his embrace.

"Damn, that's a sexy ass look." He let out a short laugh. "But it's okay. I know how to hold a baby."

He tried to move past Sanora but she stood firm. Fat Ed sneered. "Why you acting paranoid?" His attention back on the baby, he noticed the hospital bracelet wrapped around the baby's ankle. "Damn, he a brand-new baby. Where's his mother?"

Sanora peeled from Fat Ed's embrace. Rushing over to the bed, she tossed the blanket around Lil' Kevin and scooped him in her arms.

"I got him. I got him, baby. Now go back in the room and get ready." She threw her hand to her mouth to quiet the trembling in her voice as she gently bounced the whimpering baby in her arms. "Please, baby. Just go get ready."

Fat Ed glanced around the room. "Yeah, we need to hurry up and get on the road so you can tell me what the fuck is going on." Turning to leave, his eyes fell upon the picture of Felicia with Sanora and a handful of her half-dressed dancers.

"Whose house is this?" Without waiting for an answer, he added, "I know this ain't that bitch's house. I know damn well you ain't bring me over here."

Sanora went to him as she continued to shake Lil' Kevin in hopes of silencing his cries. "Look, baby, please. Grab your coat and wait for me in the room." Her sea-green eyes pleaded with him.

Lil' Kevin's wails heightened as he squirmed in Sanora's arms. His arms and legs peeked from openings in the sloppily wrapped blanket.

"Hey, baby." Fat Ed cooed. "You don't even have him wrapped up good. His feet..." His facial expression hardened. "This baby's bracelet says Kennard," he mumbled to himself then grabbed Sanora by her wrist. "Please tell me why the fuck this baby's bracelet says Kennard?"

He released Sanora's arm as he thought aloud. "Damn, hold up. Is that why Kevin ain't meet me? Shit. Is that why he ain't answering his phone? Did Simone have the baby?" Then it hit him like a ton of bricks. The AMBER alerts. A baby had been kidnapped from a hospital.

Sanora laid Lil' Kevin back in the middle of the bed. "Oh my God, Ed. Listen." She rushed to him but he shoved her with more force than he intended, sending her to the floor.

"This shit here ain't feeling right." He pulled his cell from the clip attached to his waist and dialed Kevin.

"Hey, Kevin —"

"Ed, no, baby! It's not —"

"Shut the fuck up," he growled at Sanora before proceeding with his message. "Look, Kevin. I really need you to call me. Did Simone have the baby? I'm with a baby and the bracelet around his ankle says Kennard clear as day."

"Ed, it's not what you think!" Sanora cried from the floor.

"This some spooky shit. Call —" Fat Ed's body jerked. His eyes laced with shock and then fear.

"Ed?" Sanora scrambled from the floor into his embrace. His body went limp. She struggled to hold him but the weight of his body sent them both crashing to the floor.

"Ed?" She cried, pinned beneath his weight.

A warm gooey substance oozed from him. Sanora lifted her hands and gasped at the sight of his blood. Like a fish out of water, she flopped about, struggling to free herself. Her body covered in blood, she rose from the floor screaming hysterically.

Felicia stood in the doorway, clutching the baby's bottle and her 9mm with the attached silencer.

Sanora screamed, jumping around like she was demented. "WHAT DID YOU DO? WHAT DID YOU DO?"

Felicia stormed across the room and stomped Fat Ed's phone with her foot.

"Bitch, calm the fuck down! What did you expect me to do?" Felicia shot back.

Her adrenaline on high, Sanora collapsed to the floor. She flipped Fat Ed's two hundred and forty pounds over to his back. She lifted his head and kissed his face over and over again.

"No, baby. No," she cried.

She rested his head on the floor and checked his pulse. There was none. She opened his mouth and performed CPR while Felicia picked up the cordless phone from the cradle on her nightstand.

"No, no, no." Sanora sobbed. Her chest heaved. Seconds later, she vomited over the floor.

"Hey, old man. Sorry to wake you. I got myself in some major bull-shit," Felicia said. "Need the boys at my house as soon as fucking possible."

Chapter Twenty

T he news trucks had moved on in search of their next story. The mob of police officers that once roamed the halls of the hospital had dwindled down to the one lone uniformed officer who stood guard outside of Simone's room in ICU, where she lay with no change in her condition.

Close family members and friends were allowed to visit Simone two at a time. With Kevin a permanent fixture at her bedside, the rest of the family took turns visiting one at a time. Everyone came. Everyone except for Fat Ed.

For days, Kevin called him from the hospital phone, leaving urgent messages on his cell and at the studio for Fat Ed to call him at the hospital, but his calls remained unanswered and unreturned.

"Look man." Kevin said again in the voicemail, "I've called you a million times. I know you ain't tripping 'cause I didn't show up at the bar. Shit, I've left this message a hundred times. Just call me, man. It's important."

Now, Fat Ed's voice mailbox was full. Kevin shared his concern with Stan, Simone's brother and Fat Ed's business partner. Both wondered if he'd taken an impromptu trip out of town but even that was unlike Fat Ed. Yet, for the last few weeks, Fat Ed hadn't been himself anyway. So, neither knew what to think.

"You still haven't heard from Ed?" Beatrice asked as she stood at Simone's bedside.

Clutching Simone's hand with his face buried in the bed, Kevin shook his head.

"Hmm, I know you don't want to hear this, but I wonder if we should file a missing person's report."

"Stan filed one yesterday," Kevin said with his head still buried in the mattress.

The sharp chirping from the heart monitor mixed with the ventilator's dull hum filled the silence.

"I don't know what I'm supposed to do." His eyes glossed over with tears, Kevin lifted his head and stared at his wife. "I want to go look for him, but I can't leave her like this. I left her once, and I'm not leaving her again."

Beatrice studied her son: sunken raccoon eyes, wrinkled clothes that were at least three days old, and a shadow of gray stubble sprouting from his face that hadn't been shaved since the ordeal occurred. The hair on his head, just as gray as the hairs on his face, grew in patches around a receding hairline.

Beatrice asked, "Have you eaten anything?" Kevin shook his head.

"Why don't you go downstairs to the cafeteria and grab something? When Simone comes to, you won't be any good for her if you're in a hospital bed, too."

Kevin didn't budge.

"She's going to be okay, son."

Kevin looked up at his mother, staring intently as if to check the authenticity of her words.

"She's going to make it. Just like she's made it through everything else. Simone's a fighter and you know that."

"But the doctors said —"

"Boy, I don't want to hear what the doctors said," Beatrice spoke adamantly. "All they know is what their textbooks told them. They don't know this child right here. You shouldn't be sitting here worrying about if she's going to pull through, because she will. What you need to be worrying about is what you're going to tell her when she asks for her baby. Still no leads?"

"None," Kevin mumbled.

"Have they issued the warrant yet?"

Kevin shrugged. He had no idea.

"That's just insane. We know you didn't have anything to do with it. Will the warrant interfere with your parole?"

"I don't know, but what am I supposed to do? I'm not going to the station."

Beatrice sighed. "Why don't you go downstairs to the cafeteria and grab you something to eat?" she suggested again. "I'm right here. The cop is at the door. Won't nothing happen. And ask the nurse for a toothbrush and toothpaste so you can take care of your grill. You got green fog coming out of your mouth, boy."

Kevin smiled for the first time in days.

"When I leave here, I'll swing past your house and pick you up some more things. I'm going to bring a radio up here, too. You know Simone loves her music."

"Okay," Kevin mumbled.

"Oh, and here. Jordan charged your cell. I'm sure you have a ton of messages, probably one from Ed. Now go. Get to getting before you end up in the hospital from dehydration or a dirt rash."

*****

Kevin sat at an isolated table in the cafeteria, fighting to ignore the chatter that buzzed around him. It amazed him to see people continue with their daily routine, when in his mind, the world should have come to a complete stop.

He stared down at the dried-up French fries, the questionable looking hamburger patty on top of the sesame seed bun, and the piping hot cup of coffee, with no desire for anything but the cup of Joe. But like his mother said, he had to eat something. He picked up a pack of ketchup and shook it. He couldn't help but smile as he pictured Simone doing the same thing with the Taco Bell seasoning packet before sucking out the contents.

Tossing the condiment back on his tray, he powered on his cell. It was no surprise to see the voicemail icon. He dialed into his messages, silently praying that one of the messages offered a breakthrough. Maybe the police had some news about the baby or maybe Fat Ed had surfaced and returned his call.

Don had called the night Simone went into labor. Kevin recognized the excitement in Don's voice. He had good news for him but it wasn't the news Kevin needed. He skipped the message and moved on to the next. The sound of Fat Ed's voice made him gasp. But the three messages one behind the other were old, left the night they were supposed to meet at the Gentleman's Bar. There was comfort in the sound of Fat Ed's voice. For a brief second, it took Kevin back to when things were okay.

Kevin listened to Fat Ed's lengthy messages hoping he'd mention something that would shed some light on his current whereabouts. But the messages were absent of any clues.

As the messages played, Kevin turned his attention to one of the plasmas mounted on the walls of the cafeteria. The local news was on. He took a sip from the hot cup of black coffee and scanned the room. He envied the hospital employees laughter as they ate lunch a few tables away for all seemed right in their world.

Angela, Beatrice, Lavon, and Melanie had all called the night Simone went into labor. Each left a message, requesting a status on the baby's delivery. With the cup of coffee at his lips, the next voicemail caught Kevin off guard.

"Hey Kevin —"

"Ed, no, baby! It's not —" an unknown female said in the background.

"Shut the fuck up." Fat Ed barked at her. "Look, Kevin, I really need you to call me. Did Simone have the baby? I'm with a baby and the tag around his ankle says Kennard clear as day."

Hot coffee spilled from the cup, burning Kevin's hand as he sprung from his seat, knocking over the chair, unfazed by the burn or the stares his abrupt behavior caused.

"Ed, it's not what you think!" the female cried in the background.

"This some spooky shit. Call—"

Call where? Shit, where are you? Kevin thought. Then he heard the woman say Ed's name. The haunting scream that followed sent shivers through Kevin's body.

Trembling, he hung up from his voicemail and called Fat Ed's cell. Nothing. His mailbox was still full. He called the studio. Nothing. The mailbox was full there, as well. On the verge of panicking, Kevin dialed back into his voicemail to listen to Fat Ed's message again while silently praying another followed. Antsy, he tapped his foot and searched around the room. Kevin's eyes locked with the uniformed officer's standing in the entrance. The officer pointed at him. Hidden by the officer, Beatrice stepped into view. Her face was drenched with tears as she followed the officer's direction.

Coffee splattered across the table as Kevin dropped the cup and collapsed to his knees. Beatrice hurried to her son, with the uniformed officer on her heels as she yelled across the cafeteria.

"No, Kevin. No, it's not Simone." She kneeled beside her son. "It's not, Simone, baby."

The uniformed officer tapped Beatrice on her shoulder and nodded toward the plasma. Fat Ed's picture was plastered on the screen. Beatrice pulled his hands from his face.

"Listen son," and pointed toward the television screen.

Slowly, Kevin lifted his head.

"A black Lincoln Navigator belonging to Edward Michael Jones, an area music producer and promoter, was found scorched and riddled with bullets. No body was recovered at the scene; however, Mr. Jones has been reported missing by his family and friends. If you have any information about Mr. Jones whereabouts, please call Crime Solvers."

Beatrice struggled through her tears. "That's what we came to tell you, baby."

Chapter Twenty-One

A gentle breeze danced across Simone's face, awakening her as she rested curled up like a baby. There was something special about the bed. Never had she endured such a peaceful night's slumber. Stretching the kinks from her limbs, she smiled and filled her lungs with the fresh morning air, thinking, *Man, I feel good. Feels like I've been asleep forever.*

Prepared to greet what was sure to be a glorious day, she opened her eyes and looked out into the massive, heavenly, blue majestic skies. Her mouth agape, she clutched her chest and rose to her feet on rubbery legs as her heart thumped.

"Oh my God." The peaceful slumber had taken place amidst a white fluffy cloud. "I must be dreaming."

Thick massive clouds populated the skies for miles. The gentle winds offered the purest of air without the slightest hint of impurities. Glancing down at the cloud beneath her, Simone dug her toes into the fluff, amazed by its cool, misty softness. It felt exactly how she'd imagined when she gazed in awe from the window of a plane.

"I know I'm dreaming," she repeated to herself.

Unsure of her footing, Simone stretched out her arms to ensure her balance and slowly eased into a squat. She scooped up a handful of the cloud and studied how it clung to her hands like bath bubbles. She blew the puff from her hand and watched it sail out into the heavens until it made its home with a nearby cloud. Bracing herself, she stood to her feet. Up and down she rose on her toes to test the clouds durability. It seemed to hold her fine, just as it had cradled her while she slept. She leaped into the air. Like a trampoline made of cotton, the cloud supported her bounce.

Filled with playful energy, Simone looked off into the heavens. Then she took off running. She ran across the clouds, hopping from one to the next. She giggled like a child at recess as she bounced from her butt to her feet. Leery of the grayish colored clouds off in the distance, she stopped to catch her breath.

"Whew," she panted as she stared out into the storm clouds. "I bet y'all full of water, too." A huge grin covered her face as she envisioned the splash. "Why not?" she said aloud and sprinted towards the clouds.

To spice up her fun, Simone figured she'd belly dive into the gray cloud. With her arms and legs stretched out like Superman, she dove into the storm cloud, prepared for a soaking. But this time, she fell through.

Gone was the Superman form she'd modeled. Wildly, her arms and legs swung in search of something to latch onto to stop the fall. She reached for clouds but they slipped through her hands. The wind roared through her ears, whooshing through her hair as she belly flopped towards Earth at 120-mph. Then she remembered—she was dreaming.

Her eyes squished shut; she ignored the wind's howl as she told herself over and over again, "I'm dreaming. I'm dreaming," as she continued to fall. She stole a quick peek and gasped. Land approached. In her dreams, she never, ever landed. Before panic could resurface, her bare feet graced the stone terrace of what appeared to be a quaint French café.

I thought landing meant you died, she thought to herself. She patted her chest, stomach, and butt. She was still intact, dressed in a white gown that resembled that of a Greek goddess.

"Where'd this dress come from?" she wondered aloud as she studied the dress.

White patio furniture in its classical wrought-iron form was positioned around a stone patio. The guitar and accordion sounds from Daniel Colin's "Trois Petites Notes De Musique" played off in the distance and offered the café graceful elegance. Despite the storm clouds hovering about, everything still seemed so perfect, so peaceful...so heavenly.

An elderly, sophisticated white couple sat at one of the tables, sipping tea from porcelain cups. Their attire—her soft pale pink suit with a satin lapel and his white three-piece-suit—reminded Simone of Easter Sunday. The woman smiled sweetly at Simone as she returned the teacup to its saucer.

"Well, hello dear. You must be Thomas' daughter. Your father told us you were coming."

"My father? Oh my goodness, so I did die," Simone said as she glanced around the café. "This is heaven?" she asked the elderly woman.

The quaint little café was beautiful but didn't mirror the images of heaven that had been planted in Simone's head since childhood. There were no pearly gates, golden streets, or angels hovering about draped in the purest of whites and wings.

"Goodness no, darling. This isn't heaven." The woman chuckled. "This is where we meet our loved ones that are stuck between their earthly and heavenly form. It's the in-between. The crossroads. We're waiting here for our son."

Simone chuckled. *Okay, I'm still dreaming. Falling from the sky must not count. I guess I need to find a cliff to jump from. Then I'll wake up for real.* She stepped back and gazed up at the café's roof.

"That ain't tall enough. Plus, how will I get up there?" she said aloud.

"What you looking for?"

And there was the voice. That old familiar voice so strong, yet jovial and carefree. The voice of security and love. Tears swelled in Simone's eyes as she slowly turned to greet the one person who'd been her absolute everything no matter the consequences or circumstances.

"Hi, Daddy," she whispered.

*****

The doctor shared words Kevin didn't want to hear. Simone had been in the coma for two weeks. If she were to pull through, it wouldn't be without some form of brain damage.

An emotional wreck, Kevin stood at Simone's bedside, unable to cope with the news. His son was gone—dead as far as he knew. His best friend was missing and the person he loved most in the world lay in the bed lifeless. Her chances of pulling through decreased with each passing day. He needed Simone more than ever, for life would have no meaning without her. If she died, Kevin would take his own life, too. This he knew for sure. Be it a bullet to his head, a bottle of pills, or both. If his wife were to be buried, he would surely rest alongside her.

The doctors had encouraged them to talk to Simone. Jordan read poems she'd written just for her mother. Lavon read stories from her Kindle. Melanie read scriptures from the bible, and Angela and Beatrice each took turns reading from the newspaper. Kevin didn't need a script. He talked to her the way he'd always done. But tonight, after the doctor's report, he couldn't muster up any words. So, he turned on the radio his mother had left.

The timing couldn't have been more perfect. As if on cue, the introduction to the ballad Kevin wrote and sold to Don Brandon when he was first released began to strum through the radio.

Kevin's voice quivered as he stood before his wife, battling his emotions. It was the moment they'd been waiting for. But instead of celebrating the airplay, Kevin remembered the words he'd carved into paper as if it were yesterday. Words that had poured from his heart the day Simone shared that she loved him.

"They playing the song, baby." He reached for the radio and turned the volume up slightly. The artist's voice was too high for what he'd envisioned in his head. Jordan would've sung the song perfectly.

Every day of our lives, I'll try to make it like the first day,
When we fell in love from the words love made us say.
I have faith that we'll both do our part,
A permanent fixture in each other's heart.
I will share my life with you.
And I will be with you, for the rest of my life, always.
I will dream of you. Thinking how I'm gonna love you,
For the rest of my life, Always.

"I love you, baby," he whispered in her ear, then planted tender kisses to the parts of her face the million and one tubes left exposed. "Please come back to me." Tears began to creep from Kevin's eyes.

*****

There he stood, unchanged. Smooth, wrinkle-free, absent of gray and dressed in the suit that Simone and Mae had selected for his funeral. Thomas was as debonair as ever. He smiled and opened his arms.

"Ain't you going to hug your daddy?"

Without hesitation, Simone grabbed her father and squeezed his heavenly form that felt just as real as her own.

He grabbed her hand. "Come on here, baby girl. Let's talk."

Thomas led Simone to one of the wrought-iron tables.

"I can't tell you how proud I am of you," he said as he slid a chair from the table for his daughter to sit in.

Simone wiped away the lone tear she couldn't prevent from falling. "You've always been proud of me, Daddy."

"There were a few times you made me scratch my head, though."

Ashamed, Simone turned away and sighed. "I know."

Thomas held his daughter hostage with his eyes. "Now is one of those times."

"What do you mean?"

"You don't know why you're here?"

Taken aback by the question, Simone said, "I'm dreaming."

"It's no dream, baby girl. You're torn between life and well...,"

Thomas said with a shrug of his shoulders, "heaven. You've lost your will to live."

Simone sat at a loss for words. Since Thomas died, life had seemed so different. His absence left a void that had yet to be filled.

"I was worried about you when I first left. I thought you'd gotten it together but I guess you haven't. Otherwise, you wouldn't be sitting across from me."

A blast of thunder cracked the gray sky. Specks of rain began to fall. A drop splattered on Simone's hand and sent a tingling sensation through her body. Thomas watched her shiver. He reached out his hand and caught one of the drops. He rubbed it between his fingers as another drop landed on Simone, causing her to shiver yet again. Thomas rose from the table.

"Come here. I want you to see something."

Following Thomas inside the café, Simone froze in disbelief as the elderly white couple from earlier ascended through the sky on a seemingly transparent elevator hand-in-hand with a young man who had to be their son.

"Daddy, look—"

Thomas grabbed Simone by her hand and pulled her along. "C'mon Simone," he said. The incident was nothing he hadn't seen before.

Nothing could have prepared Simone for what she was about to witness. The ride amidst the fluffy white clouds; the elevator ascending the family of three into the cosmos; her unexpected visit with her dad. None of it could compare to the miracle unfolding before her.

A huge 92-inch flat-screen TV hung from the wall. In front of it, a small wooden step stool. Thomas picked up the remote resting on the stool and brought the television to life. Simone gasped as the image of her lifeless body stretched out in a hospital bed, tangled in cords and plugged to machines came into view. Kevin sat at her bedside, weeping.

"I don't know what I did, God," her husband cried, "but please don't take her from me."

"It's not rain, Simone. Those drops are the tears from your husband."

Through the transparent wall, Simone watched Kevin shower her lifeless body with kisses over and over again as he prayed aloud through his tears. It pained her to see him hurting but why was she in the hospital?

"Simone, you're only thirty-nine years old. You have a lot of living to do."

Simone's voice trembled with fear. "But look at—"

Thomas hushed her. "You've always gone after everything you wanted in life. Some things took you a little longer than others but eventually you did it, and you did it well. But you aren't going after life."

"But Daddy, what's wrong with me?"

"Simone, don't worry about that. If you wanted to live, you would live. You could wake up but you've lost your will and I know it's because of me." Thomas studied Kevin's every move. "Do you see that man right there? Look at how he loves you. He'll do anything for you, Simone. But only you can make the choice."

"I don't know how to get back anyway. So, maybe I'm really supposed to be here."

"This is the in-between, Simone. Getting back is an option and it's easy. All you have to do is walk up the stool and step inside."

"Step inside the television?"

Thomas smiled. "Once you step on that stool, it's no longer a television."

Simone sighed. "You can't come with me?"

Thomas wrapped his arms around his daughter. "I've never left you." Holding her by her shoulders, he smiled. "I'm happy where I am, Simone. I've told you that in countless dreams. You have a lot of living to do. Now get going, baby girl." He planted a kiss on her forehead and scooted her toward the wall.

"Are you going back?"

"No, not yet. I'm waiting for someone." Thunder cracked the sky. Thomas had revealed too much.

Simone's eyes got big as saucers. "No, Daddy, who?"

Thomas grinned. "No need for you to worry, baby girl. I love you."

With a deep sigh, Simone uttered the words, "I love you, too, Daddy."

*****

The machines began to beep. Simone's eyes started to flutter. Alarmed, Kevin stood and backed away from the bed as Simone began to gag on the breathing tube. He managed to muster the strength to yell, "Nurse! Doctor!"

"It's okay, baby." He laughed and cried all at once as he ran toward the door. Before he could yell out into the hallway, doctors rushed inside the room. Simone was conscious. Kevin's wife was alive.

Chapter Twenty-Two

Kevin tried to hold his baby's image hostage in his mind. But newborns changed daily. Had he darkened? Had his hair grown or thinned? Was it curly or straight? Had his eyes changed colors? No picture had been snapped. Few had a chance to glance at him but even worst, Simone didn't remember having him.

Just as the doctors predicted, the two weeks Simone spent in the coma weren't without consequences. Her short term memory had failed and she suffered from violent migraines that caused her to pass out. Ironically, she remembered everything and everybody, but nothing pertaining to her pregnancy or her hospital stay. For now, the doctors suggested the family keep it that way until Simone grew stronger and the migraines had subsided.

"I'm sorry, Doc. I don't think I can do that," Kevin said as he and the rest of their immediate family sat in the doctor's office. "I can't lie to her."

"Mr. Kennard, how long have you and your wife been married?"

"Not even a year. We dated almost twenty years ago and recently got back together."

"How long have you been back in each other's life?"

Kevin looked at Jordan. "Guess like two years, right?" Jordan said.

Kevin grabbed Jordan's hand and gave her smile.

"Yes, 'bout two years."

"Interesting," the doctor said. "It appears that Mrs. Kennard is suffering from anterograde amnesia which is the inability to remember recent events in the aftermath of a trauma. It's often times brought on by a traumatic brain injury." His eyes on Kevin, he said, "In addition to the somewhat lengthy comatose state, we have to remember that your wife flat-lined. There's no easy way to say this, but clinically, she had died."

With his eyes on the floor, Kevin immediately turned to Jordan, who pulled her hand away. It broke his heart to see Jordan dabbing at her eyes. Kevin reached over and rubbed his daughter's back.

"So what now, Doc?"

"Well, I must commend your wife. She's doing remarkably well. She's beaten the odds a few times over."

"But what about her memory loss?"

"It's a mysterious ailment, Mr. Kennard. The precise mechanism of storing memory isn't well understood. Her memory may come back gradually. More than likely in bits and pieces. But we don't want to force feed her too much too fast. Especially something as devastating as what took place. We don't know nor can we predict how the news will affect her. So, my suggestion is that you monitor her visits with people and instruct everyone who may come in contact with her to keep everything hush hush."

"But physically, won't she be able to tell she's had a baby?" Angela asked.

"Well, she was in the coma for two weeks and she's been conscious now for a week. The bleeding has stopped. And according to her file," the doctor said, "she's lost a lot of weight. Close to thirty pounds. How much did she gain with the pregnancy?"

"Forty," Kevin replied.

"There you have it. There's nothing like an IV diet." The doctor smiled.

"But what about her breasts?" Angela asked.

"Mr. Kennard shared that they had no plans of breastfeeding." The doctor looked at Kevin for confirmation.

Kevin dropped his head in his hands, rubbing his temples. "Right, we didn't," he confirmed without looking up.

"And I brought in some cabbage leaves and had the nurses apply them to her breasts," Beatrice shared.

Angela was shocked. "Cabbage leaves?"

"Yeah, you never heard of that?" Beatrice questioned. "I had the nurse wrap the leaves around her breasts with an Ace bandage. Dries the milk up in a matter of days."

The doctor added, "I must admit, I was a little apprehensive as well, but the nurses were quick to remind me that I never had a lactation issue. So..." He rocked back in his chair.

"I told them to go ahead and do what was best," Kevin added as he sat up.

Beatrice shared, "The cabbage leaves mixed with a little Benadryl that they gave her intravenously stopped the lactating."

Angela looked at the doctor for confirmation.

"It worked." The doctor smiled. "Lactating hasn't been an issue."

Jordan, who sat there listening to everything asked, "What about when she comes home? There's baby stuff everywhere."

"And the nursery," Kevin added. "How do we hide the nursery?"

Beatrice reached over and squeezed Kevin's hand for support. "We'll just lock the door."

"Mr. Kennard, I know this may be a huge pill to swallow, especially after what you and your family have gone through. You guys want the old Simone back, and I understand that. But she may not be able to retain the information being forced on her. It could also trigger a negative response. And with the complexity of the migraines, I really must advise that you take it slow. Let her memory return naturally. She's already beaten most of the odds, and in due time, I'm sure she'll remember everything. Hopefully, by then," the doctor added somberly, "you'll have your son back."

Chapter Twenty-Three

In the wee hours of the morning, Kevin sat at Simone's bedside, tapping his feet uneasily while his heart and mind played a treacherous game of Tug-of-war, haunted by the police's seemingly lackadaisical attitude.

In a matter of days, Simone would be released, heading home to live a lie. How in the world would the family explain their uneasiness or frequent tears? Not only was their son missing, but Fat Ed was, too.

Kevin watched Simone's chest heave up and down from a seemingly peaceful slumber. With a deep-hearted sigh, he rose from his chair and kissed her on the forehead. He cared more than the doctors or the lazy donut-eating detectives who rested comfortably in their beds at home. Havoc had been wreaked on his family's life and Kevin couldn't sit still a minute longer.

Kevin had promised everyone he loved that his gun toting days were buried in his past. But he was reneging on that promise. He was going to find his son and the person responsible for the devastation planted in his life.

Forty-five minutes later, Kevin arrived at the Gentleman's Bar. The parking lot was kind of empty, which wasn't really a surprise considering the hour and the fact that it was a Thursday. The loud music confirmed something was going on inside.

After paying the hefty twenty-dollar cover, Kevin stepped inside the dimly lit club and surveyed the crowd. True to Fat Ed's standards, half naked women lingered about the place.

"You want a lap dance, baby?" one purred.

"Naw, I'm good," Kevin replied as he made his way to the bar.

Pushing back the dirty glasses in front of him, Kevin planted himself on a vacant stool. The bartender cleared away the glasses, then whisked a wet rag across the counter.

"Last call was a few minutes ago," he said as he wiped the counter. "No more mixed drinks, but I can pour you a shot of something."

Tapping his finger along the granite, Kevin asked, "What's the best cognac you got?"

"We got some VSOP."

"Damn, that's the best you got? No XO?"

"Not too many people come in here asking for XO."

"Yeah, my brother got me drinking the stuff. Maybe you know him."

The cloth stopped. The bartender stared at him from the corner of his eye. "You Kevin? Ed's brother?"

"Damn, man, you so know him?"

"Hell yeah, I know Ed. That's my man," he said while reaching across the counter to give Kevin a hug. Kevin leaned across the counter to exchange shoulder taps and fist pounds. "Have you heard from him yet?"

"Naw, man, nothing," Kevin replied as he plopped back in the stool. "I was supposed to meet him here."

"Yeah, I know. Saturday night, April 7th," the bartender replied matter-of-factly. "Yeah, I was working. Hell, I'm working every night."

"Have you heard from him by chance?"

"Naw, man. And he normally stops in here a couple times out the week. I'm praying his truck was just stolen from the airport or something and that he's on vacation with that piece of hotness he left here with. That's what I tell myself every day."

"So he left here with a female," Kevin said to himself. "Did you know her by chance?"

"No, but a lot of the fellas at the bar seemed to. They kept asking me if she was going to dance but she didn't. She came and sat here with Ed. If I ain't know any better, I'd think something was up. They seemed like a couple."

"How so?"

"I mean, they were touching all over each other. And it wasn't some, 'you a freak and I'ma grope your ass' type of touch. I'm talking about light, little rubs. Then they got to kissing." He shook his head and chuckled. "Things got heated. They stayed 'til after the place closed. I saw them sitting outside in his truck. I didn't think too much of it. I blew my horn, he blew back, and I left."

"Damn. Do you remember what she looked like?"

The bartender chuckled again. "Man, do I? The girl was bad. She had a body for days. A tight-ass black leather dress, titties sitting out."

Kevin laughed. "Man, her face. What about her face?"

"Shit, did she have a face?" Slapping the counter, the bartender roared in laughter from his own joke. "Whew, naw, but all jokes aside, she was a red-bone. Had light eyes. Think they were hazel or something. I really can't remember. You know I wasn't all up in her face. I mean, you know how we do, right?"

"Yeah, yeah," Kevin responded.

"One of the dudes called her by her dance name. I don't follow the strippers too tough so I can't remember what it was. But I want to say it was Coochie or Poochie. Some shit like that."

"What about cameras? Y'all don't have any cameras in the club?"

"Naw, man. Not yet. We've only been open for about two months. It's a lot of things we still need to get."

Kevin nodded while mentally dissecting the information. The bartender broke into his thoughts. "Hey, you still want that shot?"

Kevin glanced at his watch. He needed to get back to the hospital. "Naw, man. I'm good." Feeling the need to give the bartender something, he reached inside his pocket. The bartender noticed the gesture.

"Man, what the hell is up with you and your brother?" the bartender asked.

"I feel like I owe you something."

"Naw, man. You don't owe me a thing."

"Alright, thanks man." They slapped hands, exchanging the brotherly handshake. "Just let me know the second you hear from Ed, please," the bartender said before Kevin walked off.

"Yeah, yeah. I will." The female's haunting scream replayed in Kevin's mind. His voiced riddled with uncertainty, he mumbled, "Can't wait to buy him a drink."

Kevin trotted down the steps, heading towards the parking lot when a voice dripping with authority yelled out his name. "Kevin Kennard!"

He glanced over his shoulder, then hastened his steps as two uniformed officers hurried in his direction.

"Yeah, what's up?" Before Kevin realized what was happening, one of the officers grabbed him. "Hold up, man. What you doing?" he asked as the cop smacked on the handcuffs.

"Parole violation," the officer said, shoving Kevin in the backseat.

"This is not happening."

A small crowd had formed at the entrance of the club to watch the excitement. Peering through the noisy group of spectators, Andre watched with a devilish grin as Kevin was hauled back to jail.

Chapter Twenty-Four

F elicia's place glistened like a model home. Linwood's team of contractors had her townhouse looking like something out of a decorator's magazine. Dark mahogany wood replaced the carpet that once graced her steps, upstairs hallway, and mostly importantly, her bedroom that had been saturated in Fat Ed's blood. She took advantage of the helping hands and snatched the floral-printed curtains from her living room windows and installed plantation blinds. Her screen door no longer swayed from the hinges and a new garage door had been installed. Her four walls of loneliness looked absolutely marvelous.

Now, what the hell was she going to do with Sanora and Lil' Kevin? She couldn't keep them trapped inside Linwood's condo forever. Part of her contemplated tying a note to the baby and dropping him off at a firehouse a hundred miles away like Sanora kept suggesting. But then, what would she do with Sanora?

Days after the kidnapping, the police had come to the spa to question Felicia just like she knew they would. But she fed them a dead end. She told them that Sanora Greenwald, the missing nurse from the hospital, hadn't worked for her in months. The girls working at the spa that day confirmed it. As far as Felicia knew, Sanora had moved to Richmond to live with her mom. She told the detectives that they chatted on occasion, but that was it.

The situation hovered over Felicia's head like a violent tornado capable of destruction. But it was a storm she welcomed with open arms if it guaranteed Kevin's suffering. After all, he'd ruined her life, her plans. It was only fitting for her to do the same to him.

For sixteen years, Felicia thought to herself. *And you just sneak home and don't say shit.*

The anger inside began to stir about. She contemplated blazing up a joint but for now, it had to wait. She had a meeting at the Gentleman's Bar that she couldn't afford to miss.

Felicia strolled inside the club a little after four for her meeting with the manager. Her pockets were feeling the heat from Sanora's absence, the thousands spent on her new body, and the recent renovations to her place. She needed money and if it meant she had to recruit and manage more strippers, then so be it. She had to do what she had to do to keep the flow of cash she'd grown accustomed to.

Vacuums hummed across the deep burgundy carpet, and glasses rattled together as chairs were taken down from the tabletops. The crew scurried about to get the club ready for happy hour. As Felicia proceeded down the steps that led to the club's lounge, she heard the haunting static of a police radio. Standing at the bar were two plainclothes detectives.

Damn, she thought. Her heart raced. She knew they were probably investigating Fat Ed's disappearance. Quickly, she turned to tiptoe back out. Beads of perspiration formed on her forehead. Before her foot could grace the last step, someone spotted her.

"Felicia?"

Shit. She stopped.

"Felicia? Dag, girl. Is that you?"

Felicia glanced over her shoulder. Andre Perkins approached with a wide grin, dressed in a navy blue suit that screamed law enforcement. She turned to face him.

"Dag, girl. Look at you!" He chuckled, obviously impressed. "Where's the rest of you?"

"Funny," she replied, not the least bit amused.

"Where you going? The manager just said he had a meeting scheduled with you. Said he needed you to bring him a better class of dancers."

"I was taking my purse out to my truck. I'm coming back," she lied.

"Come on," Andre said. "I'll walk out there with you."

The twosome walked across the parking lot in complete silence until they stood before Felicia's Range Rover. She disabled the locks, opened the door, and tossed her Louis on the floor of the backseat.

Andre leaned against the truck with his arms crossed. "Damn. New truck, new body, and a high-class brothel."

"It's not a brothel. It's a spa."

Andre chuckled. "Yeah, whatever. I've been meaning to swing by and check out your, ah, spa. Just haven't had the chance."

Felicia hated the cockiness that conveyed with his badge. Closing the door, she sighed. She threw her hand on her hip, shifting her weight.

"What do you want, Perkins?"

"Damn. Can't we have a friendly conversation?"

Felicia shot daggers through her evil eyes. "Okay, friend. Talk to me about that muthafuckin' pedophile."

"What pedophile?"

"The one who raped my daughter. That pedophile."

"Oh, so now he raped her?" Andre didn't bother to hide his smirk. "He told me he was just getting his dick sucked. And since your daughter was eighteen, what can I do? I mean, the police told you the same thing. There's no law against getting your dick sucked by a consenting adult. You of all people should know that."

Felicia sucked her teeth and attempted to walk past him but Andre grabbed her by the arm. She snatched away. Her wicked glare dared him to touch her again.

"Did you know he was a parole officer?"

"Muthafucka, I don't care if the bitch was the President of the United States." A droplet of spit flew from her mouth, just missing Andre's cheek.

"Chill out. He's not in the clear. Turns out he gets sexual favors from a lot of teenage girls who are out here dating these fake-ass thugs. Whenever one violates their parole, the P.O. calls in a sexual favor. No one's ever reported him because they didn't care. They had their freedom."

"You mean to tell me that you know this shit and you the muthafuckin' Feds!? You 'pose to throw his ass in jail for that bullshit." Felicia was heated. "Move out of my way, Perkins."

Andre ignored her demand. "You know your boy got locked up last night," he shared as he absentmindedly kicked about a few pebbles along the asphalt parking lot.

"So what you telling me for? He has a wife, a mother, hell, a grown-ass daughter, too. Go tell one of them." She took a step to move around him but he stepped in her way, yet again.

"His wife can't help him this time."

"And so what, I should?"

Andre didn't respond.

"What he get locked up for?"

"Parole violation. He failed to report to his parole officer and provide proof of employment. You should go see him."

Felicia studied Andre. Then it hit her. "You know what? You a sneaky ass. I still think it's fucked up that he ain't in jail. But I see you had a plan for his ass."

"Oh, I have a plan. Trust me," Andre said as they turned to head back to the club.

"You just might be an a'ight muthafucka after all."

Chapter Twenty-Five

Noon on Friday, Kevin was finally allowed to make a phone call. A new day had begun and he knew Simone was probably looking for him. But he couldn't call her. He couldn't tell her that he was behind bars. There was no telling what kind of trauma the information would've inflicted.

"My God, Kevin." His mother sighed into the phone. Kevin knew she was pissed. "And Simone has been asking for you all morning. What do I tell her?"

Kevin was frustrated. "Ma, I don't know. Tell her I had to rush out of town to New York to meet Don or something. Just don't tell her I'm here."

"And this is from the Kevin who didn't want to lie to his wife," Beatrice said. "And just how long are you supposed to be out of town?"

"Ma, you act like I'm here because I broke the law."

"No, I'm acting like I never wanted to get this kind of phone call. Is there an 'S' on your chest that I don't know about? Why aren't you letting the police handle this any damn way?" Before Kevin could answer the question, Beatrice added, "I know you're hurting, Kevin. Hell, we all are. But the last thing any of us need is for something to happen to you! Have you thought about that?"

"It's been weeks and the police haven't done shit! They haven't found the baby. They haven't found Ed. I call the detective every day, and they never have anything new. So what am I supposed to do, Ma, huh? You heard the message. Shit, they heard the message."

"Well, entertain me, Kevin. You find the person responsible, then what?"

"What you think? I'm sending them straight to hell."

Kevin was annoyed. No one knew his level of pain. This was his wife, his son, and his best-friend. How could he sit back and wait for the police who didn't even care?

"Kevin, once again, you're not listening. I guess you wanna spend another—"

"Look, Ma. I love you." Kevin interrupted. "Just please, let Simone know that I love her."

Beatrice sighed. "Don't try to rush me off the phone, boy. How do I get you out of there?"

"You can't. I have to go up for a revocation hearing. Once the judge hears why I didn't go back to see McPherson, everything will be straight."

"So when do you go up for that? Do you need an attorney?"

"I don't know. I'm going to talk to the prison counselor on Monday."

"Mmm, mmm, mmm." Silence followed Beatrice's moans of disappointment.

"Can you do me a favor?" Kevin asked. "Can you send Simone some flowers for me?"

Beatrice sighed. "I will, son. I'll send them to the house."

"No, send them to the hospital."

"No, I'm sending them to your house because the doctors told her she can go home today." A lump grew in Kevin's throat.

"Kevin, the revenge you're seeking may get you a casket. For once in your life, son, let the police do their job."

Kevin whispered, "Ma, I love you. Please don't forget to send the flowers."

*****

Laughter and chitchat filled the tier as the inmates headed to the recreation hall. Lying across the cot, Kevin had no interest in mingling with anyone. He needed to get from behind those bars.

"Damn."

Kevin glanced towards his open door. He recognized the young dude, but couldn't place his face.

"You don't 'member me?" Immediately, his voice registered. Kevin rose from the bottom bunk.

"Damn, yeah. You the rapper from the group. DJ, also known as Smooth, right?"

"Yeah. Sorry to hear about your partner. We'd called him a couple of times. I was actually pissed that he never called back. Then I felt bad when I heard he was missing. They find him yet?"

"No, not yet."

"Damn. I see McPherson's bitch-ass got you back in here."

"How you know I'm in here 'cause of him?"

"I heard his fat ass on the phone telling somebody he was going to find a reason to violate you. Guess he did."

"What you mean you heard him on the phone?"

"I was coming back in when you and your wife were leaving. I went back in his office. He was watching y'all out the window, I guess, and didn't know I was standing there. I heard him tell whoever the fuck he was talking to that he was going to violate you." Smooth had Kevin's undivided attention. "I was gon' tell your partner but," he said with a shrug, "I didn't have a way to reach you. For real, I know McPherson violated me because I heard him. Any other time he'd be asking me to hook him up with some ass."

"Some ass?"

"Yeah, man. McPherson is a big ass freak. But he got it in for you."

Chapter Twenty-Six

F elicia hadn't slept a wink. Five in the morning, she used her key and opened the door to the upscale condo Linwood let her use. Linwood's sons took turns watching over Sanora and the baby inside the quaint, furnished two-bedroom condo just across the Woodrow Wilson Bridge.

Linwood's oldest son, Big L, lay across the couch in front of the television, snoring with both hands inside his pants. Part of Felicia feared Sanora would be able to convince one of Linwood's sons to let her run. While Linwood, Sr. had assured her otherwise, the mountains of balled up toilet paper stacked on the table caused Felicia to grow suspicious.

Never underestimate the power of twat.

The condo door closed and Big L didn't even flinch.

Now ain't this some shit, Felicia thought to herself. Sanora could've waltzed out the door easily.

Felicia dropped the bags of formula on the table in front of the couch. Big L shot up awakened by the loud crash, looking around wide-eyed as if he'd been spooked.

"Good morning. So sorry to wake you," Felicia said, irritated. She nodded toward Sanora's bedroom. "Is she in there?"

Big L threw his hand to his nose, rubbing feverishly as he snorted and hawked like a hog. "Yeah, she in there. Her and that crying-ass baby."

Felicia opened the door. Sanora was sitting on the bed, feeding Lil' Kevin with a towel wrapped around her. Water dripped down her back from her freshly wet hair. The dark circles under her red eyes made her look sick.

"Damn, that baby looks just like his daddy. Just a little chocolate version."

"You here to take him to the fire station?" Sanora asked without looking up.

Felicia sucked her teeth. It was too early in the morning for Sanora's whining. Besides, she was too excited about the day. "No, but soon," Felicia whispered as she entered the bedroom and closed the door. "I'm going to see Kevin today."

Sanora stared up in disbelief. "What? So now you love him again?"

"I know, I know," Felicia said with a wave of her hand. "It's a long story. But if things work out, we'll be giving the baby back within the next few days. Then I'll just get you a ticket and send you to Jamaica. That's where your dad is, right?"

"Yeah, but my mom has to go with me."

"Girl, your grandma can go for all I care."

"This needs to happen soon, Felicia or somebody needs to get him to the doctor. I'm serious."

"Aren't you a nurse? Just tell me what you need to treat him and I'll bring it."

"I need my prescription pads."

"I don't know about that."

"He needs some meds, Felicia. I'll scribble another doctor's name on it. Ain't like they call to verify the signature. They only call when it's expensive drugs. I need something, too. I think Fat Ed gave me something."

"Alright, look, I'll have somebody drop off one of your prescription pads. Write out the prescription, and I'll get somebody to fill it." Felicia prepared to leave.

"Felicia, I –"

"Look, got-damn it, I told you. A few more days and you'll be on a plane to Jamaica. It's coming together better than I imagined."

*****

By noon, Felicia was ready. Her weave flowed down her back in loose body curls. Her nails and toes had been freshly manicured and her lashes extended. The twenty-minute makeover at the MAC counter was the finishing touch she needed.

Standing before the full-length mirror on her closet door, Felicia smiled. She looked just as good as any of her girls. No, her skin wasn't as light as some of her dancers and her eyes weren't green like Sanora's, but for the first time in her life, Felicia stood before a mirror and actually felt beautiful.

Her halter dress accented her new body perfectly and the strappy high heel sandals gave her an extra dose of sexy. Physically and mentally, she was ready for her Prince Charming. From top to bottom, the house looked and smelled marvelous. This time, she hoped it wasn't in vain.

*****

Keys jingled outside of Kevin's cell followed by a thunderous knock.

"Kennard," the guard's robust voice called as he opened Kevin's door, "you have a visitor."

Kevin followed the guard down the corridor that led to the visiting room. He took a seat behind the glass of a small booth, surprised that his mother had bothered to come. He heard voices. The visitors were approaching. Resting his elbows on the counter, he dropped his weary head in his hands and ignored the shadow that slid into the booth on the opposite side of the glass.

I don't feel like hearing this mess, he thought as he looked up. Shocked, Kevin gasped as he stared at Felicia. *Damn,* Kevin thought with mixed feelings. *She gotta be pissed at me.*

Kevin took a good look at Felicia. He couldn't help but grin. Nothing about her seemed the same. Not only was she half the size that he remembered but she was made up like he'd never seen before. Shiny black European hair, a weave no doubt, hung down her back. No, this wasn't the Felicia from back in the day, or the one that use to visit him in prison. The Felicia before him actually looked good.

Matching Kevin's smile, Felicia rested her curvy frame in the chair and picked up the phone. Kevin followed suit.

"What's up, stranger?" she greeted, playfully curling the cord with her finger. "What you smiling at?"

"You," Kevin said. "So what? I get two visits today?"

"Two visits?"

"Yeah, I figured the other half of you would come in after this visit."

"Ha, ha, ha. You still a fake-ass comedian," she replied bashfully. "You looking rather old."

Kevin ran his hand along the gray hairs on his chin. "Yeah, I bet."

"So what's up? You got home sick?"

"Naw." Kevin's shoulders slumped and his smile faded. "How'd you know I was here?"

"You wouldn't believe the people I know and the ones that know me. So what's going on?"

Kevin sighed. "I mean, what's not? Hey, sorry about not calling you when I came home. I wasn't trying to let everybody know."

"Yeah, your ass snuck home and didn't even bother to send me a fuckin' smoke signal. But I ain't tripping. You don't owe me no explanation. I was crushed, but I'm over it now. Ever since you told me you were focusing on your daughter, I knew things wouldn't be the same. Congratulations on your music, though. I didn't know you had it in you."

"Thanks," he uttered softly, wondering what else she'd heard.

"Why you sitting there looking crazy?" she asked. "I know about you and your baby momma. I saw y'all picture in *Jet*. You got a lot going on."

"That's an understatement. I know you watch the news."

"Sometimes." She attempted to seem uninterested.

"You heard about the kidnapping and attempted murder at Wakefield Hospital?"

"Yeah, I did." Then she gasped. "Don't even say that shit happened to you!"

Kevin lowered his head to hide his tearful eyes.

"Damn." His head shot up. "Shit, man, you know what? You may be able to help me."

Felicia placed her manicured hands on her new double D's. "Me?"

"You still managing dancers?"

"Boy, no. I told you I was getting out of that mess. No more strippers. No more prostitutes. I'm focused on my massage parlor," she lied with a straight face.

"Yeah, but you still know 'em, right? I mean, you know where they hang out, right?"

Felicia was puzzled. "Possibly. Why? What you need strippers for?"

Kevin glanced over his shoulder to make sure no guards were hovering about. "Look, Ed is missing. I got a crazy ass call from him, too. He was with my son and some dancer named Poochie, Coochie, or some shit like that."

"What kind of stage name is that?"

"I don't know. It may not be Poochie or Coochie but it's something like that and I need to find her."

"Look, Kevin," Felicia said as if trying to lighten the mood. "However I can help you, I'll help you. Ain't shit changed wit' me. I always had your back, and I still do. I'm already working on getting you outta here. If you want, I can pick you up and take you wherever you need to go. I'll help you find Poochie, Coochie."

Chapter Twenty-Seven

Feeling like he'd sold his soul to the devil, Kevin walked out the county jail with his keys and dead cell phone in his pocket at six o'clock Monday evening. Part of him wanted to go curl up in the bed with Simone, and just hope and pray the police would find both his son and Fat Ed. But he wasn't built like that. He wasn't that passive guy and couldn't just sit idle. He needed to find them. If he went home, the chances of him getting out again would be slim to none. His mother would personally see to it.

A horn blew. Parked in the sparkling Tonga Green Range Rover was his guarantee back to heaven. No one knew the streets or strippers better than Felicia. The door to the truck opened. Dressed in tight, yellow booty shorts, a colorful halter top, and high heel sandals, Felicia rounded the truck and leaned against the hood. Easing her hands in the pockets of her shorts, she crossed her legs at the ankles and struck a pose as Kevin headed in her direction.

"Thanks, Felicia. So now what's up?" Kevin asked nonchalantly. "Were you able to find out anything about this dancer?"

"No, I was too busy getting you out."

Kevin's body deflated with his sigh. "So now what?"

"We going to my place."

Kevin froze. He didn't want to seem ungrateful but he had to make sure they were on the same page. "Look, Felicia... Hell, I don't even know how to say this."

Felicia shook her head. "Boy, if you don't climb down off your high horse. I ain't thinking 'bout your married ass. You my nigga and I'm always going to have a special place in my heart for you. But that's it." She strolled around to the driver's side door, seemingly surprised that Kevin still hadn't move.

"Look, you said you needed my help so, I'm going to do like I've always done. I'ma help you. Now if you don't want my connections, then take your hen pecked ass home." She hopped inside her truck and closed her door. Rolling down the passenger window, she added, "But if you want me to help you search the streets, then come on. I need to go change my clothes. I got a spot we can hit tonight."

"Twenty-four hours, Felicia. That's all I have."

"Twenty-four hours, Kevin. That's all you get."

For close to an hour, Felicia raved on about her spa. Kevin pretended to care by offering her an occasional nod or smile. From the corner of her eye, Felicia watched for Kevin's expression as the guard opened the gate, allowing her entry into the ritzy community. And there it was. The smile of approval she'd longed for.

Felicia pulled into the driveway, next to Kevin's Hummer.

"Surprise," she said as she climbed from her vehicle. "I had your truck towed here. I wanted you to see that I'm not holding you hostage. Whenever you ready to roll, you can roll."

"Damn, thanks," Kevin said. He looked up at the four-level brick monstrosity with the two-car garage and whistled the theme song to the 70's television sitcom, *"The Jeffersons."*

"Funny." Felicia smiled as she led the way up the flight of steps to her front door.

Kevin followed behind her. "How come you don't park in your garage?"

"I normally do. One side is loaded with boxes and junk. It's like my storage. Your truck is blocking the side where I would normally park."

"Then let me move it."

"No, no. It's cool," Felicia responded. "We won't be here that long anyway. Come on inside."

Kevin had to give Felicia her props. It seemed as if she'd done a 180 with her life. Her place was immaculate, unlike her apartment back in the day. Contemporary-style furniture in unique shapes and bold colors were situated throughout the place. Abstract wall hangings graced the walls, accenting the furniture perfectly.

"I gotta give it to you. Your place is nice," Kevin commented, standing awkwardly in the living room. He laid his cell and keys on the coffee table. "Where's your bathroom?"

Felicia tossed her purse and keys on the couch and headed into the kitchen. "If you gotta release that weekend prison food, take your funky ass downstairs to the basement."

Ten minutes later, Kevin emerged. "Damn, your basement is set up nice."

Purple, green, and yellow painted walls decorated with various costume masks, beads, and black art gave the basement a jazzy Mardi Gras type of feel. A pool table, a bar with four stools, and about five pub tables and stools were scattered through the enormous space that screamed 'party over here.' Two gold poles situated dead center in the room gave a hint of the entertainment.

"Thanks. Make yourself at home. I'ma get us something to drink."

Kevin sat on the edge of the couch. Getting comfortable was the furthest thing from his mind.

"What you drinking?" Felicia yelled from the kitchen. The cabinets opened and closed. "Name your poison and I promise I have it."

"I'm straight. What time are we leaving?"

"C'mon, Kevin. With everything that's going on, you gotta want something."

"Water is cool."

"Water? Yeah, okay."

"So, what time tonight are we going out again?" Kevin asked.

Felicia strolled into the living room with a bottle of Patron tucked under her arm, two shot glasses clutched in her fingers, and a glass of wine in her other hand. After sitting everything on the table, she slithered to the edge of the couch inches from Kevin and filled the two shot glasses. Tossing one of the shots down her throat, she growled from the burn.

"Whew," she squealed. "We'll probably head out about nine."

"Don't you have some friends we could be talking to? I mean, we ain't gotta wait for the clubs to open."

Felicia poured herself a second drink. "We can head out earlier, that's cool. But in the meantime, drink your shot. You need to calm your nerves." She tossed back the second, then reclined into the comfort of the couch while enjoying the slow burn. Kevin didn't budge.

"Can I ask you something?" she questioned as she crossed her legs.

"Go 'head."

"Do the police have any suspects?"

"Naw, not really. They were thinking maybe it was somebody I was locked up with or something. I don't know."

"You must've really pissed somebody off."

"No, we sent one of the lieutenants a letter in the mail with some pictures. They're thinking maybe she shared it with another officer who shared it with an inmate. So, if you know anybody messing with a nigga who just got out, that would help, too." Kevin was getting antsy and restless. "I feel like we could be doing something."

"Interesting choice of words. I feel like we could be doing something, too." Felicia chuckled to soften the sexual innuendo. "Look, you're too uptight. How much information do you think you're really going to get like that? You're going to scare everybody away. You have to seem like you cool and the freakin' gang, Kevin. You can't go in there like you the po-po trying to interrogate every damn body. You get more flies with honey, baby."

Impatiently tapping his feet, Kevin rested his head on the back of the couch. He couldn't help but wonder what Simone was doing. It had been three days since he'd heard her voice. He knew she was going crazy. But in a few more hours, Kevin hoped to have information that would bring a piece of normalcy back to their lives.

Felicia's eyes traveled up and down Kevin's lengthy frame. Swinging her leg back and forth, she said, "You look like you wear about a 38. Am I right?" Kevin didn't respond. With a deep sigh, Felicia pulled herself up from the couch.

"Mercedes' room is empty. It's upstairs. The first door on the right."

"How's she doing anyway?" Kevin asked.

"She's fine. Away at school. There's a brand new set of clippers on the bed. Please cut those patches of hair sprouting all over your head and do something with that gray bread. There's an outfit on the bed for you to wear tonight, too. And some smell goods. I'm going upstairs to get ready. You should do the same."

Kevin called out after her. "Felicia, I need to run out and use the phone."

"Why can't you use your cell?"

"The battery's dead."

"We don't have time for that. Look in Mercedes' room. She has every charger imaginable."

*****

Felicia pulled the prepaid phone out her purse and fell back on her bed. Kevin was pissing her off. She had to get away from him for a second to regroup. Staring up at the dust the cleaners forgot to remove from her ceiling fan, she dialed Andre. Obviously, Andre had gotten Kevin's parole officer to do whatever it was he needed to get Kevin released. Felicia had done her part by picking Kevin up. Now the ball was in Andre's court, and he needed to move faster than planned. Kevin was too anxious and antsy.

Andre answered his phone. "You got him?"

"Yeah, I got him."

"Why you sound like that? Everything okay?"

"Yeah, yeah, everything a'ight. So what's next?" Felicia asked.

"Well, I talked to my daughter a little while ago and Simone was released Friday. So, I guess we can think of something. Just give me a few more days."

Felicia sat up. "Uh, uh, Andre. That ain't gonna work. I told Kevin I was hooking him up with someone today. If I tell him I need two days, he'll leave."

"I knew getting his truck was a bad idea."

"We'll it's here, so too late. We need to make something happen today, and you only have two hours."

Chapter Twenty-Eight

Cuddled up on the couch under the warmth of two fleece throws, Simone scanned the cable guide in search of nothing in particular. Timone scampered about the house while Jordan fiddled about in the basement studio. Kayla was in the kitchen, helping Angela scrape up something for dinner. Finally, Simone was home and life seemed normal. Well, as normal as it could be without Kevin.

"Simone, I think it's time for you to take your medicine," Angela yelled from the kitchen. "You don't want one of those migraines to sneak up on you."

"I'll take it before I go to bed," Simone replied. She couldn't take the medication now and risk dozing off. Not until she heard from Kevin.

"It takes a minute for it to work. You sure you don't want to take it now?"

"No, maybe in like an hour."

"You wouldn't be more comfortable upstairs?"

"No, Ma. I'm alright down here," she barked. Without Kevin, the bedroom lacked the warmth and passion she'd grown accustomed to.

For three days, no one had come to poke her for blood or take her temperature. There hadn't been a room full of visitors to annoy her with their constant, "Do you need anything?" But her mother had taken up the slack and irritated her more than the room of visitors and hospital staff.

Another day had nearly ticked away and not once had she heard from her husband. She'd called him a couple of times, but each time his voicemail greeted her. Even if his phone had died, there were landlines that he could've used, especially considering the circumstances. Something wasn't right and Simone needed a distraction from the gnawing in her stomach.

The house phone rang. Simone perked up, silently praying it was the call she'd longed for, but no such luck.

"Oh, hey. How you doing?" Angela greeted. "No, no. This is her mother."

Simone sighed and tried her best to relax back into the couch.

"Yes, I think she's up. But hey...." Angela's voice faded as she disappeared inside the laundry room. Ten minutes later, she reemerged. "Yes, I know. It's hard but we're trying. Hold on for second, here she is."

Angela moseyed to the couch.

"Ma," Simone mumbled through clinched teeth as her mother extended the phone. "No phone calls or visitors, remember? I don't feel like talking." She pulled the covers over her head. Just then, the doorbell rang.

"Simone, it's Don," Angela whispered.

The cover flew off. "Don?" Simone questioned as she reached for the phone. "Hey, Don."

"Simone, hey, how are you? I just heard about your, umm, car accident. My goodness. I don't know what to say. I'm still shocked. Are you okay? Do you need anything?"

"No, no. I'm okay now. Just wish somebody would tell me what happened. Guess it was bad. They said I totaled a rental car."

"Yeah, I heard," Don replied.

"I'm surprised Kevin didn't tell you."

"Wow, Simone. And actually, I've been calling Mr. Songwriter. Is he around? I have some unbelievable news for the both of you."

"I thought he was meeting you to clear up something with some money or a contract?"

"With some money?" Don questioned. "That check should've cleared by now. It's been well over a month."

Simone's head began to pound. Where the hell was Kevin and what check was Don talking about?

"Okay, yeah," Simone said, attempting to play it off. "I'll check our account."

"Yeah, let me know if there's any problem and please, have Kevin call me when he gets in. I want to share the news with both of you at the same time."

"Your office or your cell?"

"Have him call my cell. I'm in Cali right now. Should be flying back to New York within the next few days."

"Okay, Don. Thanks."

Simone hung up the phone, baffled.

"Ma, look who came to see you!" Kayla chanted as she practically pulled Andre into the family room.

"Hey, Angela, how you doing?" Andre waved to his ex-mother-in-law. "Whatever you got cooking over there smells good. You can smell it outside."

"It's just chicken breast stewing in the Crockpot. Not sure what I'm going to make out of it just yet. Need to get some meat back on Simone's

bones. See how much weight she lost? Don't even look like she—"
Angela threw her hand to her mouth. She'd almost slipped.

"Yeah, that's what an IV diet will do to you. How you feeling?"
Andre directed his attention to Simone. "You okay?" he asked as he
welcomed himself to a seat on the couch.

"I'm good, I guess."

"Simone, everything okay in New York?" Angela yelled from the
kitchen.

"Yeah, everything's fine," she lied. Simone and Kevin had vowed to
keep their family out of their personal affairs.

"What's in New York?" Andre asked.

"Kevin's in New York."

"Hmm..." Andre said with a nod of his head.

Simone studied the dumbfounded expression on Andre's face as he
sat on the couch, looking like the cat that swallowed the canary. It was
obvious he had something to say.

"Don't be scared. Say it."

Andre chuckled. "What?"

"It's obvious you have something to say, so say it."

"No, I mean, you just came home from the hospital, what, two or
three days ago? Seems like New York could've waited."

"Hey, Daddy," Kayla interrupted. "Grandma said I can make
Mommy a cake if you take me to the store to get the stuff."

"Kayla, no, that's okay," Simone intervened. "I don't want any cake,
baby."

"It's cool. I can run to the store." Andre rose from the couch.

"You don't have to go."

"Simone, your mother's cooking and you just got out of the hospital.
So..." He looked around the room and shrugged his shoulders. "Considering how nobody else is here to go."

"We actually could use a few things. I'll make a list if you don't mind
picking the stuff up," Angela volunteered.

"No problem. I mean, I have a child here who needs to eat, right?"
He smiled and turned his attention back to Simone. "You look like you
could use some air. Want to ride? I mean," he chuckled, "if your husband
won't mind."

Simone failed to recognize the humor. Nevertheless, it was the
distraction she needed. She tossed back the throw.

"Actually, I think I will ride. I could use some air. Feels like I haven't
been outside in years."

Angela yelled from the kitchen. "I don't know if that's a good idea."

"Ma!" Simone yelled. Angela's peskiness was more reason for her to take the ride.

"What? I'm talking to Andre," Angela said in her defense. "Andre, she gets dizzy spells and really bad migraines, so…"

Andre threw up his hands. "Oh no. I'll make sure she stays in the car."

"And don't be long because it's time for her to take her medicine."

Simone ignored her mother and took note of her printed pajama pants and the oversized Victoria's Secret nightshirt. "Guess I should throw on some sweats or something."

"Not to sit in the car," Angela added.

"It'll only take me a minute to toss on some sweats and fix my pony-tail."

Chapter Twenty-Nine

The pulse of the bass shook the walls. Snapping her fingers, Felicia danced around her bedroom as she put the last dab of gloss on her lips.

"Go 'head girl."

Her confidence soared as she admired the flawless image staring back at her from the bathroom mirror. Her satin mini-halter dress purchased specifically for Kevin's impromptu party flattered her new sculptured curves.

She opened up her medicine cabinet and poured a handful of roofies from the falsely labeled prescription bottle into toilet tissue, then smashed them with her hairbrush.

"Now go get your man," she said to her reflection as she hid the tissue between her boobs. Turning off the bathroom light, she pranced to her room and grabbed her 5-inch peep toe booties just as the music stopped.

"Hey!" she screamed from the top of the steps. "That's my song!"

Barefoot, she headed downstairs to the living room with her shoes and clutch in hand, ready to reveal her sexiness to Kevin.

"Why you cut the music off?" she asked when she reached the living room.

Strutting to the couch where Kevin sat, she noticed that he'd not only cut his hair and trimmed his beard, he also put on the threads she'd picked up from Men's Warehouse. She wanted to spoil him by getting him something from Niemen's or the Hugo Boss store, but there would be time for that later. Tonight, her focus was on making sure she looked her best.

"Damn, don't you look nice," she said. "So how you like?" She spun around to give Kevin a view of her voluptuous curves from every angle.

"You look alright, I guess. You ready?"

"What?" Felicia was insulted. "First of all, Kevin, this outfit ain't just alright. It's fierce and I look fierce in it. You don't think it's sexy?"

"C'mon now, Felicia. It don't matter what I think no way."

"'C'mon now, Felicia,' nothing. I know you married but your ass ain't blind. Damn."

Swinging her hips like a contestant on *"America's Next Top Model,"* she strutted to her cd player and decided to give Kevin something a bit mellower. She turned the volume down and allowed jazz to serenade the room. She swayed her hips seductively to the music and waltzed around to the back of the couch. Gently, she laid her hands on Kevin's shoulders to knead the kinks from his muscles.

"Man, you tense."

Kevin glanced over his shoulder. There was no need for him to utter a word. His expression said enough. She threw her hands up in the air.

"I was just trying to help you loosen up, damn. That's okay. I got something for you."

She went into the kitchen and popped open a bottle of Moet.

"Hey," she hollered from the kitchen, "I meant to tell you. I put my extra key on your key ring when you went downstairs to funk up the bathroom. So if ever you need to swing by here or whatever, you can."

"I don't need a key, Felicia."

"You never know. It's there if you need it."

"Are you ready yet?" Kevin hollered from the living room.

"Yeah," she hollered back from the kitchen. "But you ain't. You too uptight."

But I'm about to fix that shit, Felicia thought as she pulled the tissue from her cleavage and poured it in Kevin's champagne glass. After filling the flutes with Moet, she waited to make sure Kevin's drink didn't change colors.

Perfect.

"Kevin, these are strippers. Most of them are hood-rats. I told you, you can't just go in there asking a bunch of questions like you the po-po. They ain't gon' take to that shit just like we wouldn't. You gotta pretend like you there to have a good time. Drink a little. Tell a few of your extra corny jokes. Once you show them how cool you are, you can ask them damn near whatever."

She strolled into the living room with two glasses of champagne and the bottle tucked under her arm.

"If you want some information, you gotta show them the old Kevin."

Seated on the couch, she passed Kevin his glass, prepared to make a toast. Kevin sat his glass on the table.

A ceramic case appearing to be nothing more than another knick-knack sat next to the crazy centerpiece. The little boxes scattered throughout Felicia's house served a purpose far greater than decoration. Felicia flipped it open. Inside: another bag of cocaine, a razor, two blunts, a lighter, and a few pills. She sparked one blunt to life, pulled back a drag and blew the smoke in Kevin's face.

"You know, the old Kevin would smoke this muthafucka."

"I ain't the old Kevin, just like you ain't the old Felicia."

Felicia took another hit and filled the room with a ring of circles. "You didn't hear shit I said from the kitchen."

"Yeah, I heard everything you said."

She shrugged her shoulders. "You know what? Going out is going to be a complete waste of time. These bitches ain't used to uptight, henpecked muthafuckas."

"Why I gotta be henpecked?"

Felicia took another hit from the blunt. "I don't know. Why do you?" She glanced at her watch. "They should already be there. You gotta do something to loosen up or I'm going upstairs to go to bed and you can hop in your truck, head home to your wife, and hope the sorry cops find your son. I mean, they've been doing a great job so far, right?"

Felicia extended the blunt to Kevin but he pushed it away and reached for his glass.

She grinned. "That's fine. Either poison will do."

Chapter Thirty

Simone's mind worked overtime as she and Andre rode in silence. Over and over, she weighed the odds of calling Don back to drill him for more information but decided against it. Sure, Kevin hadn't returned any of her calls, he wasn't where he said he would be, and then there was the check Don referenced. But Kevin had never given her reason to doubt any of his actions or words. He was her real life Prince Charming and she his Princess. To avoid implying that something was off in their seemingly perfect relationship, she wouldn't call Don. She would wait to hear from her husband.

"Hey," Andre said as he hung up his phone. Buried in her thoughts, Simone never even realized he was on the phone. "You feel like riding with me to go pick up my check? It's only 'bout twenty minutes away."

"Hmm, I'm kinda waiting for a phone call."

"Oh, so what, you want me to turn around and take you back home so you can sit by the phone and wait?" His salty comment was full of bitterness. Still beneath the sour tone laid some form of the truth. Simone sighed. She was in no mood to argue with Andre.

"It's only going to take a few minutes. I just have to run in and pick it up. Besides, you have your cell. He knows that number, too, right?"

"Go get your check, Andre."

It was a little after seven o'clock in the evening, and the club's parking lot was almost full.

"Dag," Simone said as Andre pulled his car up to the door. "It's packed for a Monday."

"Yeah. Male and female dancers perform here on Monday nights. They picked Monday so they wouldn't have to compete with the other venues for the weekend crowd."

"It's packed."

"This is one of the hottest clubs in town. The women walk around topless. You can touch them and everything."

"Hmm." Simone yawned as she rested her head on the passenger window. "I'm surprised you're not working. You still do part-time security for the strip clubs?"

"Naw," Andre said as he opened the door. "I work a few nights during the week but not the same night as the dancers. Guess I had to learn the hard way, huh?" He said before closing the door.

The car door slammed, startling Simone from her nap. She glanced at the clock. Andre had been inside for close to twenty minutes.

"Dag." She yawned and attempted to stretch in the tight space. "I didn't even know you'd been gone that long. I need to hurry up and get home. Feel a migraine coming."

Andre sat in the driver's seat with his head against the headrest staring blankly at nothing.

"What's wrong with you?"

"Where's your husband again?"

Simone hesitated before she answered. "He's in New York, why?"

Andre started his car and sped off.

"What's wrong?" she asked as Andre began to circle the parking lot.

"How you feel? Can you go inside for a second?"

"Go inside for what, Andre? Plus, I have on sweats and a t-shirt."

"Simone, I need you to come inside with me. Just for a second. We're not going to party and I'm not going to introduce you to anybody or nothing like that."

"So what am I going in for?"

Andre stopped in front of Kevin's truck. "Recognize this truck?"

Simone stared at the monster truck. Andre could tell she had no recollection of the vehicle. "It's your husband's truck, Simone."

"What?"

Andre stepped on the gas and sped back around to the club's entrance. "He's not in New York. He's inside the strip club."

Simone's door was open before the car shifted into park. Andre raced behind her.

"Hey, excuse me," the cashier called out to Simone.

"It's alright. She's with me," Andre said as he followed Simone.

The music thumped. Through a cloud of fog, a male dancer performed center stage. Flashing lights bounced from his muscles, which were glistening from the baby oil. Female dancers dressed in nothing but a few strokes of body paint danced in cages positioned to the left and right of the center stage, while male and female dancers worked the floor. At the bar, mingling throughout the crowd, and everywhere you looked were dancers.

"Hey, Andre," a female dancer purred and licked her heavily painted lips as she strolled past him. She teasingly skimmed her finger across his chest.

"Hey, La La." His hungry eyes followed her as she sashayed through the club.

Feeling the start of a migraine, Simone grabbed her forehead.

"You okay?" he asked over the loud music.

"Andre, where is he?"

Andre grabbed Simone by the arm and led her toward the wide set of steps that descended down to the dance floor directly in front of the center stage. Tables were scattered around the dance floor with booths alongside the wall. "First booth closest to the stage."

"I don't see him."

"You don't see that dancer giving that man a lap dance? See, he's feeling all over her breasts right at the very first booth. He has a mob of dancers around him."

On the tip of her toes, Simone searched to see what the hell Andre was talking about. She spotted the table and when the man smiled, Simone's heart stopped. She stormed down the steps, bumping into whoever was in her way. Andre was on her heels, offering apologies on behalf of her abruptness.

He tried to yell over the music. "Simone, don't make a scene." But she ignored his warning.

All day she had awaited Kevin's call. The call that was supposed to come from New York. However, that had proven to be a lie as Kevin sat a few feet away surrounded by a table full of half-naked women as he fondled the breasts of the dancer in his lap. Then there was the woman next to him with her arm draped around his shoulders, massaging the nape of his neck. Consumed with their drunken chatter and giggles, no one noticed Simone as she stood before the table. No one noticed her, that is, until she snatched a cup from the table and slung the contents at Kevin, the bulk of which landed on the dancer grinding in his lap.

The topless stripper jumped up. Ice cubes fell from her cleavage. "Bitch! No the fuck you didn't...."

"Hold up. Hold up." Andre stepped in between the potential brawl as the females at the table stood. "It ain't even that type of party."

"This bitch threw a drink on me!"

Kevin sat, bewildered. His eyes glossy. He blinked a few times and staggered to his feet. "Baby, what you doing here?"

"I'm in New York with you," Simone screamed. She tried to wiggle from Andre's grip but he tightened his hold.

"Get your muthafuckin' hands off my wife," Kevin slurred.

"YOUR WIFE? Did he just call me his wife?"

A small crowd began to gather, enticed by the commotion. Security caught wind of the spectators and headed toward the table. The uniformed officers working security summoned Andre's attention.

"Perkins. What's up? Everything cool?"

"Yeah, yeah. Everything's cool. I got it."

"He ain't got shit!" the dancer yelled. "This dumb-ass bitch threw a drink on me. Got my titties all sticky and shit."

Simone's fight began to fade as the pain from her migraine intensified. She grabbed her head. Her knees wobbled. Andre supported her weight.

"We good," Andre reiterated to the security guards. "I'm taking her out. C'mon, Simone, you've seen enough. We need to get you out of here."

She could hear Kevin calling for her as best he could considering his drunken stupor, while Andre practically carried her from the club. Once outside, she pulled from Andre. Her footing unstable, she stood still, took a deep breath, and headed toward his police car to grab her purse. She closed his door, reached inside her purse, and pulled out her keys. Andre walked beside her, his hands out to support her in case she fell.

"Simone, what are you doing?"

"Looking for the truck," she said barely above a whisper in hopes that the banging in her head would stop.

"The Hummer?"

"What other truck would I be looking for Andre? You said it belonged to me, right?"

She stood still in the parking lot, held up the keys, and pressed the alarm. Nothing happened. She headed deeper into the packed parking lot.

"I guess it belongs to both of you."

"Well, I'm going home," she said as she repeated the ritual with her keys. An alarm sounded. Tucked away in the back corner of the parking lot was the Hummer.

"I can't let you drive, Simone."

"I'm not asking your permission," she continued to whisper.

"Simone, you're not supposed to be driving. You almost fainted in the club."

"I wasn't supposed to be in the club either, Andre, but you made sure I was. So don't let my health concern you now."

"What was I supposed to do, ignore the fact that he was in there?"

Simone was speechless. She couldn't blame Andre. This time, he wasn't the one she caught cheating or lying.

Using the remote, Simone unlocked the truck, climbed inside, and slammed the door. The smell of smoke lingered. But it wasn't the scent of cigarettes. This scent was different. She pulled out the ashtray, shocked to find it filled with ashes and a tip of a blunt. There, undoubtedly, was the reason for Kevin's glossy eyes. In the cup holders of the center console were two shot glasses, one laced with lipstick, and an empty bottle of Patron.

"What the fuck, Kevin? You lying, drinking, getting high and had them bitches in our truck," she said. She rolled down the driver's side window and tossed the shot glasses and the empty bottle to the asphalt where it shattered.

Andre watched, shaking his head. "Didn't you just take your medicine?"

"No, which is why my head is killing me. I'm not going to fall asleep behind the wheel if that's what you're thinking." The engine hummed to life.

"Simone, you sure you okay to drive?"

"Yes. Plus this is easier than getting boxes."

"What?"

Frustration was etched across Simone's face. "Just go to the store for my mother. I'm going home." She placed the monster truck into drive. Andre jumped back as she sped from the parking spot.

"Hold up! I'ma follow you!"

Twenty minutes later, Simone pulled the truck into her driveway. She hopped out and stormed up her walkway with Andre on her heels.

"I thought I told you to go to the store." She hated that any of this had to take place in front of her mother, but it's what had to be done. The second she opened the door, the dog started barking.

"I called your mother and asked her to take Kayla out to dinner. And don't worry, I didn't give her any details."

"It doesn't matter what you told her, Andre," Simone replied as she opened the door and headed up the steps to her room. Andre was still on her heels even after she entered the bedroom that they once shared.

"What are you doing?" he asked as she marched inside her walk-in closet.

Seconds later, she dragged out a huge suitcase, one that Andre was sure to recognize. She unzipped the suitcase and left it in the middle of the floor. She marched back inside the closet and returned with an armload of clothes.

"Okay, but what are you doing?"

"What does it look like?" she asked, then dropped the load inside the suitcase and went back for more.

"You sure you really want to do this? You don't want to talk to him first?"

Paying Andre no mind, she dropped another load inside the open suitcase.

"Okay, Simone. As much as I don't want to touch his stuff, please let me do whatever it is you call yourself doing."

"Fine. That's his closet. Everything in it needs to come out."

Andre headed inside Kevin's closet and returned with a gun box.

"What is this?" he asked.

"What does it look like?"

"You know parolees aren't supposed to have guns."

Simone threw up her hands, frustrated with Andre's nonsense. "I'll do this myself, thanks."

"No, I got it," he said as he placed the box inside the suitcase. "I was just letting you know. What about his shoes and the things in his drawers? Everything's not going to fit in one suitcase."

"Whatever doesn't fit in the suitcase can just get tossed inside the truck or in a trash bag. I don't care. I just want it out."

"And then what?"

"Just load the fucking suitcase for me, please," she begged.

While Andre busied himself with packing, Simone grabbed the Yellow Pages from her nightstand drawer and began making calls. Barely, ten minutes later, she slammed the phone book close and pushed it aside.

"The tow truck should be here in fifteen, twenty minutes."

Andre was baffled.

"I told you it was better than getting boxes."

"Damn," was all Andre could muster at the moment. "Where are you sending the stuff?"

"I don't know. They can store it on their lot as long as it's not in here."

"I know the girl who called him baby. She works with the strippers. I have her address, I mean, if you want to send his things over there."

"Perfect."

Her mind and heart fluttered with emotions. In need of a distraction, she turned on the iPod housed in the Bose dock on her nightstand. Donnie Hathaway and Roberta Flack's "The Closer I Get to You" began to play. She grabbed the remote and skipped to the next song. The Commodores "Just to Be Close to You" played. She skipped again. "The Lady in My Life" by Michael Jackson followed. Prince's "Adore You" followed Michael Jackson. Simone gave up. A love song was the last thing she wanted to hear.

"Damn. That's why y'all made that —" Andre caught himself.

"What you say?" she asked as she snatched the cord from the wall.

The iPod and the dock were something else she would send to Kevin. Next, she headed to his dresser drawers.

"Nothing," Andre replied. "I was thinking out loud."

*****

Simone paced back and forth on her front stoop, waiting for the tow truck. A flyer of some sort danced in the wind, tucked in the side of her mailbox. *I bet nobody's checked the mail,* she thought to herself. She cut across the lawn to the box. Just as she'd suspected, the box was jammed with a few letters and the typical pesky advertisements no one bothered to read. One envelope stuck out from the others. Simone opened the envelope addressed to Kevin from the District Court Office of Child Support Enforcement. Yolanda Moore was suing Kevin for child support.

Andre walked out of the house with the last of Kevin's things dangling from hangers. He tossed the jackets into the truck and noticed the wrinkles etched across Simone's forehead.

"What's wrong?"

She passed Andre the letter as the tow truck crept down the street.

"Whoa," he said. "Who's this?"

"Yolanda. I think it's the prison guard he dated when he was locked up. The summons must've been in the box for a minute cause the court date is tomorrow." Andre was speechless.

The greasy, white tow truck driver dressed in a filthy looking t-shirt and dirty denim jeans climbed from his truck. "You folks called for a tow?"

"Yes, I did," Simone spoke up, eager to rid herself of Kevin's belongings.

"What cha' got?"

"This truck and," she turned her attention to Andre, "can you get that yapping ass dog from the laundry room?"

Andre was shocked. "You sending the dog too?"

"Yes, it's his dog. He bought it."

The truck driver snatched off his hat and ran his filthy hands through his rumpled dirty-blonde tresses as he walked around the Hummer loaded with Kevin's things.

"Wow." He shook his head. "I thought I'd seen everything but in my twenty two years of driving, I ain't never had a situation like this."

"Well, it's a first time for everything," Simone said. Andre came out of the house with the dog in the cage and passed it to the driver.

"The dog, too, huh?"

"Yes," Simone answered without hesitation as the Yorkie yapped nonstop from its cage. "Oh, and this." She handed the driver the open piece of mail.

Andre couldn't help himself and chuckled at the driver's expression.

Reaching inside her pocket, Simone pulled out a check and the post-it note containing the address Andre had given her.

"This is the address and here's the check for three hundred. You said two-fifty, but I'm giving you an extra fifty."

The driver shrugged his shoulders and stuffed the check along with the envelope in the pocket of his dirty t-shirt. Heading to his truck, he paused and asked, "Who do I ask for?"

"Kevin Kennard, but whoever answers the door is fine."

Simone headed inside. As she crossed the threshold, she noticed a small envelope.

"I thought I saw something fall from one of those jackets."

She picked up the envelope and headed back inside the house towards her office. Shadowing her, Andre rested against the door frame as Simone tossed the envelope on her desk and sank into her high back chair. She powered on her computer and waited for it to come to life.

"Why don't you head upstairs and try to relax? Plus, you have to take your medicine."

"No, I need to send my attorney an email. I want a legal separation as soon as possible. Like tomorrow." As she waited, her eyes fell upon the white envelope. Curious, she opened it and pulled out the sonogram. Andre gasped.

"Ain't this some shit." She turned on her desk lamp and held the transparent image to the light. "He knew about the baby. He was carrying the shit around in his pocket."

"Simone, give me that." Andre pulled the sonogram photo from Simone's hands without any protest from her. "Why don't you go upstairs and run yourself a hot bath or something?"

The weight of the day finally registered with Simone and took its toll. Tears splashed against the desk as she held her head in her hands. "I don't feel like taking no bath, Andre."

"But you need to relax. You've been through a helluva lot."

Wiping away her tears, she replied, "What else is new?"

"Simone," Andre pleaded. "You just got out of the hospital and none of us want you to go back. So please, go upstairs and get in the bed. I'll bring you something to eat."

"My fucking head is killing me."

"Go 'head upstairs and take your medicine. I'll bring you something to eat and I'll hang around a bit just in case he decides to come over. Last thing you need is more drama."

Simone got up from her chair and headed upstairs to her room. Andre took her place in the high back chair and shook the mouse, bringing the desktop to life.

"Damn," he said aloud as an image of Kevin and pregnant Simone illuminated the screen. Kevin's hands were wrapped around Simone's belly as she cheesed a lotto grin.

"Damn, if you had touched this mouse —," Andre said under his breath as he tossed the sonogram picture in one of the desk drawers.

Luckily, the computer was password free. Simone hated them. As much as Andre wanted to delete the pictures that symbolized Simone and her new life, he figured a password would suffice for now.

"You'll be deleting them yourself in the long run."

He added a password, then searched the internet. "A 24-hour locksmith and a handyman. That's exactly who I need."

Chapter Thirty-One

K evin felt something gnawing at his ear. He smacked at it with his hand and sent it yapping off in pain. He tried to open his eyes but the slightest hint of light made his head throb.

"Shit," he moaned. He grabbed his head with both hands and squeezed his eyes shut.

He heard water running in the bathroom. Moments later, the water was off and the bathroom door swung open. Out walked Felicia, dressed in a thong and carrying a glass of water.

"What the fuck?" Kevin said.

Ignoring the pain, he tossed back the covers and shot up from the bed. The room spun. His body rejected the sudden movement. Unable to find his balance, he fell back on the bed, fighting the urge to vomit. He closed his eyes and threw his arm over his head to stop the spinning.

"Oops," Felicia's singsong voice said playfully as she waltzed from the bathroom topless. She placed the glass of water on the nightstand and flipped her knick-knack container closed. She opened the nightstand drawer and grabbed a bottle of painkillers.

"Damn, nigga. That's a nice ass piss hard."

Kevin's hands raced down his body in search of his clothes but there were none.

"Fuck, man," he said. Knowing he couldn't get up, he felt for the comforter and tossed it over his nakedness.

"Let me put your mind at ease. We didn't do anything, Kevin. Now here." She shoved two aspirins into his hand, then passed him the glass of water. "Take these."

"Felicia, where the fuck are my clothes and why am I in your room?"

"You don't remember?" Kevin didn't respond.

"Well...." she plopped on her side of the bed. The bounce made Kevin moan. He sat up long enough to chase the two pills down with a few swallows of water.

"You started out in Mercedes' room but you puked your brains out all over the place. I'm talking 'bout on your clothes, the covers, I mean, every damn where. I couldn't let you lay in spit up, so I brought you in here about ten this morning."

"Ten this morning? Damn, what time is it now?"

"A little after eleven."

"It feels later than that."

"Eleven at night, Kevin."

"What?"

"Kevin, your ass was comatose all damn day. And sorry, I didn't mean to keep you naked but I only got you the one outfit. I mean, had I known being naked was going to make you so uncomfortable, I guess I could've forced all that into one of my thongs."

Kevin patted himself to make sure he was covered.

"Why don't you have clothes on, Felicia?"

She chuckled sarcastically. "Because I'm in my got-damn-house and this is how I do in my got-damn-house."

"Shit, I gotta get outta here." He sat up in the bed, thankful that the urge to puke didn't follow him. "Where are my clothes?"

"I put them in the dryer a few minutes ago, Kevin. Give them like ten minutes."

Kevin sighed. "I can't believe I been out all damn day. I haven't called my wife and the fucking day is gone. Shit! What the fuck did you give me?"

"I didn't give you nothing. I mean, you took a few hits from a blunt..."

"Laced with what?"

"With a coke, Kevin, damn. But that ain't what did you in. You were tossing back shots of Patron one behind the other like you was built Ford tough. Had I known your ass don' turned soft, I wouldn't have let you do it."

"I hope I didn't get this fucked up for nothing. So what happened? Did the dancer come through? Did we get some information?"

"Kevin. You serious? You don't remember anything from last night? I mean, nothing?"

A dog started to bark.

"Nothing past the Moet I drank before we left. I don't even really remember walking in the club. So what happened? Did the bitch give the information up or what?"

"Shit, Kevin."

"Shit, Kevin, what?"

"I mean, I don't even know how to tell you this."

"Tell me what, Felicia?"

"Kevin, I got the girl to come over to the table. We were chillin' and everything until Andre walked in."

"Andre? Andre who?"

"Your wife's ex-husband, Andre." Felicia paused and waited for Kevin's reaction. "He walked in with your wife."

Timone ran into the room and leaped on the bed. Kevin's heart stopped as the little dog stood before him, barking and wagging his tail. Slowly, he eased up from the bed.

"Felicia, what did she see? What was I doing?" he asked as he read the dog's tag, though it was no need. He knew the Yorkie was the one he'd bought for the girls.

"I mean, Kevin, I don't really remember. I was shocked and damn near as fucked up as you."

Kevin tossed back the cover, stood from the bed, and headed out the room, no longer caring about his nakedness. Felicia followed him downstairs to the laundry room.

"Kevin, what are you doing?" She asked as he snatched open the dryer and pulled out his damp clothes.

"I'm going home, Felicia," he said as he stepped into his white boxer briefs. "I'm doing this shit to save my family, not fuck it up."

Desperate, Felicia pleaded, "But Kevin, we almost there. We would've gotten the information last night but..." She stopped mid-sentence.

"But what?" With one leg inside his pants, Kevin turned to face her. "But what?" he asked again, as Felicia's eyes darted around the room in an useless attempt to avoid his. He bit down on his lip. "Bitch, so fuckin' help me..."

"Kevin, one of the dancers was giving you a lap dance."

"What?"

"Yeah, and you were jive enjoying it. I mean, you were playing with her titties and everything."

"Simone saw that shit?" Kevin questioned through clinched teeth.

"Kevin, how did I know Andre was gon' bring her to the fuckin' club!"

Fuming, Kevin pushed past Felicia with enough force to send her falling into the wall. "You set that shit up."

"What! I didn't set up shit," Felicia cried as she scurried behind him. "I don't go to that club, Kevin. How the fuck was I supposed to know he was going to be there?"

"I bet that's how the fuck you knew I was locked up!" Kevin tossed on the rest of his things and rushed up the steps.

"Kevin, no. I swear, I'm telling you the truth. I wouldn't fuck with you like that. I don't fuck with strippers no more, I told you that," she ranted as she continued to chase him. "I called around as a favor for you and the girl suggested we meet her there."

Kevin ignored Felicia, grabbed his coat and whistled for the dog.

"Timone, come on."

"What are you doing? Where you going?"

"Where my keys at, Felicia?"

"Kevin, you can't leave. We gon' get the information."

"Bitch, I will punch you in your muthafuckin' throat if I have to ask you again."

Felicia ran upstairs to her bedroom and returned with the keys. Kevin snatched them from her hand as she continued her explanation.

"Kevin, I can call her. We can go meet with her and get the information. I didn't know shit was gon' happen like this."

"How did the dog get here?"

Felicia sighed and looked away. "Simone took your truck from the club. We had to get a ride back here. Last night, this tow truck driver rang the doorbell. He dropped off your truck. Said the dog and your things were inside."

The evening breeze ripped right through Kevin's damp clothes as he raced the stairs but he was too numb to even care. He climbed inside his monster truck, placed the dog in his cage, started the engine and skidded off.

The street was dark and quiet but Andre's undercover vehicle stood out in the darkness.

How fucking convenient is that shit? You bring her to the club and now you in here trying to comfort her, Kevin thought. He hopped from his truck, and rushed up the walkway. Suddenly, a bright light shined on him. He shaded his eyes and looked towards the glare. A motion sensor floodlight had been installed.

Kevin brushed it off, heading up the walkway. He turned the screen door handle; it was locked, which was unusual. He inserted his key, but it didn't work. He banged on the frame of the door and cried his wife's name. "Simone!" He contemplated breaking a window to get inside but he knew Andre would have him arrested before he managed to even get inside.

Kevin's world was falling apart. *And for what?* He screamed in thought. He looked up toward the heavens. "I only wanted to find my son and protect my family."

Lost and defeated, Kevin wandered from the house and hopped back in his truck. He needed to get away, far away.

*****

In a cold sweat, Simone sprung up in bed, panting as her heart throbbed, haunted by another nightmarish dream. Like the dream earlier, Kevin had come to rescue her. This time, his voice had seemed so real, but as she eyed the empty space to her right, reality registered. Her pills sat on the nightstand. She hated the comatose state they induced and the nightmares that tackled her as a result of the deep slumber. But she welcomed the nightmare over her outlandish reality any day.

Tears fell from Simone's eyes. She grabbed the pillow from the side of the bed to muffle her sobs. She never heard the tap at her bedroom door. Without her consent, Andre poked his head inside. Seeing her cry, he closed the door and rushed to her side.

"Aww, Simone." Andre sat on the bed and pulled her from the pillow, into his embrace. "Don't cry. He'll realize he made the biggest mistake of his life. Take it from someone who knows."

"Whatever," Simone said as her tears continued to fall. "Man, I feel like such a fuckin' fool. But Jordan just had to meet her daddy."

"You remember that?"

"Unfortunately."

"What else can you remember?"

"I don't know, Andre." She sniffed. "What are you doing here anyway?"

"I stopped by around eight. You were already in bed and your mother was nodding off on the couch. I took Kayla to the store to grab some stuff. She needed a bagged lunch for her field trip tomorrow."

"Where's my mother?"

"She's asleep. I told her I'd stay up with Kayla to help her get her stuff together. I was checking to make sure everybody was cool before I left. I heard noise coming from your room, so I came to check on you. You have to stop crying and focus on getting better. Everything's going to work out."

"Really," Simone said sarcastically. "I sent him his things yesterday, and he hasn't even bothered to call me. I was in the hospital for God's sake and he just left me there. He left me there to go to the strip club?" She said through her sobs. "Man, I feel like such a fuckin' dummy. I really thought he loved me."

"Simone, trust me," Andre's voice was soft and smooth, "you're worth way more than a room full of strippers."

She rested her head on Andre's shoulders. There was so much comfort in his embrace. Inhaling her scent, Andre stroked the small of her back and kissed her on the top of her head. His words, his touch, all seemed to work magic.

Breathing gently in her ear, he kissed her face and waited for her response. He tested the waters again and applied another tender pecks to her neck. To Andre's surprise, Simone melted deeper into his embrace. He stroked the side of her face, then skimmed his fingers along her neck, her shoulders, her arm. Her eyes closed, welcoming the affection. Someone was there to love her in her time of pain.

An unexpected fervor grew. Andre noticed her nipples harden through her pajama tank top. He lifted her head from his shoulders. Her eyes rolled up to meet his and with it, a look he remembered too well. She needed to feel love, and he was more than happy to oblige.

Knowing that Simone was fragile both mentally and physically, he eased her back to the comforts of the bed as if she were a delicate flower. Gently, his lips journeyed down her body until he rested at her navel. He eased on top of the bed and made his way between her legs while applying tender pecks. He tugged at the waist of her pajama pants. Cotton tore as he tried to work her pants down from her waist. She grabbed at his hands.

"No, Andre," Simone moaned.

"I just want to taste you." He kissed her navel.

"Please don't, Andre."

But he ignored her and tugged harder despite the clawing from her nails. Finally, he unveiled her most intimate parts.

"Andre, no." She pushed at his forehead in an attempt to make him stop, but the more she fought, the more he persisted. He grabbed her hands and pinned her with the weight of his body as his thickness hardened against her leg.

"Andre, please. Stop it," she cried.

Ignoring her cries, Andre kissed her lips, then licked her center. He remembered her spot and teased it the way she liked as he hummed a tune of nothing, just to add extra vibrating pleasure. A puddle began to form as Simone's body betrayed her verbal protest.

"Andre, please. Please stop." She cried. "Please stop."

"Not until you come," he whispered quickly, then returned to his feast.

"Andre, I can't," she cried, tears pouring from the corners of her eyes.

"Shhh. Just enjoy it. 'Cause I'm not stopping 'til you come."

Simone's eyes drifted shut, her back arched as she became reac-quainted with her ex-husband. Minutes later, she released her tearful satisfaction. Andre rose from his feast, his hardness bulging inside his jean shorts. He unfastened his belt.

"My hand to God, I'll call the police. Now get out of my house."

Andre climbed from the bed with his hands still on his belt and lust in his eyes. Simone grabbed the bottle of pills and chased two down with the bottle of water on her nightstand. In minutes, she'd be sleep. She welcomed the nightmare with open arms.

Chapter Thirty-Two

A gentle breeze danced through the crack left in Felicia's bedroom window and waltzed across the pillow where Kevin had rested his head, awaking the scents he left behind. Frustrated, she grabbed the pillow from the other side of her bed and filled her lungs with Kevin's sweet scent. In an immediate rage, she tossed the pillow to the floor and burst into a tantrum, kicking and screaming.

"I had you! I had you in my bed!"

She smacked away her unexpected tears and sprung up from the mattress, glaring down at the now empty spot. Yesterday, she'd fed him pills, passing them off as aspirin just to keep him there. While he was out, she had her way, loving him the way she'd fantasized about for sixteen years.

She kissed Kevin's lips then traveled down his sculptured body, leaving a path of kisses that she traveled over and over again. She toyed with his manhood, sucking and stroking, never caring that he wouldn't get fully erect. She managed to get him inside of her a few times but he kept slipping out. If she wanted to get her man, she had to slow down. With Kevin inside of her, she used her fingers until she arrived at ecstasy's threshold. She grinded deep into Kevin and showered him with her joy.

"I love you so much," she cried as she showered his face with kisses. "You just don't know what you missing, baby."

Dismounting him, she went to the bathroom for a warm washcloth but cleaning him ignited another frenzy. This time she decided to record it with Kevin's phone.

She iced him with strawberry flavored motion lotion and went to town. After another round of pleasure, she lifted his arms and drifted off to sleep, resting soundly in his forced embrace.

Hours later, she woke. *Shit,* she had mumbled as she stirred from his arms. She hadn't meant to sleep long. She waltzed to the bathroom, to fill a glass with water, ready to feed him another dose. But Kevin had awakened.

"Damn. I bet your ass went flying back home to your wife."

Felicia had to give it to Simone. Packing up Kevin's things and sending them to him on a tow truck was a thorough ass move. A move that had Felicia's insides tap dancing with joy while on the outside, she fought to remain that supportive friend with the shoulder for Kevin to lean on.

Or grip tight with both hands, she thought. The image of Kevin gripping her shoulders while he worked her deep from behind made her shiver.

"Man, I hope you didn't go back home."

Haunted by the thought, Felicia grabbed her purse from the floor and fished around for the prepaid phone. The red message light flashed. Two people had the number - Andre and Sanora. It didn't take a rocket scientist to figure out who'd left the messages. Felicia knew what Sanora wanted and she'd give it to her just as soon as she had Kevin where she wanted him, which was there with her. Hell, since Simone had put him out, he may as well be where he should've been from the beginning. Somehow, everything would work out. Felicia would have Kevin, Andre would have Simone, and Sanora could fly the hell on to Jamaica. Until then, Sanora had to stay put and be thankful she was even still alive. After all, her phone call had started it all.

Andre's phone rang six times. Glancing at the clock, Felicia wondered if he was even up.

"Hello..."

"Who's with your wife? You or Kevin?"

"I am. I'm heading to the office. I can discuss it with you then."

"Yeah, whatever," Felicia mumbled as she ended the call. "Now ain't that some shit. If Andre's in your bed this muthafuckin' early, he got to be dicking your wife. Hell, I should send her ass this muthafuckin' video," she said with a sinister laugh. She grabbed Kevin's phone from her nightstand drawer, searching through his videos. "But I'll wait. For now, I'll just email it to myself."

Chapter Thirty-Three

S even o'clock in the morning, Sanora sat on the bed with Lil' Kevin cradled lovingly in her arms as if he were her own son. The son she and Fat Ed had created. Tears flowed freely as she gingerly rocked the sleeping baby back and forth, longing for her own child. The baby she hadn't held in close to a month.

Sniffing back tears, she closed her eyes and tried to imagine how life would've been had she and Fat Ed lived out the fantasies spoken minutes before his senseless death. But Felicia's fatal attraction killed Sanora's future.

"And now I'm supposed to stay locked up, babysitting a baby your crazy ass kidnapped?" she cried.

Her son would never know his father and the way things were going, he probably wouldn't know his mother either. The remorse dwelling inside of Sanora grew into hate more and more each day.

"You a selfish bitch, Felicia. All of this just for some fucking dick?"

She had to do something to make it right. She owed that to her son, Fat Ed, the baby cradled in her arms and his parents.

"Lay right here for a second, sweetie," she said. She laid Lil' Kevin in the center of the queen-size bed and unwrapped his blanket. "I'm sorry but we gotta do this again."

For the second time in less than an hour, Sanora wiped the needle she found inside a sewing kit with alcohol, swabbed Lil' Kevin's heel, then poked him just enough to ignite his wails. Pacing the floor, she nibbled on her ragged nails. It killed her to watch him cry but his wails justified her lie and irritated the hell out of Linwood's sons.

"Aww, come on." Big L screamed from the couch. "Can you shut him up? Got damn, that's a crying ass baby."

Sanora swaddled Lil' Kevin in the receiving blanket then scooped him up in her arms. She snatched open the bedroom door and said, "I told you he's sick. He needs medicine. Felicia was supposed to bring my prescription pad days ago."

Frustrated, Big L sat up on the couch and grabbed his cell. "There's a pharmacy inside the grocery store across the street. At this point, I'll just call it in under another doctor. I know his control number."

"What the fuck ever, man. If it'll stop that baby from crying, just call the shit in, please."

A few hours later, Big L opened Sanora's door. The smell of greasy bacon, toast, and onions waltzed inside the room. His eyes roamed her body as she sat on the bed in her bra and panties, patting Lil' Kevin's back as he lay in the middle of the bed. Her heart raced as she prepared to answer questions about the three bottles of medication. She prayed they would be none the wiser to the prescriptions but there was always that chance that whoever picked it up would inquire.

"Here. I had Big Daryl pick up the prescription and some breakfast, too." Big L placed the brown bag with the round grease stain on the nightstand with the pharmacy bag. "Whatever you don't want let me know."

"Okay," Sanora replied.

"And you got me on dessert, right?"

Sanora rolled her eyes up to the ceiling. She didn't bother to answer. After all, it wasn't like she had a choice.

Big L and his brother, Daryl, Sr., each took turns as the watchdog. During either shift, they got horny and took turns reminding Sanora that she was a high class hoe. She lied and said she had an untreated sexually transmitted disease. Daryl, Sr. used a condom but Big L's nasty ass said she was worth a shot in the ass. He wanted the full sha-bang, raw dog. In his eyes, sex wasn't sex if he had to wrap up.

Once the bedroom door was closed, Sanora silently rejoiced. She grabbed the bags and headed to the bathroom. Locked inside, she poured four sedatives into a piece of toilet paper. She grabbed an unopened can of formula from the cans stacked on the bathroom vanity and rolled it across the pills until she felt the crunch. Folding back the tissue, she approved the powdery form. Next, she unpacked the bag of grease.

Wrapped in plastic was a sandwich - bacon, egg, and cheese on toasted white bread. She flipped back the top of the small white styrofoam container and savored the smell of the hash brown potatoes and onions. She stuffed her mouth with forkfuls of the potatoes, disappointed that they smelled better than they tasted, and peeled apart the sandwich. The powdery sedative in hand, she sprinkled it across the fried egg.

"Damn," she mumbled as she glanced inside the tissue. She'd poured more than half of the powder on the sandwich. *Oh, well,* she thought. The medication was tasteless. Inside the potatoes, she sprinkled the remaining portion of the powder and a pack of salt and pepper, then stirred them just a little. Big L normally ate and drank everything she left behind. She hoped today would be no different.

Inhaling strength and nerves, she wrapped the sandwich back up, closed the styrofoam container, and carried it out to the living room. Big L sat on the couch, sucking his teeth with the remote control in hand. Sanora parked the sandwich and the potatoes on the table, next to his trash.

"You ready for me?"

"Let me hop in the shower real quick."

"Naw, you good," he replied as he made his selection.

"I probably smell like your brother."

He sat the remote on the table and reached for the sandwich. "Then get your ass in the shower."

Sanora's heart thumped inside her chest as she closed her room door. She turned on the shower, letting the water run while she gathered the bare necessities.

"The second he falls asleep, I'm snatching his keys and we're out of here. I'm going to get you back to your parents."

Chapter Thirty-Four

The realization of life's most recent devastation greeted Kevin in the morning as his shabby motel room came in to view. The slow jams that once rocked him and Simone to sleep or serenaded their lovemaking, played in the background. All night long, the melodies played in his head while his heart spilled out lyrics. He needed a tablet or something. He had to put his lyrics on paper.

Yesterday had been one of the worse days of his life. He wanted to tell Simone everything, regardless of the doctor's warning. She needed to know what had happened to her and their baby, the baby she'd barely held. She needed to know Fat Ed had stumbled across some information that had ultimately cost him his life. And most importantly, she needed to know he loved her beyond measure. His lies were simply a means to keep her safe and out of harm's way both physically and mentally. But the changing of the locks coupled with the removal of his belongings from the only place he cared to know as home, screamed how bad his actions had hurt her.

Defeated and lost, Kevin had driven until he couldn't drive any more. He stumbled across a rinky-dink motel in God knows where with a neighboring liquor store.

All night long, he tossed back shots of Remy, one behind the other, while he thought about everything. Felicia's actions had appeared so genuine, but Simone popping up in the club with Andre was too much of a coincidence. The shit was planned and he knew it. Everybody thought their bond had weakened in the crisis. Kevin had to find a way to show them otherwise.

Pulling himself up from the floor, he accidentally kicked over the bottle of liquor. Timone's doggie instincts leaped into action. Yet, despite Kevin's massive headache, he reached out and caught Timone before he could sample from the small puddle.

"Shit, you probably already had some," he said to the little pooch as he licked Kevin's face. It was the only act of love that he'd received since Simone went into the hospital.

Grabbing the bottle from the floor, Kevin was surprised to see he'd only consumed half. His head throbbed as if he had drunk the entire store. He put Timone down on the floor and sat the bottle on the three legged table, right next to the infamous letter.

"Aww, man," Kevin said as he picked up the opened letter to read it again. "Damn, what's today?" He scanned the room in search of a calendar or something with the date, but instead of the date, he caught sight of his reflection.

His damp clothes, wrinkled from the dryer and the night spent on the floor were covered in white specks of lint. He was a drunken mess.

With a heavy sigh, Kevin knew the last thing he needed was another bench warrant. He patted his pockets in search of his BlackBerry to check the date.

"Damn, where the hell is my phone?" He reached in his pocket and pulled out the receipt from the motel. He'd checked in at 11:58 on the 30th of April, making today May 1st. "Shit, it's today."

He had to hurry. He had to be there by ten o'clock and the courthouse was at least two hours away. It was already after eight.

He headed into the bathroom to take a quick leak. As he relieved himself, a fruity scent waltzed about in the air. Baffled, Kevin fixed his clothes but hesitated when he spotted the reddish stain against the waistband of his white boxer briefs. Though he hadn't felt a pinch or sting of any sort, he checked his shaft to make sure he hadn't accidentally snagged himself with the zipper. But as he examined a little closer, he not only spotted specks of glitter but caught a better whiff of fruit: strawberries. He tore the wrapping from the no-name bar of soap and snatched one of the rough cloths dangling from the towel holder. With a vengeance, he washed his private parts.

*****

Kevin's shoes clicked along the floor as he proceeded in the direction of the muffled chatter and baby wails. The high-pitched voices of women screaming at both their children and alleged baby daddies grew louder as Kevin approached the Family Court division.

"Geez," he hissed. The place was swarming with people. Kids ran amuck climbing over the wooden pews serving as the reception area for those individuals waiting to see the magistrate. Fathers stood at the counter pleading their cases to the poor receptionist who couldn't do a thing for them.

"But sir, the test says you're the father. There's nothing I can do."

In the background, a mother growled, "Sit down, Latierra," while another unashamedly yelled, "Lamont, if I tell your black ass one more time...."

Kevin stood in line, waiting his turn.

"Your name?" the receptionist asked with little patience.

"Kennard."

"Oh. I think they already called your case." She picked up a yellow highlighter and drew a line through the case, indicating the presence of all parties.

"I hope not. I don't even know if the child is mine."

"Well," the receptionist responded, "if you don't think the child is yours, you can request a paternity test for seven hundred and ninety-five dollars."

"And who pays for that?"

Annoyed, the receptionist looked up. "The one disputing it."

"So if it comes back that…"

"Kevin!" A female called his name off in the distance, distracting him.

Kevin looked out toward the crowd until he spotted a heavyset woman making her way from one of the back pews.

"Excuse me," he said to the receptionist as he headed in Yolanda's direction. Her smiley face slowly turned upside down.

"Hey," she greeted him somewhat hesitantly.

"What's this about, Yolanda? I haven't spoken with you in over three years and out of the blue I get this letter. You told me you were on the pill."

"Kevin, it's a…"

"Mommy, Mommy!" Running full speed, a little boy darted through the crowd seemingly from out of nowhere and charged into Yolanda's legs like a bull.

"Whoa, baby. Don't knock Mommy down." She chuckled as the little boy wrapped his arms around her legs. "Kevin, this is my son, Patrick. Patrick," she said as she stared down into her son's hazel eyes, "this is Mr. Kevin."

Stunned, Kevin stared at the little boy tangled around Yolanda's leg. Patrick didn't share his mother's mocha complexion, dark brown eyes, or hair. Instead, his complexion was light and his eyes were hazel, just like Kevin's. And if that weren't enough, his light brown, almost dirty blonde hair reminded Kevin of the pictures he'd seen of himself back when he was a toddler.

Oh my God, Kevin thought to himself realizing there was no need for him to waste seven hundred and ninety-five dollars.

A blonde haired, blue eyed white man, professionally dressed in a suit and tie approached. "Hey, there you are." He extended his hand to Kevin and smiled.

Damn. She got an attorney, Kevin thought, wondering if he should've sought representation.

"Is this Kevin?" he asked as he kissed Yolanda on the lips.

"Yes." Yolanda smiled. "Kevin, this is my husband, Patrick Collins. Patrick, this is Kevin Kennard, the songwriter."

"Nice to meet you," Patrick said as they shook hands.

"Yeah, you, too," Kevin responded as they exchanged pleasantries. "So you know about the songwriting?"

"Yeah, we saw your picture in *Jet*. Congratulations. And Simone? She's the mother of your daughter, right? The one you were looking for all those years."

"Yeah, yeah," Kevin said, rather antsy as his eyes fell upon the face of the little boy.

"Wow, what a love story."

Yolanda stared at him intently. Her eyes questioned his wrinkled lint-covered clothes. She reached out and rubbed Kevin's arm. There was comfort in her touch.

"Is everything okay, Kevin?"

"Far from."

"You know, drinking won't help."

Kevin sniffed his shirt. "Damn, it's that bad?"

With a simple smirk and a squinted up nose, Yolanda slowly nodded her head.

"I'm going through a tough time, Yolanda, so this right here doesn't help. How come you didn't notify me while I was locked up?"

"Hey, everything's okay, Kevin. I spoke to the clerk of the court and confirmed that everything's been taken care of."

"What do you mean everything's been taken care of?"

Patrick sighed. He placed his hand in the small of Yolanda's back and nodded up the hallway. "You got a minute? Let's go somewhere and talk."

*****

Kevin sat in the booth alongside little Patrick, thankful that one burden had been lifted.

"I mean, I wish you coulda read what I was thinking when I first saw him. I was like, man, it's a wrap. It's a done deal. I knew for sure," Kevin said, doing his best to talk in code.

"Yeah, so imagine how confused we were," Yolanda confessed as she and her husband held hands on the table.

Squeezing his wife's hand, Patrick said, "Initially, I didn't want to know for fear that the results wouldn't come back in my favor. But we owed it to him, you know, for medical reasons if nothing else. I took the test but it didn't come back the way we wanted. So, we had no choice but to file the papers," Patrick shared.

"Then we got a phone call saying there had been some kind of mix up with the lab results. Something about the barcodes. We went back in and well," Yolanda giggled.

"He's mine," Patrick finished. "We were so happy that we forgot to cancel these proceedings."

"Patrick and I met a week after I got transferred and we've been together ever since. He actually helped me get over you."

Kevin was shocked. "Wow, what were you in for?"

"No, no." Patrick chuckled. "I'm a private investigator."

"Lies. He's an attorney," Yolanda added proudly. She picked up a French fry from the basket in the middle of the table and dunked it in ketchup.

Patrick shook his head.

"Well, you are. Shoot, I'm proud of your law degree," Yolanda expressed.

Patrick chuckled. "I guess for all intents and purposes, I am an attorney, yes. But I don't plead cases. Investigating behind the scenes is what I like but my dad wouldn't hear of his only son being a detective. He said I had to get a law degree and pass the bar. Once I did that, he would allow me to investigate for his firm."

Patrick picked up a French fry and dipped it in vinegar.

"So, needless to say, he was at the prison a lot," Yolanda shared.

"Yep." Patrick sighed. "I saw this beautiful woman one day when I was with my dad and fell in love with her instantly." He took another fry, dipped it in ketchup, placed a dab on Yolanda's lips then kissed it off.

"Hmmm." Kevin nodded.

"We're sorry you had to go through this for nothing," Yolanda added.

"Yeah, we'd forgotten about it until one of my dad's associates said he saw Yolanda's name on the docket for today. I tried to track you down, but your mother's number had been terminated, and I guess you have a new parole officer? McPherson, I think his name is."

Kevin chuckled. "Yeah, McPherson. If you weren't calling to say I broke the law, he wouldn't call you back."

Patrick and Yolanda exchanged glances. "Yeah, well he never returned any of my calls. So, we figured we just needed to show up here today and let you know ourselves."

"Kevin, is something wrong? Do you need some help?"

"I don't think there's a person alive who can help me," Kevin said.

"So how are you adjusting? From what we read and saw in the magazine, it seems like everything is going well for you."

"Yeah, it was." Kevin avoided their eyes for fear that his tears would rain. "Until someone tried to kill my wife and kidnapped our son minutes after he was born. He's still missing, and oh, my best friend is missing, too."

"Wakefield Hospital?" Patrick sat upright in the booth.

"Yeah, guess you saw it on the news, too, huh?"

Patrick and Yolanda sat baffled as Kevin filled in the gaps. Yolanda reached across the table to place her hand on Kevin's. Her body jerked the second she graced his flesh.

"Hallelujah!" she cried.

Taken aback, Kevin stared at Yolanda from the corner of his eyes, watching as she closed her eyes and began to speak in what he figured to be either Swahili or a variation of Tina Turner's chant from the movie, *"What's Love Got to Do With It."*

"The spirit hits her all the time and out the blue," Patrick whispered.

"The spirit?" Kevin questioned.

"Yeah." Patrick seemed surprised that Kevin had no idea what he was saying. "You know, the Holy Ghost. Yolanda's an ordained minister now. She's speaking in tongues. No disrespect, Kevin, but I thought ninety-nine point nine percent of all inmates found religion in prison."

"Most do. A lot turn Muslim. I didn't. I mean, I pray and I know who GOD is but…"

Kevin watched Yolanda rock back and forth as she prayed in tongues oblivious to the other patrons around her.

"We went through a lot trying to have our son. In the midst of it, Yolanda got her calling to be a minister." Patrick shared.

"Oh Jesus. Sweet Jesus," Yolanda chanted. "Kevin, everything's going to be fine. You hear me? God just wants you to trust in him."

Patrick pulled two cards from the inside pocket of his suit jacket. "Here, Kevin. This is my card and my dad's card. If you need my help or even my father's help, just give us a call."

Yolanda added, "Before we leave, I want to pray with you. I want to speak the power of healing over your wife's mind. She will remember, Kevin. She will." She reached for Kevin's hand again. "You keep that ring on, Kevin."

Kevin snatched his hand away and stared at his ring finger.

"Where's my ring?"

Yolanda summoned his hands with her fingers. "Find it and put it on."

She grabbed the hand of Patrick, who in turn grabbed the hand of his son.

"Let us pray."

*****

Kevin sat in his truck outside of the courthouse. He thought his morning was doomed, but it had proven to be filled with the most sunshine he'd experienced in a long time. He knew Simone had read the summons and figured he'd call and share that the only kids he'd ever fathered were the ones he made out of love with her. Then it occurred to him. He took his ring off at Felicia's and stuffed it in his pocket. In the pocket of the pants she'd purchased for him.

"The pants I left in the dryer," he said as he started up his truck. More than likely, his cell was there, too.

Kevin pulled the hotel receipt from his pocket and programmed the address into his GPS. Gathering his things and checking out would've made him late for court. An hour and forty minutes later, he pulled into the parking lot of the motel. Once inside, he caught another glimpse of himself in the mirror.

"Guess I could take a quick shower and change my clothes."

Unzipping the suitcase, the gun box caught him off guard. Inside lay a stainless steel Kobra Carry with a snakeskin textured grip. Thoughts of a bloody revenge danced inside his mind. He closed the box to turn off the images, silently hoping there was power in Yolanda's prayer.

Chapter Thirty-Five

S imone woke with a fierce headache. She was tired of the nightmares and taking another painkiller wasn't an option. If the
headache wasn't enough, Andre snored from the other side of the
bed.

I thought I told him to leave. She remembered him going to the bathroom but nothing thereafter. She felt under the cover, thankful her
pajama pants were still on.

I must've fallen asleep.

The way his erection protruded from his pants last night, she knew
the purpose of his bathroom visit. Just when she was getting ready to
kick him from her bed, his cell rang and summoned his immediate
attention. Too rushed to converse, Andre left with a generic, "I'll call you
later," which was three words too many.

Refusing to wallow in her trouble, Simone needed something to paci-
fy her heart and occupy her mind. She powered on the television.
Morning shows invaded every channel.

*Hmm, I wonder what's in the DVD player. Maybe I was watching a movie
before the accident. Ooh, maybe this will help me remember something.*

As the DVD played, there she was, as gorgeous as ever, in her white
flowing grown, standing before the priest with her ever-so-handsome,
teary-eyed husband. Laughter rang out from the guests seated in white
lawn chairs draped with tulle and flowers. She reached up and wiped
away one of Kevin's tears. Closing his eyes, he kissed her hand. The love
between the two of them shot daggers through Simone's heart.

As bad as she wanted to watch, or needed to watch, she refused to
spend her day crying. She turned the television off, and searched her
room for something else. The answer sat on top of her dresser. She
grabbed her Kindle and headed to the bathroom where she would spend
her morning reading in a nice warm bath of bubbles.

After seeing the D-cup, tiny waist, big-booty dancers surrounding
Kevin, Simone avoided the reflection her own body cast in the mirror.
Not only had she gained weight but her stomach was dark and itched
liked crazy. Silently, she wondered if her body had turned Kevin off.
How she wished she could remember what had transpired before her car
accident or even the accident itself. She hounded everyone for informa-

tion, but they constantly danced around the question each time she inquired. The most she'd learned was that she'd totaled a rental car.

But where was I going? Why was I driving a rental? The more she tried to force her memory, the more intense the migraines became.

In need of a confidence boost, after soaking in the tub, Simone decided to throw on something extra cute. She found a pair of jean shorts in her drawer but couldn't fasten them.

When she fell back on the bed, the shorts fastened but when she stood, she couldn't breathe and the mushroom top that sat above the waist of the shorts was far from attractive. She peeled off the shorts, tossed them to the floor in disgust and headed into her walk-in closet where a long, flowing strapless maxi dress in beautiful shades of summer screamed 'wear me.'

"And you're new. You still have your tags."

She tried to remember when she'd bought the dress but it simply wasn't worth the pain. Snatching off the tag, she eased the dress on. She glanced in the mirror on the back of the closet door and loved the way the dress flowed. It hid her flab well.

"Now, I need some cute little sandals."

She tore through a few boxes, found a brand new pair of flats and slipped them on.

"I need a pedicure," she said as she studied the ensemble in the mirror. Despite the chipped polish on her toes, the outfit was the perfect confidence booster.

Blessed with what her family and friends constantly called 'good hair,' Simone lathered her hair with a little mousse and then teased it into a wild, sexy ponytail. A little make-up and accessories and she immediately felt like her old self.

"Now what?" she said aloud.

Dolled up with nowhere to go, she looked around her room. With the exception of the shorts she'd thrown on the floor, the room itself was clean, thanks to the helpful hands of Angela and Beatrice. But there was one thing that had always been completely off limits to everybody: her laundry. She didn't want her mother or anyone else washing her panties or getting a glimpse of some of the kinky things she wore for Kevin.

I need to wash these sheets anyway, she thought as she snatched the sheets stained with last night's action from the bed. Guilt tugged at her heart. Dropping the sheets to the floor, she plopped on the bed, staring at her cell phone. Without a second thought, she picked it up and dialed Kevin's number. No answer. She called again. Still no answer.

Why the hell do I feel guilty when you're out there doing God knows what. She sighed.

She contemplated watching the video again but dismissed the notion as her eyes welled.

I'm not going to cry. I'm not going to cry, she told herself. The cell back on her nightstand, she grabbed the sheets from the floor and placed them on top of her laundry hamper. Without a second thought, Simone carried the hamper to the laundry room right outside her bedroom.

Jordan's bedroom door opened. Rubbing her eyes, Jordan said, "Ooh, Ma, where you going? You look pretty."

"Thank you. I just felt like putting on clothes."

"You can leave those there. I'll wash them for you."

"It's okay, Jordan. I got it," Simone said as she tossed her linens into the washing machine.

"The doctor said you're supposed to take it easy."

"Washing clothes is easy."

Knowing how stubborn and determined her mother could be, Jordan retreated to the bathroom in defeat while Simone pulled more sheets from her laundry hamper.

What the hell? There was a huge pinkish stain in the center of one of the sheets she pulled from the hamper. A sharp pain shot through Simone's head causing her kneels to buckle.

The toilet flushed. Water splashed from the faucet. She had to get it together before Jordan came from the bathroom. Shoveling the sheets inside the machine, she yelled over top of the running water, "Hey, Jordan. Where's the vacuum?"

"I don't know," she hollered from the bathroom.

Closing the laundry room door, Simone peeked inside Kayla's room. The vacuum wasn't there, but Lord knows it needed to be. Kayla's room was a mess. Jordan's room was no better despite Angela's presence. No matter how bad Simone fussed, their rooms seldom improved.

Just as Simone turned the door knob to the bedroom next to Jordan's room, the bathroom door opened.

"NO!" Jordan screamed, scaring the daylights out of Simone.

"Got-damn it, Jordan! Have you lost your mind?" Simone clutched her chest. "You scared the mess out of me. Why is this door locked anyway?" she asked as she twist the knob.

"Because you can't go in there."

Simone shot her daughter a look that clearly said, *'You must have lost your mind.'*

"No, Ma. I'm serious," Jordan said. "You really can't go in there."

Irritated, Simone threw her hands on her hip. "Why, can't I, Jordan?"

Glancing down at her bare feet, Jordan's panicked expression turned somber. "You just can't," was all she could muster. "We're, umm, hiding a surprise for you."

"Where's your grandmother?"

"She went on Kayla's field trip."

"Oh yeah," she replied. Andre had mentioned the field trip last night.

"Ma, I'll find the vacuum, and I'll vacuum the whole house."

Simone looked at her daughter from the corner of her eye.

"I'm for real. I'll vacuum. Why don't you go do some real estate stuff or something?"

"Hmm," Simone said. An overwhelming amount of flowers, balloons, and cards had graced her hospital room, thanks to her clients and business associates. "I do need to write out some thank-you cards."

"Yeah, see. You can do that while I look for the vacuum."

"You mean while you look for the vacuum, and then vacuum the whole house, right?"

"Dag, I did just volunteer for that, huh?" Jordan said as Simone headed to her office. Following her mother down the steps, Jordan stood in the doorway of her mother's office.

"Ma, can I ask you something?"

"Yeah," Simone said as she planted herself in the chair.

"You not gonna get upset, are you?"

"Oh, it's one of those kinda questions?"

"No, I mean, I was just wondering. Andre's been here a lot the last two days. He didn't leave last night, and he didn't sleep on the couch."

Gingerly, Jordan entered her mother's office and eased into one of the two chairs in front of the desk. Her hands in her lap, she toyed with her fingers and asked, "You and my dad aren't breaking up, are you?"

Simone studied her daughter who sat timidly in the chair avoiding eye contact. For the first time, she noticed the dark circles underneath Jordan's eyes and realized how scary her comatose state must have been for her girls and everyone else. Everyone else but her husband.

Though Jordan had asked a grown up question, Simone knew she wasn't ready for a grown-up answer.

Before Simone could think of an answer, Jordan said, "Things aren't what they seem, Ma. No matter what you think. I mean, my—"

"Jordan," Simone interrupted, knowing her daughter was getting ready to defend her father's actions. "Andre and I are not getting back

together. I had a bad night last night so we were in my room talking."
With a shrug, she added, "He was keeping me company."

"So, you and my dad—?"

"Jordan, please. I don't want to discuss your dad and me right now. I
came down here to work on real estate like you suggested, right?"

"Okay," Jordan said as she removed herself from the chair. "I'll find
the vacuum."

"Thank you," Simone said. "And when you finish, let me know.
We'll go get our toes done."

Jordan smiled. "Okay."

Simone fished around inside her desk drawers for her note cards. But
instead of the cards, she stumbled across the sonogram of Kevin's baby.
With so much going on, she'd actually forgotten about his baby. Though
the baby wasn't made from an adulterous affair, it hurt nonetheless.

An ounce of her being wished she'd gone through with the act with
Andre just to get back at Kevin. But for some reason she didn't understand, part of her felt like something was wrong. How she wished she
could just remember.

I wonder if it's a boy or girl, she thought as she again attempted to
study the photo from each angles. The support papers only referenced
Yolanda's name. There was no mentioning of the child. Writing note
cards went out the window. Simone had a different plan.

"Hey, Jordan!" Simone screamed. The vacuum shut off.

"Yeah?"

"I'm running to the store. We'll get our pedicures when I come back."
Before Jordan could protest or ask to go with her, Simone was out the
door.

*****

The nurse instructed Simone to undress and slip on the examination
gown. However, Simone had no intentions of being examined. Though
Dr. Covington had been her OB/GYN for years, there was no way she
could bring herself to come right out and grill her about the sonogram
picture unless she had a legitimate reason to see her. So, she lied and
exaggerated some aggressive symptoms of a yeast infection that she
didn't have just so she could bring up the sonogram in hopes of learning
a few details.

Fully dressed, Simone sat on the examination table, swinging her legs
as she waited for Dr. Covington. Her cell phone buzzed inside her purse

for what had to have been the tenth time in less than an hour. She knew Jordan had probably summoned the National Guard because she'd left the house. But Simone ignored the vibration just as she had done the nine times prior.

Simone looked around the examination room and wondered if she was actually due for an exam.

When was the last time I had a pap smear? she thought to herself.

Out of the blue, an image shot through her head like a bolt of lightning. As plain as day, she could see a doctor, not Dr. Covington, but a doctor kneeling in front of Kevin as he sat in a rocker cradling a tiny infant, a newborn. Simone's head began to pound in agony just as someone tapped on the door.

"Knock, knock."

Dr. Covington's partner peeped her head inside the door. Simone barely knew Dr. Peterson and today, she welcomed their lack of association. Still there was something about her face that seemed so familiar.

"Hi, Miss Perkins." Dr. Peterson's voice was tentative as were the steps she took to enter the room. Smiling softly, she eased the door closed as if she were sneaking inside the room to see Simone.

"Kennard," Simone corrected.

"Oh, I knew that." She laughed, goofy-like. "They still have Perkins on your file. You know I'm Dr. Peterson. Dr. Covington had an emergency at the hospital, so I'm filling in for her for the rest of the afternoon."

Dr. Peterson's eyes fell to the photo clutched in Simone's hand.

"Oh, wow." Placing her hand to her mouth, she gasped, then rested her hand tenderly on Simone's knee. "Dr. Covington told me they wanted to keep it from you. I was wondering how long it would take before you found out. How are you holding up?"

Her question shocked Simone. *Damn, they know?* she screamed inside.

"Yeah," Simone hesitated, avoiding the doctor's eyes from embarrassment. "I found out. That's the real reason I'm here. I was wondering if you could give me some information about this?"

The doctor took the picture from Simone's hands and held it up to the light.

"The baby looks to be about six months in this sonogram. I'll be more than happy to confirm it for you." She offered Simone the picture and a comforting smile. She placed Simone's chart on the counter and flipped through the pages of Simone's file.

"Yes," she confirmed. "Six months."

Simone chuckled sarcastically. "And you know that by looking in my file?"

This chick is stupid, Simone thought to herself, irritated. *This is why I only like to see Dr. Covington.*

"Why of course," Dr. Peterson responded. "I mean, I know our turn-over rate with our clerical staff is high and there may be some confusion with appointments and things like that, but Dr. Covington and I keep accurate records."

"Excuse me?" Simone sneered. "Okay, I'm confused."

Dr. Peterson held out her hand for the sonogram and compared the information with Simone's file.

"Yes," she reiterated as she flipped through Simone's file. "According to your file, you had a total of three sonograms. This was your second and it was taken when you were about twenty-six weeks. Our entire office was devastated. You and your husband were so excited about the baby, then for someone to do something that awful. My LORD. I'm just glad you recovered."

A sharp pain shot through Simone's head as Kevin's image flashed. There he was again, holding a tiny infant. Clearly, she could see him easing from the rocking chair to sit along the edge of her hospital bed. She could almost feel his lips kissing her. She grabbed her head, squinting her eyes from the surreal pain.

"Are the police getting anywhere with your case?" Dr. Peterson asked as she turned to face Simone. "Oh, my God," she cried. "Mrs. Perkins, are you okay? Who's here with you?"

Shaking her head in confusion, Simone stood from the examination table. "Kennard. It's Kennard."

"I'm sorry, Mrs. Kennard. But are you okay?"

Another sharp pain shot through Simone's head, causing her knees to buckle. She could hear the doctor's voice in a memory as she stood before her, saying over and over again, "It's a boy."

"I didn't have a baby," Simone muttered. "I didn't have a baby."

Realizing something was wrong, Dr. Peterson grew concerned. "Is your husband with you?"

Tears fogged Simone's eyes as she held onto the examination table for support.

"Wait here. I'm going to see if I can reach Dr. Covington at the hospital or see if I can get your husband on the phone." Dr. Peterson rushed from the room.

The images flashed through Simone's head like a super-model's pho-to shoot. Fighting through the pain, she grabbed her purse and her file resting on the counter and eased from the room like any other patient.

Exhaling deeply, she wiped her eyes, stood tall, and prepared to walk through the lobby with a smile.

"Have a good day, Mrs. Perkins," one of the medical clerks said in error. Simone ignored the slip-up. Dr. Peterson was right. It seemed every time Simone came to the office, there was someone new sitting behind the desk.

"Has anyone seen Mrs. Kennard?" Dr. Peterson yelled frantically throughout the office.

"Wasn't that her who just left?" another receptionist asked as she pointed at the door.

Her co-worker responded, "No, that was Mrs. Perkins."

"Oh, goodness," the doctor said, pushing her way to the computer to access Simone's patient information. "Her last name is Kennard now. Her file should've been updated months ago."

"I don't think the last girl updated anything in the computer."

"We'll worry about that later. For now, get her husband on the phone. Tell him he needs to track down his wife. I'm going to page Dr. Covington," she said over her shoulder as she hurried to her office.

The receptionist snatched up the phone and dialed Simone's hus-band.

"Hello, is this mister Perkins? Andre Perkins?"

*****

Simone drove the forty-five minute ride home like a bat freed from hell, fighting the images that continued to flash through her mind like bolts of lightning. Flying down her street, her tires screeched as she swerved into the driveway and jumped from the truck. She rushed inside the house without bothering to close the front door, heading straight towards the kitchen.

"Ma, what's wrong?" Jordan asked, frightened by the crazed look on her mother's face. "Ma, what's wrong?"

Ignoring her daughter, Simone snatched the largest butcher knife from the block on the counter and sprinted upstairs to the forbidden room.

"Ma!" Jordan cried, too frightened to intervene. She grabbed the cordless phone from the kitchen to call her father while Simone tried feverishly to pry the door open.

Andre rushed through the opened door. "Where's your mother?"

"Oh my God, Andre," Jordan cried as she hung up the phone. "She's upstairs. She got a knife and—"

Before Jordan could finish her sentence, Andre was halfway up the steps.

"Simone!"

"Leave me the fuck alone, Andre," she cried.

Like a crazed manic, she raised the knife and attacked the door over and over again. Andre caught her wrist on her third stabbing attempt.

He soothed her with his voice. "Calm down, Simone. Calm down. I'll open the door for you."

Her face drenched with tears, Simone relaxed her grip on the knife and stepped aside.

Andre stared into her face and asked, "You sure you ready to…"

"OPEN THE FUCKIN' DOOR, ANDRE."

Releasing a deep sigh, Andre slid the knife along the latch and pried the door open. Jordan stood a few feet away, crying hysterically.

Simone took zombie-like footsteps inside the nursery. Slowly everything started to come back. The sporting teddy bear border, the white and navy blue pin-striped wall paper that matched the comforter set lying in the espresso-colored crib. On top of the chest of drawers sat a sterling silver 5-x-7 frame. Inside the frame was a picture of Simone and Kevin. There she was, good and pregnant, smiling ever so happily with Kevin at her side.

Dangling from the wall above the chest of drawers was a huge frame. This one contained a collage of photos. Pictures of Kevin kissing and rubbing her bare belly. There was even a picture of what appeared to be a home pregnancy test. Dead center was another sonogram photo.

"Where's my baby?" Simone cried as she took in the room and its contents.

Feeling helpless, Jordan ran to her room, unable to watch her mother's breakdown.

Softly, Simone cried, "Andre, what happened to my baby? Is my baby dead?"

"Here, sit down, Simone," Andre said. He placed his arms around her waist and guided her to the rocking chair.

"Where's my baby!" she screamed.

Andre grabbed her, smothering her in his embrace. "It's okay, Simone. It's okay."

"Where's my baby?" she cried.

Rubbing his hands up and down her back, he hushed her. "It's okay, Simone. It's okay. I'll tell you everything."

Chapter Thirty-Six

Hispanics dressed in green uniforms were scattered throughout the community. The funk of mulch mixed with the scent of freshly-cut grass hovered in the air as Kevin made his way down Felicia's street.

"Damn," he hissed as he whipped into a space marked for visitors. There was no sight of Felicia's truck.

Heading up the steps, Kevin muttered a dull hello to the landscape guy who smiled and nodded. He swung open Felicia's screen door and pounded on it. But, as he suspected, she wasn't home.

"Damn, I never wanted to use this thing." He fumbled through the keys on his ring. "I'll leave this shit right here."

He opened the door, stood in the foyer, and called her name a few more times before trotting up the steps to the living room. He searched around the couch and under the cushions, but there was no sign of his ring. He searched the pockets of the pants he'd left inside the dryer. Nothing.

"Shit."

He turned the tumbler inside the dryer with his hand. A loose piece of metal clanked around inside. "Damn, I hope that's not a penny," Kevin muttered as he looked inside the silver tumbler. The diamonds from his platinum wedding band stared back at him.

"Yes," Kevin rejoiced with a sigh. He slid the ring on his finger and gave it a quick peck from his lips. "I bet my cell phone is in her room."

After climbing four flights of steps, he stood in the doorway of Felicia's room. He kneeled on the mahogany wood and searched under the bed but only saw a few candy wrappers and an empty Pepsi can. Seated on the hardwood floor, Kevin leaned up against the bed, his legs to his chest. He could replace the phone but his ring had sentimental value.

The front door slammed. Prepared to yell out Felicia's name, he hesitated at the sound of the unknown female.

"Felicia," she called, her voice barely above a whisper as if she were sneaking. "Felicia." Her voice grew louder, closer, as she walked up the steps, mumbling something Kevin couldn't make out. He crawled from the side of Felicia's bed and listened by the door.

"You dumb, evil bitch. Bet you out chasing behind Kevin," she ranted as she ducked inside one of the bedrooms. Kevin crawled out into the hallway. "One minute you trying to fucking kill his wife, then the next you love him again. I'm glad he got married on you."

Kevin's mouth sprung open in shock. His body trembled as he gasped for air. What the fuck? His heart thumped an unsteady rhythm as he crawled from the room and crept down the steps. He leaned against the wall as he waited outside Mercedes' bedroom.

Why the fuck didn't I bring my gun?

"Yes! Yes!" the female rejoiced from the room and hurried from the room.

A fire burst inside of Kevin. He wrapped his hands around her neck. She fought back, swinging her arms wildly. Her ragged nails ripped into his face, cutting his flesh like knives. Still despite her clawing, she was no match for Kevin. Like a rag doll, he threw her body into the wall. She sprung back violently, but Kevin connected one fierce blow that knocked her out cold.

His chest heaved up and down as he wiped beads of sweat trickling down his cheek. Out of habit, he reached in his pocket for his cell phone, then quickly remembered he didn't have it. It was why he was at Felicia's in the first place. But what he pulled out was probably more valuable than his cell: Patrick's card. He peeked inside Mercedes' room for a phone and spotted the cordless on the dresser.

"Patrick. Listen," he panted. "It's Kevin and I got an emergency, man. I know who took my baby. I know who tried to kill my wife. I'm in the bitches' house!"

"What? Kevin where are you?"

"I'm at the bitches' house in Annapolis—"

"You're at her house! Kevin, hang up now and call the police."

"Patrick, I—"

"KEVIN!" Patrick screamed into the phone. "Hang up now and call the police!"

For the first time in Kevin's life, he dialed 9-1-1 as Sanora began to moan from the floor. A horn blew. Nervous, Kevin hung up the phone and peeped through the blinds. A cab was parked in the driveway, obviously waiting for Sanora.

"Shit," Kevin hissed. He ran down the steps and swung open the front door. He waved his hand and yelled, "Go 'head." Confused, the cab driver raised his hands and hunched his shoulders. "Go 'head," Kevin repeated.

The cabby lowered his window. "Someone has to come and get the baby. And Miss Jones owes me three hundred dollars."

"Baby…" Kevin said to himself. He raced out to the cab, opened the back door and there, strapped inside the car seat was a baby.

"Oh my God," he whispered. Happy tears began to flood his face. "Oh my God."

Engulfed in his son, Kevin never saw Sanora emerge from the house.

"Miss Jones! Miss Jones!" The cab driver sprung from the car. He grabbed Sanora by her shoulders, shocked by the mass of blood and tears that covered her face. Sanora tried to pry herself from the cabby's grasp. "Miss Jones, what happened to you? Do you need an ambulance?"

Kevin unfastened the straps to the car seat and grabbed his son. Sirens wailed off in the distance. For the first time in Kevin's life, he welcomed the sound of the police.

Chapter Thirty-Seven

T he doorbell chimed, indicating potential customers. Felicia sat on a stool, behind the front desk counter, searching through Kevin's phone, reading emails and text messages. She hit the jackpot by stumbling across a text he'd sent to Simone, asking her to check his email and print papers from a Don Brandon. In that text was the password to access his email account. Engulfed in his personal affairs, Felicia carelessly pressed the button and granted access to the patrons standing outside the door.

"Excuse me." The baritone voice demanded her attention.

She glanced up and frowned at the two suited gentlemen standing before her, pissed that she'd allowed them in. She recognized Detective Ward. He'd questioned her once a few weeks ago. She forced a smile.

"How you doing, Detective Ward and company?"

"How are you, Miss Payne. This is Detective Harvin, my partner." Chewing loudly on a piece of gum, Detective Harvin nodded hello while Detective Ward flipped through a pocket-sized tablet.

"How you doing?" Felicia said. "You gentlemen here for a massage?"

"No, no," Detective Ward replied while his partner looked around, which made Felicia uncomfortable. She caught his brief chuckle at the bowl of pineapples chunks. He stuck a toothpick inside one of the chunks to examine it.

"Hey Ward, you know they say pineapples make your nut taste good. Is that true, Miss Payne?" he asked as he dropped the pineapple back in the bowl.

"Guess that's something we'd have to ask your wife?" Her bold replied shocked both men who gawked at her through wide eyes. "I'm not trying to be funny, I'm just saying." A shrug accompanied her innocent smirk.

"Edward Michael Jones. Know him?" Detective Ward asked. Detective Harvin eased his hands inside the pockets of his trench and stared at Felicia.

"Fat Ed? Yeah, we grew up together."

"When was the last time you saw him?" Detective Harvin asked.

"I see him out in the clubs here and there. We don't spoke, though. We're not friends, for real. Just grew up in the same neighborhood and know some of the same people."

"Were you aware of his involvement with your dancer, Sanora Greenwald?"

"Men come and go with these dancers."

Detective Harvin asked, "Is that a 'yes' or a 'no'?"

"To their involvement, that would be a no," she replied rather defiantly.

Detective Harvin chewed his gum and smiled. In the game of good cop, bad cop, he was certifiably the asshole.

"What about the baby?" Detective Ward asked.

Felicia was taken aback. "What baby?"

"Michael Edward Jones Greenwald born on the 22nd of February."

Detective Harvin frowned. "So you mean to tell me, you didn't know your top dancer had a baby? Sounds like there may have been issues."

Felicia fiddled about nervously, wondering if the thump in her chest protruded through her skin in 3D. *Get it together, Felicia. Get it together.*

"Miss Greenwald's car," Detective Ward flipped through his tablet, "blue 2006 BMW two-door convertible—"

"I know the car."

"Okay, okay. Well, that car and Mr. Jones' car were found scorched on the very night Mr. Kennard's baby was kidnapped from the hospital. That's not to mention what happened to his wife. You remember that incident with your friend Mr. Kennard, don't you? We spoke about it briefly."

"Yes, yes."

"I had a chance to view the prison log, and you visited Mr. Kennard often while he was incarcerated. Were you guys involved in any way?"

"No, just friends."

"Interesting. None of his other friends visited as much as you." Tapping his pen against his tablet, he added, "It's funny. I noticed your visits stopped after his wife starting visiting." He waited for Felicia to respond but she didn't. "Miss Jones —"

"Look, you're asking me a lot of questions."

Detective Ward looked around the lobby of the spa. "Oh, I'm sorry. I don't see any customers. But if you like, we could do this from a comfy, cozy interrogation room down at the station."

"No, I'm just saying. It's an awful lot of questions."

"I'm sorry, Miss Payne, but I do have one more. Where were you the night of April 7th?"

"The same place I was when you asked me weeks ago. At Linwood's."

"And what's Linwood's last name?"

"I'm not sure. I know him as Linwood."

Before Detective Ward could piss Felicia off with another question, Detective Harvin blurted, "Let's roll. We just got a break-through."

Detective Harvin rushed from the spa while Detective Ward handed Felicia his card. "Do you have a card, Miss Payne? I didn't get one last time."

She wiped her sweaty palms along her pants and grabbed a card from the holder. Her hands trembled as she passed Detective Ward the card. "Are you okay?"

She forced a smile. "Yeah, I'm fine."

Felicia stood in the lobby watching until the detectives pulled off. She was shocked. The police department had stepped their game up. But there was only one person who could prove Felicia was involved.

"So it wasn't your nephew that the parking attendant was asking about, you lying-ass bitch. And I killed her got damn baby daddy. Hmm, mmm."

There was no way she could let Sanora live now.

*****

Nervous energy flowed through Felicia's veins as she drove to the condo, barely able to keep her eyes on the road for fear that the authorities were trailing her. Inside the building, she avoided the elevator and opted for the stairs. Every few steps, she stopped to listen for footsteps. Fighting to catch her breath as she stood on the landing of the sixth floor, she searched her purse for her key and proceeded down the hall, looking over her shoulder every few seconds.

The television in the living room was on but no one was there. Where the hell was Big L or Daryl, Sr.? Felicia pushed opened the door to the room where Sanora stayed. There was no sign of Sanora or the baby. The bathroom door was slightly ajar. She kicked it open. Still no sign of Sanora.

"This shit is not happening," she said.

Covers were tossed about the queen-sized bed. Bath towels were tossed around the room. Soda cans, snack wrappers, and pissy baby diapers overflowed in the trashcan. But there was no sign of Sanora or her things.

Frantic, Felicia searched her purse for the prepaid phone. She called Linwood. Before she could say anything, he said, "Meet me at the Exxon right across the street."

Like a bat out of hell, Felicia pulled into the gas station and jumped from her truck.

"Where the fuck is Sanora?" she demanded.

"She's gone," Linwood said as he and his two sons got out of a black Escalade. "I've been trying to call you."

"What you mean she gone?"

"I came to take my shift and found Big L out cold on the couch. Took forever to wake him up. I was scared as shit. I looked around the room, and her and the baby was gone," Daryl, Sr. said.

Felicia ran her hands through her weave. "This shit ain't happening," she muttered under her breath. She lunged at Big L, but Linwood and Daryl, Sr. grabbed her. "You stupid muthafucka! Why the fuck was you sleep?" she screamed.

Customers pumping gas began to glance their way.

"Pops, you better get that ugly bitch."

"This ugly bitch saved your pussy ass!" Felicia spat.

Big L's chest swelled. Daryl, Sr. released Felicia and grabbed his brother.

"You ain't got to hold me, man. I'm good," Big L told him.

"Look, calm down." Linwood, Sr. was always cool and collected. "Y'all in hot-ass Virginia. If you fart too loud, they call the police. That's why the last fuckin' tenant moved. The residents in that building complained too much."

"Not even that, though, Pops. The baby was sick. What was I supposed to do? Let him holla all night long?" he said with his eyes on Felicia.

"How'd she get away?" Felicia asked.

"She fuckin' drugged me and took my 745. I called On-Star. My car is parked at some grocery store in Richmond."

Felicia froze. "Richmond?"

"Yeah, that's what they said," Linwood replied. "We on our way out there now."

Felicia shoved her keys inside Daryl's hand. "You take my truck. I'm riding with them."

Chapter Thirty-Eight

Sniffles filled the examination room of the pediatrician's office as Kevin crept inside, searching for Simone who was nowhere in sight. Beatrice rushed to her son, wrapping her arm around his waist, while Angela sat in the glider, attempting to calm a fretful Lil' Kevin.

Through her tears, Beatrice chuckled. "The doctor said he looks good. He's going to be alright." She glanced up at her son, quickly doing a double-take as she noticed the claw marks. "Did you get someone to look at your face?"

He eased his arm around his mother, giving her a quick squeeze, before heading to the rocker.

"I'm alright, Ma. It's just scratches." He kneeled in front of Angela to peek at his son.

The rocker stopped. "Kevin, here." Angela prepared to stand. "Why don't you sit here and hold him? Maybe he wants his daddy."

Kevin smiled, then kissed his son gently on the top of his head. The words were music to his heart.

"No, Ma. You hold him for a minute. Now that I know he's safe, I need to find Simone. Is she okay?"

"This couldn't have happened at a better time," Angela shared.

"Yeah, we've been trying to call you," Beatrice added.

Worry lines were etched across Kevin's face. "I lost my phone. What happened? She okay?"

Angela sighed. "She found the sonogram picture. None of us knew this until today though."

Inside, Kevin rejoiced. "So she remembers having the baby?"

"No, wasn't that simple," Angela shared. "She thought it was your other baby."

"You got some child support papers in the mail from Yolanda?" Beatrice asked.

"Yeah. I went to court today and the child's not even mine. It was just a mix up." Kevin mumbled unpleasantries under his breath. "See, this is why we should have just told her the truth."

"No, that's why you should've let the police be the police," Beatrice corrected.

"And then where would he be?" Kevin gestured to his son. "Look, so she found the picture. Then what? Her memory came back? She remembered having him?"

"She took the picture to Dr. Covington who wasn't in. She ended up seeing her partner, the one who delivered the baby. The partner saw her with the sonogram and figured Simone knew. Everything slipped out," Beatrice shared.

"Needless to say, she had a fit. She came home and stabbed the door to the nursery up trying to get into it," Angela added. "Andre was in the room talking to her when Kayla and I got back from her field trip."

"Andre? Why was Andre there?"

"Somebody at the doctor's office called him by mistake. You didn't have your phone, so no one could reach you anyway," Beatrice added.

"I called her doctor. He was going to phone in some sedatives. I'd just hung up the phone with him when the police called telling us to meet you guys here," Angela said.

"It was a good idea to bring him here oppose to the hospital," Beatrice said.

"Yeah, they tried to fight me on it at first. I'm glad Patrick was there."

"Who's Patrick?"

"You'll meet him." Kevin headed to the door. He needed to find his wife. "So where is she now?"

"She went to the restroom."

Kevin followed the restroom signs down the hall. He tapped on the door.

"I'll be out in two seconds," Simone said.

The water ran inside. Kevin tapped again, two times with his knuckle.

"I'm coming. I'm coming."

The water shut off. The hand dryer blew. Kevin knocked again. He heard Simone sigh and the flopping of her flip-flops. The lock unlatched, and the knob turned. Kevin stood front and center in the doorway as it swung open. Simone gasped, but Kevin couldn't decipher the emotion. But when she attempted to stroll by him without a single word, he knew he wasn't welcomed. Getting rid of him wouldn't be easy.

"I need to talk to you, baby," he said as he forced her back into the bathroom, locking the door as it closed behind him.

Kevin studied Simone's face. Her eyes were swollen from crying and laced with so much pain. Yet there was no disputing her angry expression. Never had he seen her look so worn. He imagined he looked the same way. He reached for her hand but she pulled away.

"Simone, baby, I need you to listen to me. I know how things look but you have to believe and trust in your heart. You know I would never, ever do anything to hurt you."

She inched away from him until there was nowhere else to go. Her back against the wall, her eyes glossed with tears as she refused to acknowledge Kevin.

"They said we couldn't tell you anything, to let your memory come back on its own. I didn't want your memory to come back and our son not be there. So, I went out looking."

She glared at Kevin. "And you knew where to find him?"

"Baby, listen. There's so much that you don't know. I want to tell you so bad but I can't jeopardize your health. Those raunchy ass tramps in the strip club didn't mean anything to me. It was something I had to do to get information."

She frowned, disgusted with the poor excuse. "How much information did you get from their breasts? Then you had them raunchy ass tricks in our truck smoking weed, drinking liquor."

Reliving the incidents weren't worth the headache. Simone brushed Kevin off with a wave of her hand, attempting to walk away. Kevin grabbed her by the arm.

"And I'd do the shit all over again just to get our life back to normal. You were my focus, Simone. Everything I did, I did for you and the baby." He softened his tone. "You know I promised not to lie to you and at the same time, I didn't want to live in some bullshit world of make believe. I couldn't pretend like everything was cool, waiting for you to remember having our baby while he was out there in God knows where."

An awkward silenced lingered in the air.

Simone sighed and looked at her husband. "Look, I need to get away. I'm thinking about flying out to Melanie's. I'll leave tonight if I can catch a flight."

"Simone, no."

"Kevin, I just need some space, some time to think. The baby, my mom, and the girls are going with me. Your mom is thinking about flying out, too."

"Simone, we'll get through this. Don't run."

She eased from Kevin's grip and headed to the bathroom door. "I'm not running. I just need some space."

Deflated, Kevin watched her head to the bathroom door. The spark of love that once twinkled in her eyes had been replaced with something Kevin didn't want to acknowledge. He couldn't let this ordeal be the death of his marriage.

Everything's going to be okay. Just have faith. Yolanda's words echoed in his mind.

"I'll take you to the airport."

"You don't need to do that, Kevin."

"I'm not asking you."

*****

Like a thief in the night, Felicia crept up the seemingly mile long tree lined driveway that led to Sanora's mother's house close to one o'clock in the morning. Absent of a plan, she had no idea what to expect once she stepped inside the shabby-looking house. But two things she knew for sure, she was leaving with the baby and she was leaving with a car.

A cat jumped from the darkness of the trees. Startled, Felicia snatched the gun tucked in her sweatpants.

"I outta blow you into a million fucking fur balls," she growled underneath her breath. She threw a rock from the graveled driveway at the cat but missed as he sped off into the darkness. With a deep sigh, she tucked the gun back in her sweats and continued towards the house.

"Probably all kinds of fucking animals out here," she said as she continued up the driveway.

A hint of light shined from the house as Felicia snuck around to the back door. It was locked. *Funny,* Felicia thought. Sanora always harped on how safe the country was; how she grew up with the doors unlocked. No worries.

While Linwood and Big L checked the BMW for damages, she had gone inside the convenience store and purchased a few things. She eased on a pair of latex gloves and laced the hinges of the dilapidated wooden screen door with squirts of oil, a move she'd seen on *"Snapped."* Nice and lubricated, she pulled the door open, and reached in her pocket for Sanora's keys.

After testing key after key, Felicia finally found the right one. She pushed the door open, nice and slow, and tiptoed quietly through the little country kitchen that was in desperate need of updating. All was quiet. Slowly, Felicia lurked from the kitchen to the hallway, hugging the wall as she peeked inside two of the three bedrooms. Both were empty.

A television flickered from the gap in the slightly ajar bedroom door at the end of the hallway. Ginger steps toward the room, Felicia froze when the floorboard cracked. Braced against the wall, she waited for some form of life to stir, but everything remained still. Moving past the creak in the floor, she peeked inside the room. There was no motion in the bed. She doused the hinges with oil, then massaged it into the metal that peeled from an old, sloppy paint job. Slowly, she pushed open the door. From the looks of it, only one person laid in the queen-sized bed. Inside the room, she looked inside the bassinet positioned at the foot of the bed. Empty.

Shit, she thought. She inched toward the bed and there he was, resting peacefully on the chest of Sanora's mother. She couldn't pry him from her arms without disrupting her sleep. There was only one way she could take him. An extra pillow rested next to Sanora's mother on the empty side of the bed.

You can thank your daughter for this, Felicia thought. She grabbed the extra pillow and chuckled at the pistol resting underneath it.

"Damn, guess you were expecting me."

The pillow clutched tightly in her grasp, Felicia placed it over the face of Sanora's mother and smothered life from her.

*****

Felicia was beat. Even with a pill, there was no way she'd be able to keep her eyes open. She pulled into what had to have been the shabbiest motel she'd ever seen in her life. But, it wasn't like she could stroll inside the Ritz Carlton and expect to get a room. By now, she knew she was wanted; a fugitive from justice.

Parked between cars in the parking lot of the motel, Felicia waited for her chance, but little was happening in the wee hours. Finally, a room door opened. Three Hispanics, two females and a male, chatted back and forth loudly in Spanish. With the baby sleep in the front seat, Felicia got out of the car and approached the trio.

"Hey English. Y'all speak English?" She pointed her finger back and forth between the threesome. The two females grinned, nodding their head. "Yes, you do? You don't? What?"

"I speaka little English," the male replied brokeningly.

"Y'all checking out? You go home?"

He frowned.

"Look, I need help, please," she said with her hands clasps together in prayer. "I left my purse at home. No, purse. No room. I have baby."

Her lips curled upside down as she cradled her arms and pretended to rock a baby. She pointed at the key in the male's hand. "Can I have this room?"

He pulled back the ket. "No, de uh, front desk." He nodded and pointed in the direction of the motel's office.

"No. No front desk. No I.D. No driver's license." She reached in her back pocket and counted out three hundred dollars. "Here. I'll give you this for that."

The threesome smiled. Money was a universal language that every-one understood. The male handed her the key and stretched out his hand.

"Si, si."

Felicia laced his hand with the three hundred dollars. "Gracie or whatever the fuck y'all say," Felicia mumbled. "Did y'all fuck on both beds?" she asked as she dry humped the air.

With his inflated chest poked out, the male draped his arms across the shoulders of both women and grinned from ear to ear. Giggling bashfully, the two girls curled into his embrace.

"Si, si." He nodded.

"One bed or both?" Felicia asked again.

"Naw, just the one by the door," he answered in perfect English.

Shaking her head, Felicia headed to the car for the baby. *Ain't that some shit. This bitch muthafucka speaks English.*

Chapter Thirty-Nine

S imone's feet hadn't graced Georgian soil for twenty-four hours
before Melanie had her out and about. Melanie's husband Robert
eagerly welcomed the challenge of playing host to both Angela and
Beatrice. Jordan splashed about in the pool watching Kayla as she played
with Melanie's twin girls, Jade and Jada, while Melanie whisked Simone
away for a much needed day of pampering. Knowing that Lil' Kevin was
in the best of care with both grandmothers at Melanie's, Simone leaped at
the invitation. Three o'clock in the afternoon, Simone sat in the passenger
seat of Melanie's truck admiring her new European-styled bangs and
long, straightened tresses.

"I was scared for nothing."

"Scared?" Melanie said, heading home after being out for close to six
hours.

"Ah, yeah. I'm a city girl going to get her hair done in the country."

"There's nothing country about Atlanta."

"Yeah, I see that now. I love my hair," Simone said as she toyed with
her bangs. "And my nails and toes. Gosh, this is so what I needed."

"Yes, you did. Your heels were like cinder blocks."

Laughing, Simone tossed the Starbucks napkin wrapped around her
caramel frappuccino at Melanie as she turned into the entrance of her
community. Up the windy road they traveled, passing the estate homes
that were nestled on the massive plush green lawns.

"Man, I see why you moved. I could live down here in a heartbeat.
The air is fresher, the people are friendlier, and this dang community you
live in is off the freakin' chain. Straight up like an episode of *"Cribs.""*

"Without the *"Cribs"* price tag. You wouldn't believe what we paid."

"Oh yes, I would. It had to be in the upper eight hundreds at least."

Melanie laughed. "Are you crazy?"

Simone turned her attention to her friend. "I said at least."

"No, darling. Remember, this is the south. So, mix that with the
recession, and we barely paid half of that."

"Melanie, get out of here! I might have to toss a For Sale sign in my
yard."

"Simone, I'm serious and look." Melanie pointed out Simone's window. "That house up on the hill…"

"The stucco monster behind the iron gate?"

"Yeah, that's a rent with an option to buy. It's been on the market for a minute. We looked at it, but it's too much house for just the four of us."

"Man, that house is vicious."

"The little girl who used to live there was in Jada's class. She was an only child so she kinda stayed at our house a lot. Her father is an officer in the military. They transferred to Hawaii. Poor little girl cried for days."

Simone rolled down the window and stared. An iron fence with an electronic gate surrounded the estate. Pom-pom and spiral trees were scattered about the manicured lawn that had been edged to perfection. A custom-built, three-tiered fountain was positioned in the center of the yard. The lack of water flowing from the fountain was the only telltale sign that the house was empty.

"If they want to sell it, they should turn the fountain on. It'll add more 'wow' to the curb appeal."

"It was on up until a week ago. They were supposed to go to settlement so they had everything turned off. Now something's up with the buyer's loan. I feel sorry for them. This is the second contract to fall through. That's why they're willing to entertain a rent with the option to buy."

"And to think I actually thought me and Andre were doing something back in the day. Y'all out here living like the freakin' rich and famous without having to spend millions. How's the inside?"

The iron gates were open. Melanie drove her E500 through the gate and up the long, smooth asphalt driveway. She stopped in front of the four-car garage connected to the house by a breezeway.

"Why are you teasing me?" Simone said as she climbed from the car.

Melanie jiggled her keys. "No tease."

"You have the key?"

"Yep. Robert and I told them we'd keep an eye out on the place. We swing by here at least once a week."

The twosome walked up the cobblestone walkway to the huge frosted glass double doors. Melanie unlocked the locks and opened the door. She stepped aside and smiled at her childhood friend. Walking inside, the butterfly staircase with its wrought iron railing, the huge marble tiled foyer, and the gigantic chandelier all took Simone's breath away.

"I would put some kind of round table here with a crazy monster centerpiece, or a fountain. But, something would have to go here to warm this area up." Simone's voice echoed throughout the foyer.

"Hmm," Melanie said. "This real estate agent I know once said when people start placing their furniture inside the house, it means they want it."

"Oh my gosh, Melanie. I love it," Simone said.

As she proceeded to tour the rest of the house, one of the marble tiles in the foyer clapped against the subfloor. The tapping echoed throughout the foyer. "They would fix that, of course," Melanie told her.

"I'm sure. I'm almost scared to ask how…" Simone stopped mid-sentence when she reached the kitchen. "Oh my gosh." She gasped. "The price doesn't even matter."

Chapter Forty

Propped up on three pillows, Sanora laid on the top sheet-less bunk with an ice pack to her broken nose. From her two blackened eyes, she stared at the plumbing pipes. Hanging herself would've been easy if she had a sheet to rip apart and make a noose. Her head throbbed from the hysterical sobs and the pain from her injuries. She hadn't thought of killing herself initially, but as the realization of the circumstance weighed in, what was there to live for?

Guilt hovered over her like a dark thunderous cloud, ready to strike her with an electric bolt as she worried about her mother. Baby Michael Edward was safe. Safe in the arms of Kevin and Simone. She knew they would love him as if he were their own. Heck, as far as they knew, he was their precious baby boy. The baby snatched away from them barely an hour after his birth. But by now, they should have known the truth. Their biological son should be with them, and Sanora's mom and her baby should be in protective custody. She hoped and prayed that her mother had followed her specific instructions which were to call the authorities and spill her guts if she didn't hear from Sanora within twenty-four hours. But more than twenty-four hours had passed and with each tick from the clock, Sanora worried more. She needed help. She needed Patrick Collins.

Despite the seriousness of the matter, the white guy who showed up at the scene seemed nice and highly intelligent. He almost seemed to care as he inquired about where Sanora was being taken and her arresting charges.

"Make sure she goes to the hospital first," he'd instructed.

She'd found his number in the Yellow Pages and had left three messages. Still, she heard nothing. Her lock turned. The door swung open. The guard tossed an envelope on her floor and closed the door, locking it behind her.

Sanora sat up and glared at the blank envelope resting on the dingy floor, absent of a return address. She climbed from the top bunk and picked up the lightweight envelope. Inside, there was a note: *Your attorney will be here in the morning.*

Chapter Forty-One

For the first time in weeks, Kevin felt optimistic. The production deal Don and his label offered exceeded his expectations. Financial worries would never be an issue for him and his family as long as he continued to write the way he'd been doing.

While detained behind bars, Kevin's fantasies for love and happiness fueled his lyrical flow. He wanted a wife, one who understood him and his dreams. One who would reciprocate the love he showered. Someone beautiful, witty, and intelligent, with goals of her own that stretched beyond the horizons. Someone fun-loving and gentle, with the ability to break it down when the situation presented itself. A classy, yet sexy lady in the streets, and a freak in the bed. He'd found each of those things and then some in Simone.

Kevin's emotions ran amuck. His heart and soul longed for her. With such a handsome production deal, he would release the other creations in his catalog that he'd refused to sell when he first came home. Jordan had taken her pick of the crop and now that the dollar amount was right, he'd release the rest of his arsenal and pen the songs burning inside of him as soon as time permitted. Now that Lil' Kevin was back, healthy and unharmed, he had to reunite the rest of his family.

He called Simone a few times, but her vague responses and the deafening gaps of silence told him that getting back together wasn't going to be that easy. But this time, he refused to run from the problem the way he'd done when they were teens. He had become one with the woman of his dreams and terminating their union wasn't an option. But how could he make it like it was? Where was Simone's mind? He needed to have a heart-to-heart with his wife. He dialed Melanie's number.

"Hey, Kevin. She's upstairs taking a nap with the baby. I think she and I had too much pampering. You should see your wife."

"I would love to. Right now, she's so pissed, though. I don't know what to do."

"Kevin, Simone loves you just as much as you love her."

"I don't know. I'm not feeling that."

"Trust me, Kevin. She's just as lost and confused as you are. You need to snatch her by her hair and bring her home. You rescued her heart before. Now do it again. If you love her—"

"That's an understatement, Melanie."

"Then take control. Show her that a separation isn't an option. Put your family back together. I love you guys together, so I'll help you if you want. I even have an idea. I'm going to send you an email."

An hour later, Kevin got off the phone with Melanie with an excitement he hadn't felt since his release from prison. Everything was going to work out, just like Yolanda had prophesized. He could feel it. His cell vibrated in the cup holder.

"What's up, Patrick?"

"Kevin, hey, listen. I got a message from the prison."

"What? I know she's not trying to press charges."

"You did break her nose."

"Then she got off lucky because I meant to break her muthafuckin' neck. Is this what you're calling me about?"

"No, no, not at all. Listen, call me nosey, but being nosey is what makes me good at my job. Just for shits and giggles, I plugged your parole officer's name into our system."

"McPherson?"

"Yeah, McPherson. And ironic as it is, he has a child support hearing coming up, too."

"Okay, and?"

"The mother of the child is an eighteen-year-old African American girl."

"What?"

"Yeah, I was able to reach the girl's mother who was livid."

"Damn, you work fast."

"That's why I'm the best at what I do, Kevin. She wanted to press charges against him, but her daughter wouldn't cooperate. Turns out McPherson is her best friend's parole officer. She had sex with him to keep him from violating her friend."

"What?"

"That's not all, Kevin. Turns out, McPherson was part of an assault about a year ago. Young girl's mother beat the crap out of him. Are you ready for this? The girl's mother is Felicia Payne."

"Patrick, you are bullshitting me!"

"Oh, ho ho. It gets better my friend. I went and met with McPherson. I told him I could help him —"

"Help him?"

"Hear me out, Kevin. I told him I could help him if he cooperated. Told him everything I found out. None of the young girls have pressed charges. So technically on paper, he hasn't committed any crimes. It took some convincing but he finally agreed. Turns out he was being black-mailed by someone in the FBI."

"Blackmailed?"

"Yes, when Miss Payne didn't get the justice she felt she deserved, she sought help from an FBI agent."

"Don't even tell me, Patrick. Don't even fucking tell me."

"Yep. She went to Andre Perkins."

"This is unbelievable," Kevin mumbled.

"Turns out, Agent Perkins was going to see to it that the girls filed charges. The only way McPherson could avoid jail was to —"

"Violate me."

"You got it."

"Damn, so now what?"

"Well, he's being brought in today for questioning. I'll keep you posted."

"Hey, Patrick. Look, is there any way I can flood your plate with one more thing?"

"What you got?"

"McPherson violated this young guy who goes by the nickname DJ or Smooth. He violated him because he overheard him on the phone talking about me."

"He's in custody now?"

"Yep."

"I'm on it."

Chapter Forty-Two

F elicia heard the crying in her sleep. As much as she tried to ignore it, it just wouldn't go away.

"Why the fuck do people want babies?" she screamed. She grabbed a pillow from the double bed and put it over her head. But the annoying, high-pitched whine would not go away.

"Fuck!"

She threw the pillow across the room. "Look, got damn it. You gotta shut the hell up before the police come."

She combed through the things she tossed in a bag. "Okay, look. I'ma change your lil' ass and feed you a bottle, but that's it. Please go to sleep. Otherwise, I'ma leave you right here in this room."

Lil' Kevin lay in the middle of the other double bed, kicking and screaming. Standing over top of him, ready to change his diaper, Felicia got a whiff.

"See, this bullshit right here 'bout to be for the fucking birds. Your ass gon' have to itch 'cause I don't have nothing to wipe your butt with."

Every few hours, Lil' Kevin woke. Felicia couldn't take it anymore. Daylight had peaked over the horizon. It was time to go. She folded the blanket over Lil' Kevin and headed out to the car.

*****

Lil' Kevin laid in the front passenger seat with the seatbelt jimmied around him, squirming as Felicia drove in circles, heading north, then an hour later taking an exit to head south. From Kevin to Sanora, everyone that had ever meant something to her had now betrayed her. But for now, she couldn't let the revenge she sought cloud the business at hand: her getaway. She had to find a place to take Lil' Kevin but where?

With her driver's side window halfway down, Felicia popped in the cigarette lighter and grabbed a Newport from the box resting in the cup holder. She brought the cigarette to life and blew the cloud of smoke out the window.

"Why the hell y'all doing road construction in the middle of the got damn day?" she said.

Orange construction signs decorated the shoulder of the interstate as four lanes of traffic were converged into the far two right lanes. As the cars before her had done, Felicia allowed the car to the right of her to take its turn and merge in front of her. But with that car, came a tatted up redhead white man in a red pick-up truck.

"What the fuck is this fool doing?" she said as he attempted to bow-guard his way in front of her. She stepped on the gas and blew the horn but he appeared just as aggressive and determined. She smacked the horn. "We'll play demolition derby out this bitch," she said as stepped on the gas, ready to smash the Ford Taurus into his pick-up if that's what it took.

"Yea, that's what I thought," she said as he retreated to his lane to wait his turn like everyone else had done. She watched as he rolled down the passenger window.

"You stupid black bitch!" he yelled.

Felicia took another drag from her cigarette and chuckled.

Yeah, Opie. You lucky I can't reach my purse. I'd show your ass a stupid black bitch.

From her rear view mirror, she watched as the car behind her granted the pick-up access to the lane. For every inch that the traffic moved, the pick-up revved up extra close to ride Felicia's bumper. Tempted to slam on brakes simply for the hell of it, she decided against it since Lil' Kevin was in the front passenger's seat without the proper restraints. Instead, she decided not to inch up with the traffic. With the work crews to the left of her and traffic nice and thick to the right there was no way he could get around. She glared at him in the rearview mirror as he blew the horn and mouthed a smorgasbord of obscenities. More horns began to blow as a slew of cars from the right took advantage of Felicia's little game and darted in front of her.

Let me stop playing with this cracker 'fore we mess around and have an accident for real. Last thing I need is the fucking police.

From the passenger's seat, Lil' Kevin's tiny fists began to swing in the air.

"C'mon now. Please don't start that noise," Felicia said as she proceeded with the traffic. She fished around on the passenger's seat for his pacifier and stuck it in his mouth, watching without a care as he went to town sucking away.

"I ain't got time to be pulling over to feed no damn baby. Shit," she hissed. "I need another fuckin' pill." She patted her pockets but they were empty.

She had a bottle of water in the cup holder. All she needed was the stash from her purse.

"Shit," she hissed. She tried to pull her purse from the floor of the backseat but it was stuck on something.

Traffic finally opened up.

"It's about fuckin' time."

She took one final drag from her cigarette and flicked the butt from the half-opened window, but a sudden thump and liquid splashed over the windshield startled her.

"What the fuck!"

Through her opened window, a few droplets landed on her wrist. She looked up just in time to catch the red pick-up zooming pass her on the left. Then, the smell hit her. She brought her hand to her nose.

"THIS BITCH MUTHAFUCKA THREW PISS ON ME!"

Felicia floored the gas. Like a NASCAR driver, she darted in and out of the traffic in pursuit of the red pick-up truck. Weaving in and out of traffic, the pick-up was barely two cars away from her. Unable to free her purse, she fished around inside of it for her gun.

Construction signs warned of yet another change in traffic.

"Yeah, you bitch muthafucka," Felicia yelled. Placing the gun in her lap, she accidentally knocked the bottled water to the floor.

The pick-up truck was right in front of her. Stepping on the gas, he zoomed to the next lane leading Felicia straight in to the construction. She yanked the wheel and tried to step on the brakes but the water bottle blocked the pedal.

"OH SHIT!"

*****

Thomas grinned proudly as he sat at one of the outside café tables admiring his grandson. He placed his finger in Lil' Kevin's hand and chuckled as he gripped it tightly.

"You got a strong little grip, you know that?"

Lil' Kevin cackled as if he understood.

"Now you listen to me. Your momma? Well, that's my baby girl and I'm relying on you and your daddy to take care of her for me, you hear me?" Lil' Kevin cooed.

Thomas released a light-hearted chuckle as he rose from the chair and headed inside the café. Through the television, Thomas watched the chaotic scene unfold. A helicopter was attempting to land on the highway as paramedics worked feverishly to revive the little infant.

"Look at them working on you," Thomas said. "You see that? Tell 'em you just wanted to come and see your old granddad."

Debris flew about as the helicopter landed on the highway. The pilots leaped from the aircraft, grabbed the gurney and ran toward the paramedics in the woods.

"NO PULSE!" a fireman yelled.

The paramedics from the helicopter kneeled before the baby's lifeless body and began the mask ventilation and cardiac massage. Thomas starred into Lil' Kevin's hazel eyes as he cradled him in his arms.

"Now you listen. You and your momma cost me a few favors. So don't you disappoint me, you hear me?" Lil' Kevin's toothless grin tickled Thomas. "I've peeked at your future. Yes, I have. You gon' be something, you know that?" Lil' Kevin cooed as if he were trying to talk back. "I know. You get it from your granddad." Thomas chuckled heartedly.

"Now you have to get going. I've had you a little too long. They gon' call you the miracle baby." Thomas kissed Lil' Kevin on his forehead. "I'll come play with you in your dreams, okay. I love you, grandson."

Thomas swung Lil' Kevin playfully through the television screen.

"WE HAVE A PULSE!"

Chapter Forty-Three

Full from the steaks and salad Robert prepared, Melanie and Simone sat on the deck, overlooking the pool and the lavish lawn surrounded by nature's finest. Dessert was bad news. The owners of the house had phoned, and apparently, the buyer's loan had been approved after all.

Lil' Kevin rested peacefully across Simone's lap. His chest heaved up and down in a rhythmic motion signifying his deep sleep. Though she knew he should have been resting someplace other than her lap, Simone couldn't help her yearning to keep him close.

"Melanie, you have it so good," she said as she rubbed the baby's back.

"I have it good?" Melanie chuckled sarcastically. "My husband and I are happy but what you and Kevin have is unreal. You two have a fairytale."

"Yeah, for six months it was."

"Was?" Melanie stared at her friend. "Please, it still is. You love him and he loves you. I don't know why you're out here hiding instead of making amends. Don't get me wrong, I love the company but when are you going to face your husband?"

"Actually," Simone said, "I was kind of prepared for you to tell me that the house was gone so I emailed another agent before I took my nap. She's taking me out to look at properties this weekend."

"Wow, so you're really set on moving, huh?"

"Done deal. Just have to figure out what to do with my house and the company. I have a ton of equity even in this funky market. So, I could sell it and the business and live off that income for now."

"What about your husband?"

"What about him?" Simone answered with a slight edge in her voice.

"Come on now, Simone. Are you honestly ready to throw in the towel? If Kevin wanted to run the streets, he would've run the streets when he came home. He loves you and this whole ordeal has been hard on everyone."

"How?"

Melanie sighed. "It'll come back to you, Simone. Just promise me that you won't make any hasty decisions."

"I won't."

"You've only been here three days and already you want to move. That's a bit hasty, don't you think?"

"Something about Georgia feels right. Feels like home."

"Well, other than moving, promise me that you won't make any other decisions. When your memory comes back, you just might kick yourself in the butt."

*****

Simone's heart raced as she lay in bed, naked and unable to move amidst the still darkness. Brainstorms, *"This Must Be Heaven,"* played in the background. The smell of floral-scented Carpet Fresh mixed with food — string beans, meatballs and fried chicken — all lingered in the air. She tried to move.

"Where you going?" Kevin asked through a yawn from the other side of the bed.

Simone's body began to shiver. Her body erupted in pain.

"Knock, knock, knock," a nurse chanted. The lights came on, illuminating the room. Simone's eyes squinted as they adjusted to the sudden brightness. She studied the female standing before her. Her face seemed so familiar.

The room took shape beyond its initial blur. Streamers draped the kitchen and family room, pastel-colored balloons were scattered about the floor and dangled from the ceiling. It was a baby shower. Her bed was in the middle of a baby shower?

The nurse yanked Simone's arm. She tried to pull it back but relaxed when the nurse apologized.

"I'm sorry. I'm sorry," the nurse said as she tied the rubber tube around Simone's arm. "I'm just trying to hurry up. I've been here all day." She pulled a syringe from her pocket, pushed the air from the needle, and injected Simone with the contents. She snatched the band from Simone's arm. "Bitch, fuck you."

The squeaky sound of wheels woke Simone. Panting, she sprung up in bed, thankful that the television was on as images from her dream flashed. Laughter echoed from outside her bedroom door. There were the squeaky wheels again.

"Don't wake your mother up," she heard Angela say to Kayla.

"We're trying to get this rollaway bed in our room," one of Melanie's twins giggled.

"Kayla, just use the air mattress."

"It has a hole in it."

Simone rubbed her hand down her face. As she closed her eyes, an image from her dream flashed like lightning. She gasped. Clear as day, she saw the face of the nurse who'd taken her baby and tried to kill her.

"That's what happened to me," she cried. "Oh my God, I remember. I remember."

Tossing back the covers, she scanned the room for her purse. She couldn't find it. But there on the dresser was Melanie's house phone. She picked it up and dialed Andre's number, pissed that he didn't answer.

"Andre!" she cried into the voicemail. "I remember. I remember what happened to me. I can see the nurse. I can see her face. I'm coming home first thing in the morning. I need to meet with you. Please call me back as soon as possible."

Hanging up the phone, she ran out into the hallway. "I remember! I remember!"

Chapter Forty-Four

A steady rain fell from the gray skies, greeting Simone as she arrived back in town. Immediately, she regretted the flip-flops and jean shorts she'd worn as travel clothes. It was eighty-three degrees in Atlanta but the place she'd referred to as home greeted her with gloom, which mirrored the way she felt about the place.

Strolling through the airport, she watched her fellow passengers rush off to baggage claim. There were no bags for Simone to pick up but her trip back to Atlanta would require more than suitcases. The bittersweet decision to move had been made. Hopefully, by the weekend, she'd have a place in Atlanta. A place to call home.

Dag, I have to find long distance movers, too, she thought.

With one hand on her shoulder strap and the other clutching her giant hobo purse, Simone walked through the busy airport ducking and dodging the latecomers who hurried to their gate, bumping into folks without a pardon. The atmosphere brought back memories of her trip to St. Lucia. Leaving for the wedding, some careless fool bumped Simone so hard that her purse and everything inside crashed to the floor. Luckily, Fat Ed had been there to prevent Kevin from catching another charge.

"Man, what you tryna do? You wanna go back to the joint or you wanna go to the islands and get married?" Fat Ed asked.

Kevin bit down on his bottom lip and shook off the rage. He bent down to help Simone pick up the contents of her purse.

"It's okay, baby. It shouldn't have been open," Simone had told him with a smile.

"I'm sorry. I'm just a little overprotective of you. I'll never let a mu-thafucka hurt you."

Kevin, Kevin, Kevin, she sighed as she recalled the incident. Her memory was back, which only made the circumstance more painful. How could he have loved her the way he had and left her when she needed him the most?

To keep back the flood of emotions thoughts of Kevin brought, Simone placed the earphones to her iPod back in her ear.

Surfing through the songs, Simone found her boo-boo. Her all-time favorite entertainer. She turned the volume up to a deafening level and allowed Michael Jackson's "Blood is on the Dance Floor" remixed with Herman Kelly's "Dance to the Drummer's Beat" to take her somewhere else. Seconds into the extended intro, Simone was in her own world, free of life's turmoil. Snapping her fingers and bobbing through the airport, she headed to meet Andre. She cleared her throat, ready to sing despite the uninvited audience around her until the sign in the limo driver's hand caught her attention: *'Simone Woodard Perkins Kennard.'*

She pulled the earphones from her ear and slowed her pace as she watched the driver in his black hat and single breasted black suit survey the crowd as if he knew who he was looking for.

A car, Andre? Really?

Andre had never returned her call, which was odd considering the seriousness. If she had to catch a cab to head home and wait for him, she would. But, the limo driver clutching the dry erase board confirmed that he did in fact receive her message.

"Hey, how you doing?" She greeted the driver and pointed to his sign. "Umm, I'm all of those people. Then again..." She cocked her head to the side, took her finger and rubbed away *'Perkins-Kennard.'*

"There." She pointed. "I'm her."

The driver looked Simone up and down. He smiled and handed her a card. "Maybe Queen would make you happy?"

Simone read the name on the business card. "Reginald Queen. Cute. Y'all men have too much drama. I may need a different kind of queen. Maybe like Queen Latifah."

The driver stood dumbfounded. "Don't worry about it. Where's the car?" she asked while heading towards the exit.

The driver pivoted on his heels and scooted after Simone as she walked through the automatic doors out into the chilly rain. He popped open an umbrella.

"No bags?"

"No bags," Simone replied as he opened the door for her to climb inside.

Before the door was closed, Simone raised the petition that separated her from the driver. Alone, she relaxed into the seats and welcomed the solitude. Sending the car wasn't such a bad thing after all.

A few days ago, Simone called Andre and shared her decision to relocate. Despite their incident, he was still Kayla's dad and would need to know eventually. But calling him had proven to be a big mistake. He had apologized repeatedly for taking advantage of her, blaming it all on love. In addition, instead of understanding why Simone wanted to move, he pleaded for her to stay and give their relationship another try. But reconciliation with Andre was the furthest thing from her mind. She dreaded the night she allowed him to comfort her. She never intended for things to escalate. Kevin's shenanigans had made her vulnerable. She did her best to fight Andre off but he wouldn't budge and she was no match for his strength. In the back of her mind, she wondered if it was rape. It was a question that would linger unanswered forever. Never would she mention the incident to anyone. It was something she'd take to her grave.

When the limo pulled in front of her house, a part of Simone actually felt sad. This had been her home. Her place of refuge from heartache, twice. Now, as she sat glaring at the red brick Colonial, she began to question if she was being too hasty. Her dream house in Georgia was no longer available, which meant she was giving up her home for the unknown.

No, you're giving it up for a fresh start, she told herself. *And this ain't home anymore.*

The driver stood with the car door open. "Um, Miss Woodard?"

"Oh, I'm so sorry. I'm sitting here daydreaming."

The rain had paused but the gray skies above promised that more was on the way. With her soaking wet flip-flops in hand, Simone eased from the back seat and stepped barefoot onto the damp asphalt.

"Let me give you a tip or something."

"No, no." Leaning on the open door, the driver smiled as his eyes gave Simone a final once over. "Mr. Kennard took care of everything."

"You mean Mr…. Never mind." She turned to head up the walkway, stepping over the fresh puddles. "Thanks!" she yelled over her shoulder.

The second she opened the door, she knew something wasn't right. There was an eerie silence, a haunting stillness. Slowly, she stepped across the threshold.

"Why is it so dark?" Her voiced echoed through the foyer.

She usually left a light on whenever she traveled. She flipped the light switch and when the light came on, she gasped in horror. Her house was empty.

"What the fuck?"

She rushed to check the rest of her house. The foyer, the living room, dining room, and even her office were bare: Stripped of even the pictures and decorations that once hung from the wall. The only things left behind were the impressions in the carpet from where furniture used to be.

The wood steps creaked. Her chest tightened. She'd been robbed and the burglar was still inside. She stuck a trembling hand inside her purse for her phone, quietly making her way to the garage.

"It's me, baby."

Kevin strolled into the kitchen. Simone was pissed, unable to control her trembling hands. "Kevin, you scared the fuck out of me."

"I'm sorry, baby." His voice was calm, almost tranquil.

"What are you doing here? How'd you get in?"

"You added me to the deed, remember? So, I called a locksmith."

"You called a locksmith and took my things?"

"I took our things, Simone."

She scanned her empty kitchen and family room, then brought her hand to her forehead. "Oh my goodness, Kevin? I sent you your things."

"You only sent me half of my things."

"So you did this? You took my stuff?"

She snatched open the cabinets. All empty. She turned to face him.

"Georgia works for you, baby. You're absolutely breathtaking."

"Kevin," she said as her temper began to boil. "Please undo your little magic trick and make my stuff reappear." He approached her and tucked a fallen strand of hair behind her ear. She tensed at his touch, but he ignored it. "Don't worry. I haven't stolen anything. You'll see the stuff again." He glanced down at his watch. "May take a while but you'll see it again."

Disgusted, she avoided his eyes. "It's going to the new house."

She looked up at him. "What?"

He inched a little closer, fighting the urge to take her in his embrace. Instead, he ran a finger along her hand, happy that she didn't tense up again or pull away. "The one you liked in Georgia."

She chuckled. "So you were the buyer?"

"No. For now we are the tenants. I couldn't buy it that fast and I wouldn't buy it without you. Well, no, let me rephrase that. I could have bought it, but I didn't want to invest in something like that without my partner."

"Who, Ed?" she asked sarcastically. Kevin's body stiffened at the mention of Fat Ed's name.

"No, you, Simone."

"Me?" She jabbed herself in the chest with her finger and searched around the room. "Me? Oh, I'm your partner...hmm." She nodded as the words lingered in the air. "Well, sweetheart, let me share some business ethics with you. It's bad business to lie to your partner, to hide money from your partner, and to cheat on your fuckin' partner."

She stormed to the refrigerator, hoping there was something cold to drink but the groceries were gone as well.

"The cleaning crew is coming to clean the place in a day or so."

Closing the refrigerator, Simone held onto the handles. "So now what? You walk in here, hit me over the head with a club, and drag me back to your cave after everything?"

"If that's the way you want to look at it."

"So just like that, huh?" She stared at her husband. "We're just suppose to pick up where we left off and pretend like none of this happened?"

"No, we need to talk first. Then we're supposed to stand strong, pray, and get through this together."

"Kevin, our baby—"

"I got our baby back. And now I've come for you." He watched her eyes gloss with tears as she bit down on her lip.

"I can still see your hands all over the stripper. I had just come out of a coma, our baby had been kidnapped and you were at a strip club."

Kevin reached for her, but she knocked his hands away just as the doorbell rang. Happy for the distraction, she moved past him, heading towards the door, wiping away the tears as they began to fall. She snatched open the front door.

"Yes," she greeted the visitor coldly through the screen door. "And before you start, no thanks. I read my bible."

The suited white gentleman chuckled. "No, no. I'm not a Jehovah's Witness," he corrected quickly as Simone prepared to close the door. "You have to be the beautiful, Simone."

Simone frowned. "What can I help you with, sir?"

The elderly white gentleman took two steps back to look at the numbers on the house.

"Hmm, this seems to be the right address." He clapped his hands together. "I'm Ben Flounder. Can I get you to step outside for a second, please?"

Simone was taken back. "Step outside for what?"

Kevin appeared in the doorway, a few feet from Simone. Ben spotted him. "Kevin!" He looked past Simone and greeted Kevin in glee.

"Hey, Ben, how you doing?"

"What's going on? Never mind." Simone threw her hands in the air and prepared to turn away. But Kevin placed his hand in the small of her back. "What?" she snapped.

"Ben's here to see you."

"I don't know, Ben, Kevin," Simone replied.

Ben raised a brow. "Ah, Kevin, you think you can help me get your wife out here?"

"Simone, can you go outside please? Just for a second."

"Why? Does Ben have my things? Ben, do you have my things?" she asked as she opened up the screen door and stepped on the front stoop. Kevin followed behind her.

Ben trotted down the few steps and walked out into the yard. With a wave of his hand, he announced with uncertainty, "Congratulations?"

"Congratulations?"

"Walk down the steps, Simone. Go look in the driveway."

Slowly, Simone walked down the steps and out into the grass. Parked in her driveway, equipped with a baby blue bow, was the Mercedes.

"It's your baby shower gift," Kevin whispered from behind her.

"Mrs. Kennard, I've been holding this car for a while now. Since the day of your shower. We were supposed to deliver it the very next day but, hey...." he offered with a caring smile.

"Simone, I don't know if you remember, but I missed the shower."

"I remember," she mumbled solemnly. "I was in the tub when you came in. It's the day I went into labor."

"Yesss!" Kevin was elated. "You remember that day?" She nodded her head.

"I'd been plotting for a while. I wanted to get you something special. Something just for you. I got an advance from Don and tucked it in Fat Ed's account to surprise you."

"We took extra special care of it, too, Mrs. Kennard. I had the guys drive it around a few times a week and I had it detailed again bright and early this morning. There's a full tank of gas in it, too. Here." Ben held the keys out to Simone. She stared at them for a while before reaching for them.

"Oh, and Kevin, don't forget about those items in the trunk." Ben winked.

"Thanks, Ben." Kevin reached out and shook Ben's hand.

"Hey, not a problem. Mrs. Kennard, Kevin shared your family's tragedy. I submitted a prayer request through my church and had the entire congregation pray for you and your family."

"Wow, thanks, Ben," Kevin said as Simone stood, absent of words.

"Kevin, please, it was the least I could do. You're a good guy. And on that note," he smiled, "I'll leave you guys alone. Enjoy that car, Mrs. Kennard."

"Thanks, Ben," Simone said. "Hey, and I'm sorry I was so rude. I feel so embarrassed." Kevin placed his arm around her waist.

"You owe me no explanations."

"Yes, I do. First impressions are everything."

"Simone, the way your husband ranted and raved over you, the first impression was planted long ago. No worries," he replied with another wink. "Enjoy that car."

Ben waved bye and headed down the walkway to an awaiting Mercedes S550. The horn tooted and Ben waved goodbye again as the car headed up the street.

"Come on. Check it out." Cheesing hard, Kevin guided her to the car. He opened the driver's side door. "Get in. Check it out."

Simone followed his instructions and sat halfway inside the driver's seat, melting into the cream leather seats.

"Hey, pop the truck."

"Kevin, look. The car is beautiful, but I— ."

"Simone, just pop the truck."

With a sigh, Simone opened the trunk as Kevin walked around to the back of the car, returning with that old familiar box.

"Here you go."

"Kevin, I—"

"You want my hands to fall off?" Kevin joked playfully.

Simone reached to take it and while staring at the box, it suddenly occurred to her. "Wait a second, Kevin," she said as she glazed at the box in her lap, unable to look at her husband. "So the money..."

"I wasn't hiding money from you, baby. I mean, well, I guess I kinda was. But, only because I wanted to get you something special." Kevin squatted in front of her. "Simone, I told you." He grabbed her hand, brought it to his lips and kissed it gently. "Nothing was what it seemed. Now open the box."

Simone untied the bow. She lifted up the top, folded back the tissue paper, and smiled at the ebony Gucci diaper bag.

"We're not Will and Jada."

"I know." He smiled, passing her a little blue box from Tiffany's. "This isn't really a gift. I just figured we'd frame the baby's first photo in something special."

Simone opened the box and smiled. Kevin had framed the baby's sonogram picture.

"Everybody tried to feed me a bunch of information last night when I told them I remembered everything. I heard the child's not yours," she said as she skimmed the silver-plated frame with her finger.

"No. It's her husband's. But going to court that day was a blessing in disguise."

"Really? Why is that?"

"Simone, I was lost like I've never been before in my life. You were in a coma, the baby was kidnapped, and Ed..."

"What happened to Ed?"

"Long story but he's been missing since April 7th."

Simone felt her heart stop. "What? Kevin, no. Oh my God."

Now that her memory was back, Kevin took the time to tell her everything that had happened. From the night in labor and delivery, to Fat Ed's call before his disappearance, to his arrest, he told her everything. Tears fell from Simone's eyes as she listened in disbelief.

"Kevin, I remember who drugged me. I remember who took the baby. I know I can identify her. That's why I called Andre."

"Simone, Andre never called you back because he's in custody."

"Custody? For what?"

"Blackmailing McPherson in exchange for violating me."

Simone sat with her mouth wide open. Finally, she uttered, "This is not real. We need to write a book."

"It has to end happily with me and you together forever." Kevin stood and pulled her from the car, then wrapped his arms tightly around her. He planted a kiss on top of her head, silently thanking God when her arms wrapped around him. "Being apart in anyway can never be an option for us, Simone. We're one."

Chapter Forty-Five

The spicy-colored bricks faded in the distance as the Mercedes floated down the street. There were so many things Simone hadn't fully decided and yet, it seemed as if the decisions had been made for her. Deep down inside, she kind of liked Kevin's caveman antics. She needed someone to hit her over her head and take the lead.

The house and Woodard Real Estate could be sold. With the upgrades Simone had made over the years, coupled with the fact that she'd never borrowed against her equity, she would earn at least two hundred grand from the sale. Woodard Real Estate would net her just as much, if not more. With half a million in the bank, she could take some time off and be a full-time mother to her kids. And who knows, once she familiarized herself with Georgia, she could obtain her real estate license and open up another firm there if she so desired.

"You okay?" he asked.

"Yeah, just thinking."

"Penny for your thoughts."

"I'm just thinking about everything." Kevin squeezed her hand. "Where are we going? Are we driving to Georgia?"

"Yep. I'm taking you home." He loved the sound and the smile those words put on her face. "I can't wait to see the place." He laughed.

"Oh my goodness, Kevin. You're going to love it. I swear it's—"

Simone stopped midsentence at the sound of Kevin's new cell phone vibrating in the cup holder.

"It's Patrick," he shared before taking the call. "Hey, Patrick. What's going on?"

"Kevin, where are you?" Patrick asked.

"Heading home to Georgia."

"I need you to do an about-face, my friend."

"An about-face? For what?"

"Kevin, the girl from the other night is the missing nurse."

"No, she's not. She's a dancer."

"Kevin, she's both. Where's your wife?"

"She's here with me."

"Good. Bring her."

Kevin sighed. "Patrick, look. Since she's in custody, it really doesn't matter who or what she is. Let the police deal with it. We're ready to put this behind us."

"Kevin, I don't know how to tell you this."

"Then don't. Send me your invoice and you can handle everything from this point on."

"The baby in your possession isn't your son. I have the proof."

Kevin never knew his heart could thump so loud, so hard. Simone noticed his panicked expression.

"Kevin what's wrong?"

"Kevin?" Patrick called through the phone.

"We're on our way."

Chapter Forty-Six

T he crowd in the visiting room began to thin. Kevin sat slouched in the chair, massaging his temples with Simone at his side. Patrick chatted on his phone, pacing back and forth.

"Why are we here again?" Simone asked.

"I'd rather you not even be here," Kevin muttered.

Patrick pulled the phone from his ear, "No, this is something you both need to hear."

Simone's eyes darted from Kevin to Patrick, searching for a hint. "But what is it that I need to hear?" She asked.

The officer behind the desk bellowed Patrick's name.

"Please, let me know as soon as possible," Patrick instructed quickly into his phone, then eased it into his pants pocket.

"No cell phones," the officer shared.

"He's an attorney," his coworker offered.

Patrick placed his jewelry in the tray and stepped from his shoes. Kevin and Simone both followed suit.

"Brace yourself, my friends," Patrick advised as they cleared the detector.

Ten minutes into the meeting, Kevin's heart raced as he sat before the green-eyed nurse with the broken nose. Gone were the dark contacts she'd worn the day before. Her contacts had been part of a disguise to leave the country with *her* son.

As she spilled the details of her tearful, gut-wrenching confession, Kevin felt like he'd been crowned the king of fools. How could he have been so naïve? While he hated to admit it, Sanora's plea made perfect sense.

"She's gone in the brain. I mean, you don't understand how much she loves you. The house, the plastic surgery, hell, even her business. She did those things to impress you. But, when she found out you were home and married...." Sanora shrugged. "I don't know. She flipped, I guess. Her attraction to you became fatal."

Patrick was dumbfounded. "How did she find out he was home?"

"There was a picture in *Jet*."

"Kevin, if you didn't want anyone to know you were home, why'd you advertise it in a magazine?" Patrick asked.

"We didn't. It was a wedding gift. We didn't know anything about it until it was published."

"Wow, so Sanora, you were working the night Kevin and his wife had their baby?"

"Yes, it was my second night. I had left Felicia when I found out I was pregnant and went back home to my mom's. I had no plans of returning to the spa ever again, but I hadn't found the nerve to tell Felicia. I knew she'd feel betrayed, and I knew she needed the money. Then I figured when you came home, Kevin, she wouldn't even care that I was gone. But...." She shrugged with her head hung low.

"Just when I'd got the nerve, she called me crying about you. I called Felicia and told her you guys were there, having a baby. She was so pressed for you to see the *new* her that I figured the most she'd do is stroll into your room with a gift or something. I don't know what I was thinking. I didn't drug you," she revealed to Simone, "but I still feel just a guilty."

"You should," Kevin spat.

"So should you," Sanora spat back. "You led her on for years. You bought her a ring and—"

"I never bought that bitch no fucking ring. I had no plans of being with her, and she knew that shit. Every fucking body knew it." He turned to Simone. "Baby, I never led that bitch on. I mean, think about it. If she and I were anything, how the hell did I date Yolanda?"

Patrick cleared his throat.

"Sanora," Patrick intervened, "tell him the rest. It's important."

Specks of lint covered Sanora's fingers from the wet, mucus-filled tissues. Unable to face them, she toyed with the balled-up tissue in her hands.

"Supposedly, she just wanted to hurt you the way you'd hurt her. That night she claimed she was going to check into a hotel and then take the baby to the firehouse the next day."

"So why didn't she?" Kevin asked.

"Take a deep breath, Sanora," Patrick encouraged softly. "You have to tell them."

"I needed to relax, so I went to the club to dance," she sobbed, her voice barely above a whisper. "But, I didn't dance because..." Her tears quickened.

"Because what?" Kevin asked impatiently.

"Because she ran into the father of her child," Patrick volunteered.

"Look, I'm not trying to hear about her baby daddy problems."

"Kevin," Patrick said, "Edward Michael Jones is the father of her child."

Kevin went ballistic. "What? That's bullshit. Ed ain't have no kids."

"He'd just found out a few weeks ago," Sanora told him.

"I verified it, Kevin," Patrick uttered.

"My son's name is Michael Edward. Ed's name in reverse," Sanora managed. "When I found out I was pregnant, I told Ed it was his, but he didn't believe me. After the baby was born, we had the paternity test, and well…"

Kevin sat like a stone, unable to absorb it all.

"The day your baby was kidnapped, I ran into Ed at this new place called the Gentleman's Bar. It was the first time we'd seen each other in months. We had a few drinks, and well, we left together in his truck. We were too drunk to drive to his place so since I had Felicia's key, we went to her spot because it was closer, and she was supposedly staying at the spa."

Sanora stared into space, remembering the night.

"He always talked about his brother who'd been locked up. It's funny, but I never, ever knew it was you. Makes sense now. That's why he wanted nothing to do with Felicia. I guess he blamed her for your arrest."

"Okay, what happened?" Kevin didn't want the small talk. He wanted her to move the story along.

"He got to apologizing for how he treated me while I was pregnant. He made me feel like everything was going to be alright."

Patrick asked, "Did you tell him about the kidnapping?"

"No, I didn't get the chance. We were lying in the bed, making plans to be a family. Then he heard a sound."

"What kind of sound?" Simone asked.

Sanora chuckled to herself. "A cat. He thought he heard a cat."

"He hated cats," Kevin added.

"I thought we were there alone. I got up to investigate and found Felicia in her room with your son." Sanora's bottom lip quivered. "Felicia asked me to watch the baby while she went downstairs to grab a bottle. Ed crept into the room. He saw the hospital bracelet."

"That's when he called me." Kevin replayed Fat Ed's message in his head. "So what happened?"

Sanora took a deep breath and closed her eyes. She bit down on her lip to stop the quivering.

Kevin pounded the table, startling everyone in the room. "What the fuck happened?" he demanded, unable to prevent the tears swelling in his own eyes. His outburst attracted the guards' attention.

"Kevin, please." Patrick waved the guards off and urged Sanora to continue.

"Felicia heard him on the phone and she shot him."

"Oh my God," Simone whispered.

Kevin's body shook with fury. "Where is he?"

"She killed him. He's in the freezer in her garage."

Kevin leaped from his chair and paced the room as hot tears burned from his eyes.

"No, this can't be true." Wiping away her tears, Simone refused to accept the information Sanora shared. "Ed wouldn't fit in a deep freezer."

"They made him fit," Sanora cried. "Felicia's house is stocked better than most pharmacies. I took a bunch of pills to calm down. I was really trying to OD but I guess my body is use to the mess. I was out of it for a while. When I came to, I was being held hostage in a condo out in Virginia somewhere with your son. I saw on the news a few days later that Ed's truck had been found and he'd been reported missing."

"Sanora, what made you go back to Felicia's house?"

"Ed had given me ten thousand in cash. He stuck it in my purse. I remember putting my purse on the bed pillow. I guess it fell behind the bed after, you know." She shrugged. "Felicia's a pig. She barely cleans her room so I knew she wouldn't clean her daughters'. So I went to get my money so my son and I could leave the country. The money was still there. But I took your son to my mother's."

"Wait? What do you mean you took our son to your mother's?" Simone asked. "Our son is in Georgia."

"No. Your son is with my mom. She promised to look after him until me and Mikey made it to my dad's in Jamaica."

"If our son is at her mother's house, why are we meeting here? How come we're not there?" Kevin asked.

"A warrant was issued this morning. Police should be there now," Patrick shared.

Kevin grabbed Simone's hand. "C'mon, baby. Patrick, what's the address?"

Patrick shuffled his papers in a pile, stuffed them in his briefcase, and followed Kevin and Simone. "I'll be in touch," he yelled back to Sanora.

Kevin's thoughts ran wild as they rushed out. Killing Felicia was a done deal, but how remained the question. A bullet to the head was too easy considering the measures she'd taken to inflict pain on him and his family. And for what? A crazy crush she held on to from back in the day? No, Kevin wanted her to die slowly, to endure an unimaginable pain the way he'd felt the last few months.

"Patrick, looks like I may need your services after all," Kevin shared as they climbed inside the car.

Patrick stopped to answer his phone.

"What! You have got to be kidding me!"

Inside the Mercedes', Kevin blew the horn. "I need the address, Patrick!" he yelled out the window.

Patrick dropped his phone in the pocket of his light blue button-up and ran to Kevin and Simone's car.

"No one was at Sanora's mother's house. It's empty."

"Don't tell us that, Patrick." Simone's eyes pleaded with him.

"No, no, wait. There was an accident yesterday. Woman found dead at the scene. Baby in the hospital. The car was registered to Sanora's mother. Let's get to the hospital."

Chapter Forty-Seven

T wo weeks later, boxes were everywhere. Kevin and Simone were in no rush to unpack or decorate. So much had happened and right now, they simply wanted to enjoy their family and most importantly each other.

The wishes of Fat Ed's will had been followed to the letter. To Kevin's dismay, his best friend had requested to be cremated. An urn with his remains graced the mantle of the fireplace in Kevin and Simone's family room. Once they mapped out the basement studio, a niche would be specially made to house his remains. There, he and Kevin would continue to work on music together just as they'd done before his death. Fat Ed would keep him focused, and the sadness Kevin felt every time he stared at the fancy vase containing the ashes of his best friend would keep him motivated. Hundreds had turned out for the memorial service, even the Columbian's that supplied Fat Ed with his cocaine hustle from back in the day.

Hamburgers and hot dogs burned from the poolside grill. Melanie's pool guy had serviced the pool that morning just in time for the muggy eighty-five degree temperature. Jordan sat with her feet in the pool, watching as Kayla and Melanie's twin girls splashed about. Dressed in a tank top and swimming trunks, Kevin looked at Simone like she was crazy.

"Why you got that on, baby? Where's your bikini?"

"Oh no. This body is not ready for that yet."

Beatrice and Angela strolled outside with the babies.

"They up already?" Simone asked. She kissed Little Ed on the forehead and tenderly welcomed her little curly-headed, chocolate son. Lil' Kevin was the spitting image of his dad, on down to his hazel eyes. Simone's contribution rested with his complexion, blocks of curls and dimples.

"Man, oh man, y'all gon' have trouble on y'all hands," Beatrice commented as she eyed her grandson.

"Yeah, with both of them," Kevin added from the grill. As far as he was concerned, Little Ed was staying with them.

Angela said, "We changed their butts. Lil' Ed made a stink stink. He had poop going up his back."

The house phone rang. Everyone froze in place for fear that it was Patrick calling to say Sanora's mom was ready for Lil' Ed. Jordan pulled her feet from the pool and braved the call. She picked up the cordless parked on the patio set.

"Daddy," she whispered. "It's Patrick."

Kevin and Simone exchanged worried glances. Patrick's phone calls were seldom a reason to celebrate.

"Patrick, our hearts stop every time we see it's you calling."

"Yeah, I know and I'm sorry to be the constant bearer of bad news. But," he sighed, "the body from the accident has finally been identified. It's not Felicia. It's Sanora's mother. She was dead prior to the accident. Cause of death, asphyxiation. We're guessing Felicia smothered her, tossed her in the trunk, and took the baby and the car."

Kevin was silent, unsure of the mixed emotions stirring inside of him.

"I knew a few days ago, but I needed to tell Sanora first because....Well, she has some things to think about. I met with her early this morning, and she wants to know if you and Simone would be interested in adopting her baby."

Kevin closed his eyes. The words were music to his heart.

"Yes."

"She's willing to sign over all of her rights. So, you don't have to worry about her fighting you for custody if and when she's released from prison."

"Oh my goodness, Patrick. Man oh man."

"Yep. You can change his last name to Kennard if you wanted."

"Jones Kennard maybe, but never just Kennard. I want him to know about his dad." The emotion stirring inside of Kevin was indescribable. He needed to go somewhere and write, but first, he needed to address the ominous tone in Patrick's voice.

"Patrick, is there something else that you're not telling me?"

"Kevin, I mean, the body found at the scene is not Felicia, which means she's still out there. That doesn't bother you?"

"It doesn't make me happy. I was hoping she was dead. But at the same time, I'm not worried. I mean, we moved hundreds of miles away."

"Don't get too relaxed, my friend. Not while she's still out there."

"Oh, no, trust me. I'm going to take the necessary precautions."

"Please do, Kevin. Please do."

"So what's next as far as the adoption is concerned?"

"I'll have my firm get started on those papers first thing Monday morning."

"Great, thanks, Patrick."

Hanging up the phone, Kevin headed back to the grill. "Guess what y'all. He's ours!"

"Yes!" Jordan and Kayla said in unison.

"You staying with us, grandson," Beatrice cooed to Little Ed whose sea-green eyes seemed to light up.

"So what happened with her mother?" Simone inquired.

Kevin didn't want to worry her with the details nor did he want to mention Felicia's name. "Her mom can't do it."

Simone frowned. "Really?" She replied just as her cell vibrated against the patio glass table. She picked up the phone. A new text from Lavon: WILL YOU PLEASE CALL HIM TODAY?

She showed the text to Kevin. "My clients have followed me to Georgia."

"Baby, you know whenever you ready to give it up, you can give it up."

Her lips curled into a smile. "I know, but this is a good client. He got us the mountain of diapers," Simone shared as she sent Lavon a text that simply said: OKAY.

"Here, take the baby while I go call him real quick."

"Take your time, baby," Kevin said as Simone headed inside the house.

Chapter Forty-Eight

L inwood reclined in the plushness of his recliner in search of something to watch on television. The second he found something of interest, his cell phone rang. The curse word that came to mind never rolled from his tongue. The name on the caller ID actually put a smile on his face.

"What's up, little baby Oprah?" She laughed.

"You kill me with that. How you doing, Mr. Harris? I'm sorry I'm just getting around to returning your calls."

"I was worried sick about you. I got your 'thank-you' card in the mail. I'm glad you got the flowers."

"Oh yeah, I got them. There were tons of flowers, but this one gigantic arrangement stood out from the others. I knew it was from you without even reading the card. And then the diapers. You're just too much, Mr. Harris. Too too much."

Linwood chuckled. "You know how I do. Hey, listen. I called your assistant. I found two houses I want to make offers on, but she told me that you were in the process of moving to Georgia. You closing up shop here in Maryland?"

"Haven't really decided yet. So much has happened. You heard about the baby being kidnapped from the hospital and the attempted murder on the mother?"

"Hmm, that happened a month or so ago, right? I think I remember seeing it on the news."

"Well, you're talking to the momma." Linwood sat upright in the recliner as Simone continued. "I'm not sure if I'm supposed to be talking about it, but I'm sure I can tell you. Mr. Harris? You there?"

"Yeah, I'm here, Simone. Just speechless."

"Well, now you know why I moved. It's much more complicated than that, but the bottom line is, I'm fine and have my baby so that's all that matters."

"Have they caught the bastard who did this?"

"She got the easy out. She died in a car accident a few days ago. Our baby was in the car with her. He had to be resuscitated, but thank God, he's okay." She sighed into the phone.

"I don't believe this," Linwood muttered.

"Now about those properties. I'm not sure what I'm going to do with the company just yet, but I'm still licensed. So, if you can have your secretary email me the information on the houses, I'll prepare the papers and email them back to you. Cash offers?"

"Yeah, cash, Simone."

"You okay, Mr. Harris?"

"I'm just speechless, Simone. But, I'm fine if you're fine."

"Don't I sound fine, Mr. Harris? Like my old self? Trust me. I'm cool and the freakin' gang. Sleepy, but cool."

"Okay, Simone. That's what I want to hear. But honey, if you need anything and I do mean anything, you let me know."

"Thanks, Mr. Harris."

Smooth walked into the family room but stopped when he noticed his grandfather's expression as he hung up his phone. "Dag, what's wrong with you?"

"Nothing, son. Nothing."

"Hey, I wanted to show you this." Smooth extended an issue of *Jet* to his grandfather. "This the dude I was telling you about. The one who pulled strings to get me out. He's going to help me get signed." Linwood took the magazine from his grandson and gasped.

"Oh my goodness. DJ, you know who that is, right? That's the real estate agent I use to buy all my properties. That's Simone."

"Dag, you know what? I thought she looked familiar the day I met her. Me and her husband both got McPherson as our P.O. That's how I met them. He just signed with a major label as a songwriter. One of the songs he wrote is being played all over the radio."

"He on parole?"

"Yeah. Said he got into some trouble when he was younger."

Linwood read the article while Smooth headed to the kitchen.

"Kevin Kennard." Linwood had heard that name roll off Felicia's tongue on more than one occasion.

"Pops?" Smooth yelled again. "You going deaf on me? You want me to fix you something to eat?"

"Naw, I'm good."

From a hotel suite booked in some drug addict's name Linwood's sons knew, Felicia recuperated from the injuries sustained during the car accident. A few broken ribs, a mild concussion, and a sprained collar bone. Again, she'd gotten off lucky. Linwood knew she had to be in some major trouble anytime she fled the scene of a horrific accident with so many injuries. But now, things were hot. Part of him regretted their 'no questions asked' pact. Yes, she'd saved Big L's life by shooting Harvey before he had a chance to shoot his son, but as far as Linwood was concerned, he'd repaid his debt. He was washing his hands of Felicia and her shenanigans.

With Smooth back upstairs, Linwood picked up his cell and called his son, Big Daryl, Smooth's father. "Hey, where are you?"

"I'm out and about, Pops. Why, what's up?"

"Do me a favor. Check out of that hotel, will you. From this day forth, that bitch is on her own."

Chapter Forty-Nine

"**F**uck, man. This is some straight-up prime-time muthafuckin' bullshit," Felicia said.

She sprang from the bed, still tender from her injuries. Her sudden gesture sent a surge of pain through her body. But there was no time to complain. She had to get out of the hotel room. She grabbed the plastic laundry bag stamped with the hotel's name from the closet. Well aware of the sleazy area where they'd hid her, she was prepared to take it back to her roots.

"Oh yeah. This shit right here is gon' help me. Y'all just don't know. So fuck you, Linwood and your pussy-ass sons. Y'all dumb muthafuckas did me a favor by leaving me here," Felicia mumbled.

Outside the hotel, she walked over to the storefront shops. A beauty supply, a liquor store, and carryout graced every strip mall in the ghetto. With close to five hundred in cash, Felicia hit the beauty supply store first. Two long wigs, a pair of studded shades, tons of make-up including eye shadow, lip gloss, and concealer, four pairs of cheap leggings, and five low-cut tops barely cost her a hundred dollars.

"I need to use your restroom," Felicia said to the foreigner behind the counter. She didn't know if he was Chinese, Japanese, Korean, or Filipino.

"No restroom," he said, his breath reeking of garlic.

Felicia tossed her bags back on the counter. "Then I'm returning this shit."

He nodded quickly, then pointed. "In the back. I let you use one time."

Felicia rolled her eyes before heading towards the back. Ten minutes later, she emerged and strolled from the store a new person ready for business. Outside barely five minutes, she locked eyes with an older man seated inside his pickup, a fairly new looking Toyota Tundra. He winked. She gave him her sexiest grin. He rolled down his window.

"How you doing, Chocolate Cake?"

"Chocolate Cake?"

"Yeah, you chocolate, and with all that damn bootie, I just know it's delicious like cake." He smiled a toothy grin.

Felicia could tell by the decaying of his teeth that he was an addict, but an addict with wheels.

"You need a ride somewhere?"

Felicia knew he knew the game simply from how he played along.

"Yeah, if you don't mind. My girlfriend was supposed to pick me up, but I don't know where the hell she is."

"Come on. Get in. I'll take you where you need to go."

Felicia climbed inside the pickup. Empty beer cans and liquor bottles were scattered about. A pack of Top paper and two cigarillos rested inside a coffee mug. He started his pickup and backed from the space. He nodded at the plastic hotel bag in Felicia's possession.

"You still got the room?"

"Nope."

"So what we doing? I was bullshitting about the ride. You know what I want for real."

"You can get it for free if you drive me somewhere. I'll even supply the gas."

He chuckled. "Must not be good."

"I promise it'll be the best you ever had."

"Well, how do I know?"

"I'll give you a sample."

"Some pussy?"

"No, I'ma let you sample my head skills, but it's hot around here. Go to the carwash around the corner. I'll make you cum before your truck is washed."

Tickled by Felicia's confidence, he followed her orders. "What's your name, baby?"

"Let's stick with Chocolate Cake."

"I like you already."

Inside the automatic washer, it pained Felicia to lean over and service him with her broken ribs. Still, she needed him, and because she needed him, she sucked his latex-covered penis like she'd never sucked before. Before the five-minute carwash was up, he was banging on the steering wheel and filling the condom with his semen.

"Shit." He panted. "I think I want to marry you."

"So do we have a deal?" Felicia asked, her face riddled with pain.

"Hell, yeah. If you give head like that, I can only imagine the pussy," he said as he pulled from the automatic carwash. "You okay?"

"Yeah, I'm fine. I took a nasty-ass fall down some stairs a few days ago. Fractured my collarbone, broke a rib, and got a mild concussion. But, I'm okay."

"I need to run over to the library and print out some papers. But, once I'm done, I'm yours. We can go wherever you want."

"Oh, that's perfect." Felicia said. "I need to check a few emails."

*****

A bottle of Cristal chilled in the sterling silver champagne bucket engraved with their initials. Crystal flutes with remnants of the wine rested along the tray with chocolate-covered Godiva strawberries. An array of white vanilla-scented candles in various sizes flooded the bathroom, while their favorite love songs serenaded them. In a tub filled with a mountain of bubbles, they took turns reading *Touch* by Envy Red from the Kindle. The well-crafted scenes of erotica enhanced their mood. The Kindle aside, Kevin and Simone kissed like they hadn't in weeks.

"Can you hear my heartbeat?" Kevin whispered as he planted a trail of kisses along Simone's face.

"No, because mine is beating louder," Simone whispered back.

Their passion throbbed as their lips met each other again. Pulling himself from Simone's lips, Kevin stood and stepped from the tub. He reached for Simone's hand. She accepted his hand and stepped from the tub, dripping wet. No words or instructions were needed. It was in their eyes.

On top of the faux sheepskin area rug, their bodies, soaked from bathwater and tears, became one. They had rekindled their heaven.

Hours later, Kevin laid on the satin sheets of their king size bed. Under the warmth of the plush comforter, he said, "I'm waiting on you, baby." With the remote in his hand, Kevin was ready to cuddle up with Simone and watch their wedding DVD the way they had every night since they became man and wife.

"Can't wait to make love to you in front of that fireplace."

Dressed in a short Victoria's Secret nightie, Simone waltzed over to the switch and flipped on the gas. "What's up?" She grinned teasingly.

Kevin tossed back the covers.

"No, no."

She ran to the bed and attempted to hold him down. He pulled her up on the bed and began to tickle her.

"Kevin, stop." She laughed. "Stop, I'ma pee on myself."

Mirroring her smile, Kevin stared at his wife and said, "I love your new jiggle, baby."

His hand journeyed up her nightie and massaged her bare breasts. "Your breasts got fuller, your ass got juicier." He kissed her on the lips. "Come on. We can make love in front of the fireplace."

"Are you crazy? I already need an ice pack."

"I'm sorry." Kevin smiled.

Pinned beneath him, Simone caressed his face in her hands. "Don't be. It was well worth the walker."

Kevin chuckled. "Come on," he said as he freed Simone. Returning to the pillows, he patted her side of the bed.

"I'm coming," Simone said.

Easing from the bed, she threw on her robe and slippers and headed to the door.

Kevin frowned. "Where you going?"

"To check on the babies real quick."

"They're fine, baby. Our moms and the girls have them."

"I know." She shrugged. "I just want to give them a kiss."

Simone's cell vibrated against the nightstand as she opened the door.

"Oh, check that for me. Hopefully, it's Mr. Harris sending back his contracts."

Kevin grabbed Simone's phone from the nightstand as she headed out to kiss the babies goodnight. Sure enough, she had a new email with a file attached. He opened the email, but it wasn't some ordinary file. It was a video. Kevin clicked it to see what it was, just as his cell began to chirp, announcing the arrival of email, as well.

"Damn," he said. Someone had sent him a video, too.

While his video loaded, he diverted his attention back to Simone's phone and pressed play. Unprepared for the footage, his heart thumped as he watched Felicia suck all over his nakedness. Trembling nervously, he deleted the video as sweat beaded his brow.

"Fuck, man," he mumbled under his breath. He picked up his phone. The video had loaded. He pressed play and nearly had a heart attack as Ray Charles' "Georgia" began to play.

*****

"You don't have a problem driving me?" Felicia asked from the front seat of the truck.

"I ain't got shit else to do. Plus, I'm gon' enjoy this here road trip, especially if you gon' suck and fuck me like there's no tomorrow," he said, grinning from ear to ear. "You ever gon' tell me your real name?"

Felicia smiled as she gazed out the window.

"I like Chocolate Cake. No one's ever given me a nickname before."

"Then I guess I'll call you Chocolate Cake."

"And what should I call you?" Felicia asked.

"You can call me by my real name."

Felicia frowned. "Okay, and what is that?"

"Ricardo, baby. You can call me Ricardo."

About the Author

Traci Bee is the award-winning author of the Kindle drama chart topping, *Two Tears in a Bucket*. When she's not writing, Traci enjoys karaoke and spending time with her family. She currently resides in Waldorf, Maryland with her husband and kids and is working on two novels; the final installment to the Two Tears in a Bucket Series and A Nickel for A Kiss.

Visit Traci Bee online at:
Facebook: www.facebook.com/authortracibee
Twitter: www.twitter.com/authortracibee
www.tracibee.com